7

WATERPROOF
NAVY SEALS

JO CHAMBLISS

Escapeproof

by Jo Chambliss

Copyright 2022 by Hover Press

ISBN: 9781088278147

Edited by: Flawless Fiction

Cover Design by: CK Book Cover Designs

For the people that fight for the rights and
freedoms of our most courageous heroes

I only wish that your services were never needed

CHAPTER 1

NOLAN "JUDGE" LOCKMORE

"Good riddance, asshole."

Standing in the middle of my back patio, the coroner continues his work, pretending he didn't hear me. Sweat dots the older man's brow like he's working in the hot sun instead of the middle of a mild December night. Though it has been unseasonably warm, the night air seems to have cooled suddenly, or perhaps, adrenaline kept me from feeling the cold until now.

The bag holding the aforementioned asshole is secured to a stretcher, and the medical examiner rolls the body away from the scene. The bastard is dead and gone, but my fists clench as fury builds inside me again over what happened tonight. I curse the man under my breath despite no one else being around. "A bullet was too easy a way out for you."

After threatening the lives of women and children, my family, with a bomb at my house, he deserved to be strapped to a chair and left in a room with my team instead of the quick death he received.

Well, well. I snicker at the vicious and violent thoughts pervading my mind. *I wonder what the Bar Association would think about me pondering that idea.*

As the doctor pushing the stretcher nears the front gate, the NCIS agent assigned to the case approaches me from the damaged area of the patio. "Lockmore, it's time for you to clear out of here."

I turn away from watching the coroner to stare at the shattered and bloody tiles of the patio floor. I feel no remorse for the attacker's death. I only care about the damage he caused. *That asshole just blew a hole in my patio. That was three weeks' worth of work.*

The somber agent clears his throat, attempting to draw my focus back to him. "I have a crime scene to process. You need to blow. One of my agents will escort you inside to pack a bag."

Now, he's got my full attention. "Wait a minute. Are you saying I can't stay in my own house? You know this asshole never went inside. Hell, he never got any closer than this spot."

Special Agent Tills only glares back with dark, stormy eyes over a set jaw: The high and tight signature marine cut of his gray hair and the lines around his eyes tell me he's a man who's seen it all and heard it all. He won't budge, no matter how much I don't like it.

As much as I want to argue over the asinine demand, being a lawyer by trade, I understand his need to preserve the scene for his investigation. "Fine."

He gestures to someone on his team, and I'm followed inside, where I throw some clothes in a bag. When I've gathered enough for two days, I lock the place up and stow the duffle in the trunk of my black Genesis sedan next to my SEAL go bag.

The rest of my team and commander have already cleared out, and after my eviction, I'm left standing on my driveway with the junior agent, watching the coroner load the body in his van. The doors are slammed shut, sealing the corpse inside, and the van is driven off my property.

At least I got to hang around longer than the dead guy.

The agent apologizes again for making me leave, but I wave him off. It's not like there's anything I can say about it anyway. At least the old–bat next door isn't around anymore. This kind of action would have set Mrs. Kading off, and for the next six months, she'd be convinced of me being an ax murderer and called the police every time she saw me with a shovel in my hand.

That alone is enough to have my mood lifting. Enjoying the last four months of no-crazy-neighbor bliss makes me suddenly not so miffed about finding a place to stay for the night. I slip into the soft leather seat of my car and start the engine.

The G90 purrs as I back out of the carport

and head into town, another thing my crazy neighbor would have complained about this late at night.

Driving up the quiet two-lane highway under a clear night sky, I continue my inner celebration over life post-demon-neighbor. Without the old hag's prying, I've begun spending more time outside, which has led to completing some decent garden and hardscape designs. One, in particular, would have given the old bat a heart attack, an outdoor shower. Never mind that she wouldn't have been able to see me using it unless she walked over to the back of my house.

The luxury sedan pulls into town, my plan being to stay at the closest hotel. However, when I near the entrance, I roll right by. Like the first, I also drive right past the next one. The hotels in the next towns are also ignored. *Guess I'm headed to Norfolk.*

Jasper Lockmore's driveway is empty when I pull in. My cousin and Judge Advocate General for the US Navy is probably out celebrating the close of another case. I climb out of the car and retrieve my bag from the trunk. As I close the lid, Jasper's Volvo pulls in beside me.

He kills the engine, and I lean against the passenger door of my car, waiting for him to get out. I don't have to wait long. His tall frame unfolds from the front seat, and I'm greeted with the smile juries love to be graced with. "To what do I owe the honor?"

"Some asshole just blew up my backyard."

Jasper's smile dries up in an instant. "You're not serious."

I lift my eyebrows in answer.

"Shit, you are serious."

He looks me over once and decides I'm no worse for wear. Turning for the walkway, he says, "This, I've got to hear."

Jasper leads the way inside, keying in the entry code at the front door, the same code I would have used to gain access if he hadn't shown up when he did.

My cousin tosses his ball cap and keys on the entry table and heads to the living room, where he drops into his favorite chair. Like me, he doesn't drink in uniform, preserving his and the military's reputation.

Jasper and I share a strong family resemblance, which is one of the reasons I was reluctant to join the Office of Judge Advocate General. I wanted to avoid any allegation of nepotism that other practitioners might raise. With us having the same blue eyes, dark hair, and nose, there's no denying we're related. The main difference between our appearances is the bulk I've put on since leaving the courtroom. My cousin is no lightweight, but he's also not had the many years' worth of SEAL training I have.

I sprawl on his sofa and run down the situation with Ink's woman from her first appearance to just an hour ago in my backyard. After the story, Jasper leans back in his chair and whistles. "Sounds like it's time for a transfer back to the JAG office."

Jasper stares straight at me, serious as a heart attack, and I shake my head, not quite believing what is about to come out of my mouth. "I've thought about it… but only just. I'm not ready to start making plans."

Before my cousin can start pushing, I stand up from my seat on the plush sofa and walk toward the guest room. "I'm going to crash."

"Goodnight, Counselor," Jasper calls out as I walk down the hall.

IYLA DUNSMORE

There's something magical about watching paint swirling in the sink just before the chaos whirlpools down into the drain. It's a death of sorts, the end of a labor of art. And yet, it's also the birth of a completed piece that's soon to be shared with the world.

I'm not Van Gogh with his romantic impressions, Georges Seurat placing meticulous points, or Salvador Dalí creating dreamlike surrealism. I'm just as invested in my art, but what I create will likely never end up in a museum.

My work captures the essence of and is used by some of the country's most beautiful resorts, landmarks, and celebrated companies.

The dreamy watercolor paintings featured on some of the most exclusive wine collections in the US are just a small portion of my work.

I'm what has been described as a commercial artist. Using media of all kinds, I create artistic labeling for a number of products. Another large representation of my commissioned work is regional art for resorts to display in their public areas and guest rooms.

Like any other artist, I also paint and sketch for the sheer joy of it. I've sold many paintings and illustrations over the years to feed my passion, if not my practicality. I'm one of the best at creating photoreal watercolor paintings, but my favorite pieces are made with charcoal on reclaimed wood planks.

There's life in the wood that can't be found in the pastel paper typically used. The wood breathes and speaks to me stories of its life, forming the image to be forever etched on its surface.

Bringing an end to my musing, I focus again on my current task. The water finally runs clear through the fibers of my Kolinsky Sable brushes, the fine weasel hair no longer hinting at the colors used in my recently completed work. After carefully blotting out the water from the soft bristles, I place the brushes in a protected drying rack and stare out the window over the sink in my studio.

I may not be able to see Miami's beaches

from the windows of my rented house, but I can smell the salty air, hear the call of the seagulls, and see plenty of palm trees gently swaying in the wind.

Miami has been my home for six years, but I was raised in Montrose, Colorado, where my parents still live. In Montrose, I fit in easily. In Miami, not so much. With my Scottish accent, even after years of living on the coast, people I meet tend to assume that I'm a tourist.

Having lived in America since I was four, I don't think my accent is all that thick unless I'm angry, tired, turned on, or a little drunk. As frequently as I'm asked to speak by locals, apparently, I can be sorted into one or more of those categories more often than not.

I rinse the cup and watercolor palette under the running water, set them up to dry, and finally dry my hands on my apron. Work is finally finished for the day. Now, I need to get some sleep. The movers will be here early in the morning, and I don't want to be just climbing out of bed when they knock on my door.

Stepping outside the back door for some fresh air, I close my eyes and take in a lungful of the tropical sea breeze. I've had a good run in Miami, but recent events make it clear that it's time to move on.

I need to start somewhere new, leaving behind bad memories and people I'd rather forget. My next stop is Asheville, North Carolina.

I've taken a residency commission with the Biltmore Estate to paint an extensive series of landscapes that will adorn their facilities and for the relabeling of their vineyard's wines. I'll get to paint the residence, gardens, stables, and, of course, the winery.

For the next four months, I'll live rent-free in a small cottage on the estate grounds. The house is just large enough to accommodate a decent studio and meeting space and is fully furnished. All my things here will go into storage until I decide where to go next.

My parents want me to return home but don't expect me to, and they won't push. I hate to admit I'm struggling with a bit of I-don't-know-what-I-want, which I've never dealt with before. I truly need a hard reset in life and hope to reboot with my head back on straight.

By two the next afternoon, the large moving container has been packed with all my furniture and hauled away, and all my clothes and art supplies are loaded into a tiny U-Haul trailer.

The last thing I do before pulling away from the curb is text my mother that I'm beginning the fourteen-hour drive to Asheville. It doesn't matter that I'm thirty years old; she still wants to know that I'm safe and that someone is looking out for me.

The drive is long, with the scenery and weather changing as drastically as possible. After an overnight stop and a late start to day two, I approach the Biltmore's massive gate around three, ready to begin my extended stay in this beautiful place. The security guard leans out his window to gape at the U-Haul trailer attached to my car. I guess the obnoxious orange beast is not a normal thing to see pulling through his gate.

I'm prepared for an inquisition with a printed copy of my contact's email, but the guard smiles. "You must be the artist moving in."

He looks down at his desk and then back to me. "Dunsmore looks easy enough. How do you say your first name?"

Smiling back at him, I pronounce, "Eye-luh. It's Scottish."

"Well, Ms. Eye-luh, welcome to Biltmore Estate. I'm Oscar. You need anything, you call the security team and tell them Oscar says to take care of you."

I love this place already. "Thank you, Oscar."

The older black gentleman tips his hat and hands me a map that will lead me to my temporary home. "I'll contact Ms. Dupree and let her know you've arrived. She'll meet you at the cottage."

"Thanks," I tell the smiling man. He winks in return, and I pull through the massive stone and iron gate, excited for this new adventure.

The drive to the cottage seems to wind forever through the expansive estate grounds. Through my research of the Biltmore's history,

I've learned the famous Frederick Law Olmsted originally designed the landscaping for the sprawling estate. He created the first combination of English and French styles in the gardens, and his design is proudly displayed today.

That kind of enduring impact, whether in landscaping, music, theatre, or art, is something any artist dreams of, myself included.

I finally reach the area where the descendants of the Vanderbilts still live on the estate and locate my cottage. Miranda Dupree, my contact for the commission, is waiting for me on the porch as I pull into the driveway of the quaint little house.

Pulling my purse from the passenger seat, I walk up the stairs to greet the director and shake her offered hand. "Ms. Dunsmore, I'm glad you made it safely."

"Thanks. It's beautiful here. I can't believe I've never visited before."

Ms. Dupree chuckles. "Over the next four months, you'll see enough to be sick of the place. Come on, let me show you inside. I have a pair of maintenance guys coming to help you move your things in."

Later that evening, after I've had a chance to get somewhat settled in and freshened up, I meet Ms. Dupree at the inn for dinner. Over three courses and a glass of wine, she outlines the first few pieces I'm to start with and the people who will serve as guides for the specific areas I'm to paint.

I cannae wait to begin.

Since the next day is the start of the weekend, I won't officially begin until Monday. However, I will be touring the grounds on my own, taking pictures. I've been given an all-access pass, allowing me unlimited entry into the house, stables, and all other estate features.

Half of my first morning on the estate grounds is exploring the gardens adjacent to the grand house. For starters, I wanted to catch the sunrise over the residence and gardens. I plan to photograph the sunset from the back of a horse.

My tour of the house leads to some amusing discoveries, the private bowling alley and one-of-a-kind indoor swimming pool being some of my favorites—all features well before their time.

After today's explorations, I know exactly how to start my first painting and spend all day Sunday working on the initial sketch.

By Thursday, the first of many paintings is complete. The image is from the residence's large garden from a low point of view. Of all the pictures I took of the stately home, this view angle intrigued me the most.

I take a moment to study the work from across the room and then start the process of cleaning out my brushes and other tools. Next, I pop in the shower to clean myself up and call Miranda once I've dried and dressed.

Her excitement over seeing the first work is palpable, even over the phone. She promises to rush right over to see it. Based on her reactions to the concept sketches I presented, I'm excited for her to see the finished work.

Since arriving on the estate, Miranda and I have spoken and met enough times that I've gotten to know her reasonably well. Well enough to see her as having good friend potential. We're close in age, dedicated to our careers, single, and have a shared love of art.

The friendly public relations manager arrives at my cottage a short while later, and I show her into the studio area. Miranda stops in the doorway to the room and gasps, bringing a hand to her mouth. Through her fingers, she declares, "Oh, Iyla, it's beautiful."

She steps closer and slowly drops her hand, only to put it back a moment later. "Your sketches showed such a unique perspective and were amazing, but the finished piece is just unbelievable."

"I'm glad you like it. Once it's had plenty of time to dry, I'll pack it up and deliver it to your office. In the meantime, I'll get started on some sketches for the stable. I'll call you when they're done so we can review them together."

Miranda doesn't look away from the colorful work when she says, "Sounds good. Where are you having dinner tonight? I've got a late meeting and might join you."

"Well… actually, I've been fighting off a craving all week. I was planning to go off-estate to find somewhere to get a hot dog."

"Ha. Say no more. I've got you covered."

Miranda tells me about a city park where a hot dog vendor sets up in the evenings, and just like that, I have my dinner plans.

With one last glance at the painting, Miranda leaves for her meeting, and I gather my things for a picnic in the park. My sketchpad and pencils get loaded into my CRV, along with the usual suspects: a blanket, snacks, and a small cooler of drinks.

I leave the estate grounds for the first time since arriving in North Carolina. Following GPS directions, I arrive at the park in fifteen minutes and find a lot more than a single food truck.

It seems this park is food truck central. Food vendors line one side of the parking lot, selling gyros, salads, and everything in between. On my way to the hot dog truck, I pass one selling tacos, and the mouth-watering aroma of the Mexican food convinces me I can eat a hot dog another day.

I place my order and take my steaming hot enchiladas to an empty patch of grass next to the pond. The delicious smells from the go box have me rushing to get the blanket set out and all my stuff unloaded. My arse hits the ground mere seconds before I take my first bite of the saucy goodness.

Despite my protesting stomach, I eat every delicious bite and waddle toward the picnic tables to toss my trash. *Won't do me good tae eat like this every day. I dinnae want to blow up like a balloon.*

On my way to the bin, I spot a policeman walking casually around the park. He nods in greeting as I chuck the rubbish in the bear-proof canister. As he moves, stares from other women tell me that most find him attractive. I suppose a month ago, I would have as well. Right now, Tom Holland probably wouldn't even turn my head.

I dump my rubbish in the bin, pour some water over my hands, and scrub them clean with a spare napkin. Now that I'm fully clean and in no danger of making a mess of my tools, I'm ready to sit down and draw for a while.

The policeman stands over my blanket, looking at my sketch pad when I start back. The thirteen-by-nineteen book is open to the final concept drawing of the garden scene I just painted. As I approach, I can hear the man trying and failing to pronounce my name signed at the bottom of the page. "Ill-luh... Eee-luh..."

"It's Eye-luh."

The policeman looks up and grins, testing the proper enunciation of my name. "Eye-luh. This is your work?"

"Aye."

"It's a great view of the Biltmore. Did you draw that just for the hell of it?"

"No, I've been commissioned to paint

some new landscapes for the estate to use in promos and building decoration."

His smile would qualify as a panty-dropper. "Well, you do beautiful work."

So, the guy definitely qualifies as hot, but since I've sworn off men, I'm unaffected by his classically handsome features. The officer's shiny badge gleams as he reaches out his hand. "I'm Dillan Broderick. Sheriff's deputy in Buncombe County."

"Iyla Dunsmore," I answer, accepting his hand. "From Miami."

Deputy Broderick removes his reflective aviator sunglasses and slowly releases my hand. "Miami—wow. This must be quite a change for you."

"Not so much. I grew up in Colorado. I think Miami was the real culture shock."

Flashing a smile again, Deputy Broderick replaces his sunglasses. "Time for me to get back to work. If you'll be here for a while, I might see you around, Iyla Dunsmore."

The policeman walks away, and an unexpected cold shiver crawls over my skin. I glance around the park to see if anyone took a particular interest in my conversation with the deputy, but no one is looking my way. Dismissing the sensation, I settle back down on the blanket and turn a new page in the oversized sketchbook.

CHAPTER 2

IYLA

I've completed three sketches of the stable. I'm excited to show Miranda and hop on my bike to visit the estate office. The weather here is spoiling me: cool, crisp mornings and mild evenings. I park in front of the office house and lift my bag from the basket above the back wheel. Inside are my sketchbook and sheets where I've mixed up swatches of several color samples.

For the stable, I'll be painting the selected scene twice. Once showing the emergence of spring, the second will feature fall foliage. Together, Miranda and I select the final perspective view of the barn and colors.

"I'm just as excited to see these as I was the first one," she squeals after the meeting.

I feel the same way.

Since our meeting occurred at the end of the workday, Miranda and I walk out of the estate office building together. "So, how do you like staying here?"

"I love it. Besides being the most beautiful place I've ever lived, it's peaceful."

"But not exciting like Miami, right?"

Sighing, I shrug a shoulder in indifference. "Miami left its lumps, enough that I won't be going back."

"What happened … if you don't mind me asking?"

I glance down at my ring finger, staring at the pale strip of skin. "I was almost married in Miami."

"Almost?"

"I was at the church, in the dress and everything, but he never showed. When my parents drove me home, I had a letter waiting for me on my front steps."

"Ouch. When did this happen?"

"Four weeks ago, tomorrow."

"Oh shit, Iyla. I'm sorry. I wish I'd never asked."

"Don't worry about it. I'm happy to be here, living and working in such a beautiful place. It was just what I needed to get my mind off things."

"Well, good for you." Her head tilts, and her eyebrows lift in question before she asks, "Have you met anyone here that might interest you?"

We've reached my bike, and I drop my bag into the basket before answering what I hope is a joke. "No, I'm not anywhere near ready for that. Anyway, besides you, the only other person I've had more than five words with is Oscar at the main gate."

She laughs, a light and cheery sound. "I think he's a little old for you."

"Just a wee bit."

The two of us part ways at this point, Miranda to her car and me to my bike. Once everything is secure, I peddle back to my cottage and transfer my sketching tools to my car. I'm in the mood for that hot dog and could use a little time to decompress with some people-watching.

Settling on an empty bench at the park this time, I enjoy the best hot dog I've ever had and spend a little time watching some kids toss pebbles into the pond from the water's edge. I'm about an hour into sketching when a shadow crosses the pad of paper I'm holding.

Fighting through another cold shiver, I swivel my head around and up in time to see Deputy Broderick pulling off his reflective aviators. "Iyla Dunsmore, nice to see you again."

"Deputy, same to you."

"Call me Dillan, please."

Gesturing to the empty side of the bench, he asks, "May I?"

"Sure."

Dillan drops onto the opposite side of the bench to eat his dinner of pot stickers and rice, pausing every few bites for light conversation. To be polite, I put my pencil down, taking an unexpected break from drawing. It's not that I mind; I'm just still not used to the Southern person's affinity for being overtly friendly.

"What's that you're working on today?"

I lift the sketch to show him. "It's the stable this time, a concept sketch. Once I get it the way I want it, I'll redraw an official copy to paint."

"I swear. Even your rough drafts are stunning."

"Thanks."

The rest of the exchange is mostly basic, with Dillan mentioning that he's lived his whole life in North Carolina. I talk a little about growing up in Colorado, but when his questions dive into my time in Miami, I steer the conversation back to him.

"Do you come to the park often?"

He nods. "I do. I think it helps to be seen in uniform during my shift breaks. Sometimes, I play catch or throw a Frisbee with the kids around here. Otherwise, just being a friendly face to those in the community."

"That's... that's really decent of you. I'll bet you're a popular character in the community."

"Hey, I'm just doing my part."

We talk a while longer, and Dillan leaves to finish his shift. As he's walking away, he turns around and walks backward a few steps to issue a final farewell. "Till next time, Iyla."

Over the next two weeks, I become a regular at the park. The food on the estate is fantastic, but sometimes, a girl just wants junk food. The fact that it's cheaper to eat here is a plus. Since I've decided that my next stop will be permanent, I want to save all my pennies for a down payment on a house.

And that thought serves as my daily reminder that I have no idea where I plan to live after finishing this job.

Every day, when I'm not people-watching, eating, or sketching, I'm trying to figure out my future. *Hmm. Maybe Asheville wouldn't be a bad place to stay.*

The following week, I didn't visit the park at all. I rolled an ankle walking down Antler Hill toward the Village at the estate. The resulting soreness made for difficult walking. The plan had been to take some low vantage point pictures of the Inn. The fall meant I would have to be off my feet for a few days. Fortunately, I already had enough pictures to spend a couple of weeks sketching and painting.

The time goes by quickly, and soon, I'm moving well enough to go out and invest in a proper pair of hiking boots. I don't return to the park right away, needing to spend several evenings photographing the estate at twilight and during the full moon. These paintings will go in the formal restaurants and suites for a more dramatic touch.

When I finally return to the park, Dillan is standing near the bench I usually occupy, appearing as though he's looking for me.

Too late, I wonder if my return appearances and chats with him are being seen as more than they are. Of course, I could be jumping to conclusions, but I'd be better off ensuring he knows where I stand. Hopefully, neither he nor I will be so embarrassed that he ceases speaking to me. It's been nice to have someone to chat with outside of work. While Miranda and I talk on occasion, we're getting into her holiday planning season, and she's pretty busy these days.

Deciding that I'm overthinking things but ready to quash any romantic notions he might have, I approach Dillan and my usual seat. "There she is. Where have you been?"

"Off my feet. I twisted an ankle taking pictures on a hill while wearing the wrong shoes."

"I'm glad it wasn't any more serious than that. So, what's for dinner tonight? My treat."

Damn. I hate it when I'm right. "I'm not going to let you buy me dinner for being an idiot."

"How about you let me buy you dinner because you're a beautiful and talented lady I've enjoyed getting to know these last several weeks?"

I let out a small sigh and quietly answer, "I can't let you buy me dinner for that either."

Dillan deflates instantly when I don't gush over his compliment. His eyes show that he's disappointed and a little hurt. However, he recovers quickly. "Well then, how about we get our own dinners, and when we get back, we can pretend that we've only just shown up."

I chuckle and grin, relieved by his easy acceptance. "Sounds good."

Time goes by fast after that, and soon, I'm beginning my third month of residency at the estate. Dillan and I have continued our park meetings during his shift breaks. He is a funny guy, and I can finally admit that he's easy on the eyes.

As the spring air warms, Dillan trades in his cold season uniform for one that's undeniably more fitted and with short sleeves. His broad shoulders and muscled arms fill out his fitted uniform top, which does not go unnoticed by female passersby in the park. Also more noticeable are his brilliant blue eyes that match well with his sandy-blond hair and tan skin. His long, sharp blade of a nose is perfectly proportioned and symmetrical above his chiseled jaw. As far as the principles of art go, he's a masterpiece. Just not for me. Not yet.

Today has been a day spent indoors working, and I'm looking forward to being outside. With my bag strapped across my shoulder, I walk across the park toward the row of food trucks and decide to get wings and onion rings. Usually, I eat pretty healthy, so I figure my few indulgences at the park won't kill me.

While waiting for my order, I study the

posters taped to the side of the truck. The one that catches my eye first is for a community event happening at the park this weekend—an art walk. *There's no way I can miss that.*

My number is called, and I take my wings to my usual spot where Dillan is already seated. I set my bag down, lower myself to the bench, and blurt out, "The art walk happening this weekend, how big is it?"

"Pretty big. I'm sure it's not as expansive as those in Miami, but it's a popular event."

"I think I'll check it out."

"I'd love to join you but won't be able to make it. I'm scheduled to work a double on Saturday. Speaking of art, what area of the estate are you working on this week?"

I tell him about being alone in the great room of the estate, sketching in person instead of from photos. "I swear, I could hear the raucous laughter echoing from the times the home hosted grand parties. It was a special moment."

"God, I'd love to see your work finished. Your sketches are breathtaking, and I can only imagine the life they take on when represented in full color."

"I suppose you could come to my studio on the estate. I have a few pieces I haven't turned over to the organizer yet."

"That would be great. I'm off tomorrow. Is that too soon?"

"Tomorrow is ok. Any time past nine is

fine. I'll leave your name at the gate."

Dillan looks down at his watch. "Well, back to work for me. See you tomorrow, Iyla."

At noon on the dot, there's a knock at my cottage door. I stick my brush in the rinsing cup and cover my palette. Wiping my hands on my apron, I walk to the door and open it to find Dillan standing outside holding take-out bags. He's dressed in a white t-shirt that shows off his muscular build and board shorts that expose his long, strong legs. "I brought lunch. There's plenty to choose from. I figured if I gave advance notice, you'd refuse the gesture."

I roll my eyes and lead him inside toward the small dining area. While Dillan unloads what appears to be a taco and enchilada buffet, I grab plates, cutlery, and some water from the fridge.

His company is as companionable as it has been in the park, and we spend much of the time laughing. After filling up on the Mexican feast, he helps clear the table, and we relocate to the studio.

Dillan's jaw drops over the watercolor paintings of the various estate attractions. "These are beautiful, Iyla. I swear to god, you should have your own gallery."

"I've thought about it before. The truth is, I like the way I'm working now. I get to travel to so many amazing locations to paint. Not that I couldn't do that with a gallery, but I'd have to invest a lot of time in management and making sure the place was stocked and rotated. Maybe one day, when I'm ready to trim down the time I'm on the road, I'll look into it more seriously."

Dillan studies the last piece in the room for a bit longer, then turns and looks me straight in the eye. "Iyla, you're an amazing woman. You're beautiful and a pleasure to be around. I would love it if you let me take you to dinner."

"Dillan... I can't."

His shoulders drop, as does his face. "But why? Have I done something wrong?"

"No! It's... I'm only going to be here for another month."

"And then you're going back to Miami?"

"No. I have no idea where I'm going. Probably wherever the next job takes me."

He looks like he wants to say more but only sighs. "I guess it would be crazy to start something now." He chuckles sadly. "I should have asked sooner. Then, I might have had enough time to convince you to stay."

I don't bother telling him it would have been a fool's quest. I don't say anything at all. There's no point twisting the knife.

Dillan is standing close enough that he bends down and presses a light kiss on my cheek. "I guess I should let you get back to work."

The ordinarily cheerful man walks out my cottage door dejected. I feel like a monster, though I'm not sure why. I haven't been stringing him along. In his own words, he acknowledged that.

Telling him my reason for refusing might have prevented his asking me out but at the expense of my humiliation. Anyway, hearing about my heartbreak might have also made him more determined.

Neither one of us needs what would come of that situation.

I don't see Dillan at the park at all for the next three weeks. I guess I've upset him pretty badly, but there's nothing I can do about that now.

Today marks the beginning of my final week at the Biltmore Estate. I'm driving to the grounds office to deliver the last piece I'll do for this contract. Miranda and the rest of the estate managers have been thrilled with all the paintings for their new promotional and branding series. On Friday night, there's to be a grand unveiling held at the estate's inn.

Until then, I've got work of another kind to wrap up. I've been feverishly trying to pick my next home base for the last five weeks. I've narrowed the search to three areas based on their merits and access to main travel hubs.

Of course, my mother suggested I come back home to Colorado. She knows me better than that, though. I've even considered a time or two, using my dual citizenship to spend a few years in Scotland.

The two options I'm most heavily

considering are Washington state and Virginia. I love the mountains of my home state and fell in love with the beach in Miami. Washington and Virginia have both. So, when I'm not packing or meeting with Miranda about the Biltmore series of paintings, I'm researching cities and properties.

While doing my research, my words to Dillan when we last spoke have haunted me. The more I think about it, the sadder they sound. *I have no idea where I'm going.* That was true in more ways than I'm comfortable admitting, even to myself.

I had no idea where I was going when I was engaged to Trevor. I don't think he did either. Another fellow artist, Trevor, was happy in my company, as I was in his. I now realize our problem was that neither of us had ever defined what we wanted out of life past the next canvas. That type of existence isn't much of a foundation to build a life on. It seems Trevor figured that out before I did.

He just didn't have the decency or courage to say this to my face.

At least Trevor's actions spared me from going through an eventual divorce. Now, it seems, I'm finally ready to decide what I want my life to be. I'll always be an artist, but I'm eager to see what else I can make of myself.

My attention turns back to my computer, and I spend the rest of the day researching my final two choices for my next fresh start.

After listing the pros and cons of each location, I finally settle on Virginia. Ultimately, I believe the decision came down to climate. Virginia gets snow enough that I'll experience that little touch of home, but I'll also have longer summers to enjoy the beach.

Now, all I have to do is find the right place somewhere between the foothills and the coast. After living in my little cottage on the Biltmore estate, I want something private and quiet, something in a charming small town.

It takes me until late, but I finally find what could be the perfect place. It's in a heavily wooded area and only has one neighbor. The house has been on the market for several months without a single contract, making me wonder what's wrong with it.

Some reviews of the property mention that it's a great house on a beautiful piece of land but complain about the proximity to the town's necessary amenities. *Heck, living here, I've gotten used to trips to the grocery and other simple errands taking a long time.*

I study each picture of the listing, and after each click, I become more and more convinced that this is my next home. There's only one problem. I'm moving out on Sunday.

There isn't time for the normal house-buying process to run its course, but I'm hoping for a miracle. Crossing my fingers, I contact a competing real estate agency, as my mother taught me never to contact the seller's agent.

Through the agent I'm assigned, I take a chance and make an offer on the house with one major caveat. I want to put up a deposit to rent the place pending a passing inspection and closing. Fortunately, since I can submit to them a letter of preapproval that I had the foresight to get last month, the seller agrees to the deal.

That means I'll have a place to stay for at least a few weeks, even if the deal falls through or the inspection reveals major problems. With that handled, I can enjoy my last day here without worrying about being homeless.

It's now Friday evening, and I'm walking into the grand dining room at the inn. Dressed in a navy chiffon gown and heels, I enter the part of the ballroom set up as a gallery. Tonight will be my first time seeing all of my paintings together, and it's the only opportunity I'll have. I'm grateful for the private viewing Miranda arranged for me to have before the crowds descend on the area.

I'm more proud of the work I've done here than any collection I've ever created. And this collection is certainly the most sizeable.

My fingers brush the frame of the last work in the group, and I turn to the entrance to find Miranda peeking through the door. I motion her over, and she does something I don't quite expect. The smart professional wraps me up in a brief hug. "I'm so glad you came to our village, Iyla. I don't think anyone else could have captured the spirit of Biltmore as well as you have."

"Thank you, Miranda," I reply, touched by her words.

A short while later, guests mill around the area, enjoying hors d'oeuvres, dancing to the five-piece band, and admiring the paintings. I've just collected a chilled glass of champagne from a passing waiter when a familiar face appears beside me. "Dillan, I didn't expect to see you here."

"What can I say? I am a lover of all beautiful things, and I couldn't abandon a friend on such an important night."

Before I can respond, Dillan directs his attention to the Biltmore collection. "These are phenomenal. You have a gift that blows me away."

"Thank you. Would you like me to show you around?"

Dillan lifts a hand to his chest and bows slightly. "With the artist as docent? How could I refuse such an offer?"

He holds out his arm playfully, and I wrap a hand around his bicep. We proceed to the gallery area, and I have to say, it feels nice to have someone around that I know.

The time soon comes for the program to begin, and Miranda introduces me to the crowd, which answers with enthusiastic applause. Also mentioned are the estate manager, the mayor of Asheville, and two notable benefactors.

After the introductions, the crowd is seated for dinner, me being assigned to the dignitary table. Dillan trails behind me, surprising Miranda with his presence. Her cool reception of Dillan surprises me, making me wonder if there's history there. "I wasn't aware Ms. Dunsmore had a guest."

Unfazed by her chilly greeting, Dillan responds cheerfully, "She didn't. I'm merely escorting a friend to her table."

His friendly smile is firmly in place when he turns his focus back to me. "Enjoy your dinner. Perhaps we'll catch up again for a dance."

He gives a little bow and turns to find another seat.

The rest of us take our seats and enjoy the best dinner I've had to date on the estate. Speeches are made, pictures are taken, and the crowd is finally dismissed to enjoy the traveling desserts, drinks, and dancing.

During a rare moment when I'm not engaged with dignitaries, a gentle grip on my elbow pulls my gaze to a tall figure at my side. "Could you stomach a dance with a lowly policeman?"

"Oh, haud yer wheesht," I answer while rolling my eyes.

"Huh?" Dillan asks, completely

bewildered.

"It means shut up."

I accept Dillan's offered hand, and we join the twirling crowd on the dance floor. The man is surprisingly graceful, somehow able to compensate for my lack of skills. Before long, I'm even enjoying myself instead of worrying about where to put my feet.

Halfway through the song, Dillan's graceful steps sweep us out onto the stone patio. The night is clear and calm, and millions of stars twinkle above. Though we can still hear the music, Dillan halts our momentum, pulls me tight against his firm body, and takes my mouth in a fiery kiss.

I recover quickly from the shock, work my hands into the tight space between us, and push Dillan away. "What are you doing?"

"Whatever I can to change your mind and make you stay."

Taking a staggering step back, I shake my head forcefully. "No, Dillan. I can't."

Dillan holds his ground, and I plead with my eyes for him not to ask why. At first, he looks hurt as he did that day in the cottage, but then his expression darkens. He's angry. "You know, I should say that I understand and walk away like a gentleman. But I can't do that because I don't understand."

Part of me is hurt by his anger, and part is angry in return. "You don't have to understand.

It's enough that I said no."

"Then that's it. All these months have meant nothing."

"Are you saying my friendship has meant nothing? Your friendship meant something to me."

"I don't want another friend. I want you."

I take another step back and look away from his eyes. "I'm sorry then. I cannae be what you want."

An angry hand works over his jaw, and Dillan storms off the balcony, leaving me staring after him in disbelief.

CHAPTER 3

NOLAN

"Fischer, you still got your good luck charm?" Commander Timothy O'Reilly's voice booms as he blows through the open doorway.

"Yes, sir. Always."

"You want a shot at the men that supplied it?"

Ink and the rest of us sit up a little straighter in our chairs. The commander has our full attention. Ink pulls out the resin pendant containing the mangled bullet that had been meant for his head. "Hell, yes, I do."

"I thought you might. Thanks to your lovely and intelligent Dallas, the FBI, ATF, and CIA have gotten a bead on the arms dealer working with those assholes from Chicago that tried to take down this unit. Even though they probably shouldn't have, the Pentagon asked if we wanted in on the takedown. I assumed you would and told them yes.

"There's not much to go on yet. We're in on the ground floor here. All we have at this point is a whisper of a shipment set to be delivered toward the end of this week. To find the next step up the ladder, this team must intercept the delivery and capture the guys making it.

"By itself, this mission won't take us far, but as these things go, each step takes us closer to the top. Your objective here is a simple one. Ambush the shipment, detain the shippers, and destroy the merchandise, minus just enough to be traced back to its origin."

The seventy-five-inch display activates, and a map of our attack zone comes on screen. *Libya.* "Your target will be delivering to an unknown location about five klicks south of Hinshir Kantrar. Being in the mountains, this leg of their journey will have to be slow and careful. Three roads go up that side of the mountain. Two merge about halfway up, and the other joins in just south of the city. I want you positioned at the steepest, narrowest part of the three roads. That's the path these guys'll take, not for fear of being caught by government officials but to avoid being ambushed and ripped off by locals.

"As soon as you capture the shipment, gather samples, set charges, and start back down the mountain. At your command, a non-military bird will be dispatched to a point of your choosing to pick up the detainees. You'll need to ID a secondary zone for your extraction far enough away and later enough to avoid association with the civilian craft."

"Sir," Fish speaks up. "What if locals get to

the couriers before we do?"

"Then yours becomes a rescue mission... temporarily. We need those couriers and a sampling of those guns."

Commander O'Reilly tosses a folder on the table in front of our squad leader, Fish. "Study up, gentlemen. You leave in two days."

The commander walks out, leaving the rest of us looking around at each other. I'm guessing we're all thinking the same thing, but no one dares voice it. *This seems easy. Too easy.*

Lieutenant Christopher "Fish" Hill opens the folder and begins passing out intelligence reports to the various specialists in our group. Dr. Bowie "Bandaid" Myers is given weather reports to aid his provisions calculations. With one eyebrow raised, he studies the information.

Like me, he's probably thinking this should only take a few hours. We shouldn't even need a potty break, but I know the good doctor will be prepared anyway. Every SEAL lives by the same mantra: leave nothing to chance.

Nixon "Wrench" Delano, our resident mechanic and explosives expert, reviews the estimated shipment inventory to determine the amount of explosives needed to destroy it.

Our snipers, Gunner "Devil" Murphy and Tyler "Hawk" Morgan, will be scouting shooting and defensive positions while Hagan "Ink" Fischer and Fish evaluate possible threats from locals.

I glance at Leo "Skin" Ramsay, who was given a chart of the region's topography. Thinking no one is looking, he shrugs a shoulder and drops the paper on the table surface. He shrugs again when he notices me watching. "What? We won't be doing any climbing. The slope is nothing to worry about."

It seems my particular expertise, land navigation, isn't paramount to this op. We aren't going very far. Still, I study the image on the screen, grabbing the control and panning/zooming around the image. Snagging Skin's topo map, I form a 3D image of the surrounding area in my head. I don't consider structures or trees but the lay of the land, natural access points, proximity to inhabited areas, coordinates, and distances to certain geographic formations.

All of it is information we're not likely to need for this mission, but I'll never be accused of being ill-prepared.

The flight to Libya two days later went fast, with our squad splitting the time between sleeping and reviewing the most recent intelligence reports and satellite images of the area. Priority one is to make sure the landing zone for our HALO jump is still clear.

High altitude, low opening insertions would generally be considered excessive caution for a mission as simple as this. But all precautions are being taken because of the importance of achieving a favorable result. No one wants to spook the couriers by coming in on a low-flying military plane.

All mission parameters are re-confirmed by go time to be without obstructions, and we mask up and leap off the jump deck. Feet hit sand three minutes later, and all freefall gear is stowed in place to be retrieved upon extraction. Unless something drastic changes between now and then.

It's pitch black when we start the short hike to the ambush point. So far, there's been no indication that locals are staging a holdup for the weapons delivery, which is excellent news. Even reaching our designated ground zero, we register no signatures bigger than a small mountain goat on our thermal scopes. We move quickly into position and sit in the darkness on the side of the dusty mountain road, waiting for our target to arrive.

Periodically, throughout our long wait, I hear Fish's voice in my earpiece. It sounds like he's communicating with mission support to get status updates. What he reports back to us is that our target is about three hours late, slowed down by the mountain. This is less than ideal.

We're about an hour out from sunrise, and each man is completely blacked out in tactical clothes and face paint. Once the sun rises, we'll stick out like neons under a black light on this sandy mountainside.

As the inky black sky begins to lighten to a dark purple, Hawk's whispered voice carries through my earpiece. "Vehicle on approach. Size is a match for our target."

"It's showtime, boys," Fish announces.

I glance out over the road and can just pick out the tetrahedral road spikes that were fabricated after the design by Adam Savage on Mythbusters. These hollow spikes are painted to match the dirt from this region to be perfectly invisible in the dark. With sunrise beginning to lighten the surface of the road, it's a toss-up as to whether the driver will spot them or not.

If the spikes are made, the driver will likely stop and call for backup. We need the driver completely oblivious to our ambush or be freaking the fuck out past the point of reason.

An old movie I love to watch comes to mind and gives me an idea. In the film, underground monsters find prey using their sensitive hearing. At the end, the main character sets off a bomb behind one of the monsters, sending it racing away from the noise, unknowingly toward its death.

Knowing I'll catch hell for bringing it up, I key over the radio to suggest this strategy to the rest of the team. However, I do not mention anything about the movie. "Wendigo One, we're in danger of the driver spotting the spikes in this light. I suggest we set off an M84 behind them when they're within thirty yards of the spikes.

The blast should engage their flight response and have them looking for danger instead of watching the road."

"This is from that stupid movie, isn't it? How long have you been waiting to use that?" Wrench asks.

"It's a good idea. Let's do it." Fish says and adds, "Wrench, you're in position. Get ready, but wait for my signal."

All SEALs divert their eyes when the flash bang goes off. Just as I'd hoped, the blast gives the couriers the impression that the danger is behind them, and the driver is no longer concerned about slow, careful progress up the mountain. The truck accelerates toward the spikes, and it's only a matter of time before the vehicle is dead on the road.

Within five minutes of the detonation of the M84 grenade, all four men in the truck have been subdued, and Bandaid works to patch up the hole in one of the idiots' legs from their hasty and failed firefight. Wrench walks over and slaps me on the shoulder. "I guess I can't make fun of your taste in movies anymore."

While Fish contacts O'Reilly, Skin, our weapons expert, is checking the crates and pulling one each of the different types of weapons represented. To be thorough, I suggest he also collect some of the ammo.

As soon as we're all clear of the truck, Wrench cracks a big smile. "God, I love my job," he says as he sets a shit ton of C4 in the back of the truck.

"Calm down, asshole. We need to be able to outrun this one," Fish warns him.

All traces of humor leave Wrench as his mind returns to the mission that nearly killed us all last year. I glare at Fish, who seems to regret his choice of words. Wrench quietly wraps up his work, shoves the remote trigger into Fish's hands, and walks away from the truck.

Fish swears under his breath and jogs after our friend. "I'm sorry, Wrench. I was out of line."

Wrench doesn't stop, and Fish gestures toward the prisoners before chasing after him. I speak in Arabic to the couriers, commanding them to move down the road. Ink herds them with me as we all move out of range of the deadly shrapnel.

The ensuing blast is powerful and concussive and will attract the attention of anyone within a five-mile radius. Those outside the Navy monitoring the mission would have picked up the explosion, so we double-time it to the rendezvous point to offload our prisoners. It's a thirty-minute hike to level ground, and we can see the helo coming long before we reach the bottom.

"Well, that was…" Skin begins as the chopper lands a short distance away.

Bandaid quickly interrupts him. "Don't say it."

"But we're done." Skin argues.

"Shut up!" the rest of us yell in unison.

The CIA people out of Khartoum step off the bird to handle the human cargo once we're within thirty yards. One of them approaches to greet us before calling the rest of his associates over. "Nice work, men."

He shakes Fish's hand and hands him a piece of paper. Fish reads it and shoves it in his pocket without comment. Whatever the news, his face gives nothing away. The leader of the transfer team grins. "I'd offer to take you with us, but we're at capacity."

"We've got this," Fish tells him.

The couriers and transfer team load the prisoners and confiscated weapons into the helo, and we back up as the rotors pick up speed to lift off. "We've got what?" I yell over the bird's loud engine.

The next thing I know, Fish pulls the paper from his pocket, wads it up, and throws it at Skin's head. "What we've got is a hell of a long walk."

Skin retrieves the paper and unwraps it, reading the information to himself. "Locusts? What the fuck?"

He looks up to Fish for an explanation. "It seems there's a swarm of locusts making its way east. All non-civilian rotary craft are being recalled and retrofitted with a dispensing system to spray pesticides. We're out a ride back to base."

I quickly go over the maps in my head and calculate our distance. *Damn, Wheelus Air Force Base is nearly eighty miles from here.* I'm sure we won't have to hike the whole distance, but we still have a long way to go on foot. With only one course of action available, we turn north to head back up and over the mountain, as Wheelus is on the other side of the peak near Tripoli.

The start of our journey is an easy one. We've had longer hikes, and the weather isn't complicating our situation. However, it isn't long before we're singing another tune. The eight of us are overtaken by the coming swarm before reaching the top of the small mountain.

It occurs to me that while I've heard the term swarm before, I hadn't given it any real thought. I'm thinking about it plenty now. I mean, shit! I was unprepared to see or feel millions and millions of locusts taking up all available air and ground space. Their density is enough to darken the sky like a partial solar eclipse.

Within minutes of being overtaken by the hoard of bugs, I'm ready to draw and start firing just to see if I can get some relief. Two hours later, I'm having even more explosive thoughts. Apparently, so is Wrench, as he threatens to start throwing out C4 like cherry bombs.

Amid our torment, Devil's low growl is heard in a rare moment of teasing. "Look on the bright side; we've only got to deal with them for another forty-five hours or so."

I look his way and throw up one finger on each hand even though he won't be able to see them. When I do, another fucking bug crawls into my uniform sleeve, and I swear a blue streak that would put Wrench to shame trying to get the damn thing out.

Ink's voice over the radio sounds equally optimistic about our road ahead. "Forty-five hours? Screw that. Skin, I'll give you a hundred bucks if you'll shoot me."

"No way, asshole. If I have to live through this, so do you," he responds.

Near nightfall, Bandaid calls for us to make camp. Because the good doctor is always so careful, we have enough water and food for three days. We stop to set up camp but quickly learn that our efforts are wasted and set out again less than ten minutes later.

With only mylar shelters on hand, there's no flap to close and shut out the storm of insects. Finger-sized grasshoppers crawling all over us means there's no chance of anyone sleeping, so there's no point in stopping for more than a few minutes at a time.

When we do stop for a calorie break, eating or drinking anything has to be done with a towel covering your head, or else you end up with one of the bastards on your food or, worse, in your mouth.

A vicious string of expletives comes from

Fish during one of our stops. We all look his way to see him beating his meat. Everyone immediately knows what happened, but no one laughs. Fish rejoins the group, shaking his head. "I swear to god I'd rather piss in my pants than have those bastards crawling around on my junk again. One of them bit me."

At the sound of laughter in his earpiece, Fish turns to glare at each of us with a homicidal intensity. Now is probably a good time to get moving again. We hike off and on for more than twenty-nine hours straight before we're finally met by a transport truck from Wheelus.

I waste no time closing my eyes once my ass hits that truck. I'm filthy, covered in bug parts, and still in black field paint. Though we're not completely sealed off in here, the bug-to-SEAL ratio is significantly reduced. I get a tickling sensation as one crawls over my leg, but I'm just too tired to care anymore.

When the truck finally rolls to a stop on base, I'm buzzing with the idea of being inside a building where these damn bugs can't get to me, peeling this uniform off, and taking a shower. Food will be next.

Colossal disappointment hits me like a gut punch when the flap is lifted, and I see where we are. "What the hell?"

"This doesn't look promising," Bandaid offers.

"Well, at least we've left the swarm

behind."

Each man reaches over to strangle Skin for jinxing us when an Army lieutenant marches up to us, looking less than impressed at our appearance. Even less so, that we've messed up his schedule. His apathetic greeting bears this out. "Your transport couldn't wait, so they've gone on without you. I have a loaded plane leaving for Norfolk in thirty minutes. There aren't any seats on it, but that's the only ride out this week."

Fish jumps down from the truck without comment and lands beside the self-aggrandizing lieutenant. The rest of us follow our leader and end up surrounding the Army man.

Taking in the sight of eight SEALs towering over his five-foot-five frame, the sniveling little man clears his throat and squares his shoulders.

Fish opens his mouth to speak, and the guy jumps at hearing his voice. "Are there showers in that hangar?"

"Only one, but you don't have time. Your plane leaves in" — he glances down at his watch — "twenty-eight minutes."

He points to a plane about ninety yards away just before jumping into an air-conditioned car and driving off.

"What a dick," Ink says.

Fish shakes his head and blows out a

frustrated breath. "Come on. Let's get the hell out of here."

The conditions on the plane are about what I imagined, not that any of us would complain. The cargo area is full, right up to and blocking the lavatory door. We aren't allowed access to the cockpit facilities for some bullshit reason, so a bucket has been brought on board for us to fill. Yep… a bucket and a roll of butt tickets sit against the fuselage between two eight-foot-tall pallets.

The eight of us are instructed to bunch up in a two-foot aisle for take-off and left alone for the long flight. Cramped in the confined area for take-off, we all turn to glare at Skin for jinxing us. "What? I didn't actually say it."

The plane levels out upon reaching cruising altitude, and we spread out to find any comfort possible in these less-than-ideal conditions. Like the rest of the squad, I strip out of as much uniform as is suitable for the situation. We only have the water we carried for drinking, so there will be no washing off the field paint or bug guts.

Each man finds a spot clear of tie-downs and stretches out to get some sleep. Off and on for the next fifteen hours, I lie in my chosen aisle, in the sweltering heat, leaning against my pack. I eventually strip down to socks, boxers, and t-shirt. When I'm at my lowest, I replay my last conversation with my cousin, Jasper. *"When will you have enough of playing Captain America and return to JAG?"*

I've never been more tempted than I am right now.

The awful flight finally ends at Naval Station Norfolk, where a SeaHawk waits to taxi us to Little Creek. I've pulled my pants and boots back on but haven't even bothered to secure them before walking off the plane that smells of piss since the bucket didn't survive the rough landing. My only regret is that the lieutenant that stuffed us in the plane isn't the one having to clean up the mess.

It's mid-morning when we make the transfer to the Seahawk. The flight was timed right for us to sleep and be awake and ready for the day after landing, but none of us look like we are. I must doze off during the short ride to Little Creek as I'm jarred awake by the helo's landing.

The right-side door slides open, and Commander O'Reilly looks wide-eyed at the shape we're in. "Damn. You guys look like shit. Go home. We'll debrief in the morning," he orders.

Thank god.
We all walk silently to the parking lot, some of us barely remaining vertical during the

trip. I hate getting into my car as filthy as I am, so I strip down to my boxers in the parking lot and change into a clean tee and track pants. I dig some flip-flops out of the spare bag in my trunk. Only a shower will remove the bug parts and face paint, but I don't want to risk passing out on the locker room floors. That means I get to drive home looking like the swamp thing.

I don't remember the drive to Chesapeake, but I somehow make it there safely. I'm nearly to my driveway before noticing the massive moving truck at my only neighbor's house. It looks like Mrs. Kading's house finally sold after being empty for the last five months. I briefly hope whoever is moving in will be decent neighbors, but hell, even if they're not, there's no way they could be as bad as Mrs. Kading.

I ignore the mailbox in favor of a long, hot shower and an eighteen-hour nap. As soon as I've parked in the carport, I kill the engine and climb out of the luxury sedan slowly, dragging my shit on the concrete on the way to the door.

I punch in the code to disengage the lock and start stripping before the door closes behind me. Leaving my filthy uniform and everything else on the mud room floor, I stumble through the house and my bedroom, not stopping until I reach my outdoor shower and turn on the water.

The water heats quickly, and I scrub the

remnants of field paint off my face first. Once the water pouring down my chest runs clear, I go in for my standard head-to-toe wash.

I've just finished scrubbing down and rest my forearms against the wall as the water runs over me. Showering took a lot of energy, and I'm recharging for the short trip to my bed when a feminine voice yelps behind me. "Oh shit!"

Jolted out of my relaxed state, I wrench my head up and locate the intruder. The sight not more than ten feet away is that of a woman's backside who's just copped an eyeful.

I turn the water off, not quite sure I'm in my right mind. Just in case the woman's not a hallucination brought on by exhaustion, I reach for the towel I brought outside, wrapping the soft cotton around my waist. "It's safe to look now," I announce.

The woman slowly turns but doesn't immediately lower her hand from her eyes. Her cheeks are flushed a deep crimson, her reaction making me chuckle. Oddly enough, I'm rather anxious to see the eyes she's currently hiding.

If they're half as gorgeous as the rest of her, I'm in for a treat. "Ma'am, are you going to be ok, or should we switch places?"

That comment draws her head upward and her jaw downward. It would seem that I've shocked the lady. She still has yet to state her purpose for wandering around my house, and I'm more than a little curious. "Is there something I can do for you, Miss?"

Did I imagine it, or did that Miss part sound a little too hopeful?

"Um… your… your…"

The woman shakes her head and diverts her gaze as if looking at me is frying her brain cells. "I am so, so sorry. I saw you drive up and knocked on the front door. When you didn't answer, I thought you might be in the backyard… with clothes on. My name is Iyla. I've moved in next door. I hate to tell you this, but the moving truck just left and took out your mailbox. I don't think they realized it because they didn't stop. I'll call the company to take care of it, but I wanted to bring your mail to you instead of leaving it scattered on the street."

The woman hurriedly side-steps to me, hands over the mail, and turns to rush away. Watching the beautiful woman leave brings on a sudden and powerful urge to stop her. "Iyla!"

Iyla cringes, but she does turn around. "Thank you for gathering my mail. I'm Nolan. Welcome to the neighborhood."

"Thanks."

Iyla hurries away, and I stare after her, not

quite as tired as I was just a short while ago.

ESCAPEPROOF

JO CHAMBLISS

CHAPTER 4

IYLA

Oh my god. My face is on fire as I walk back to my own house. *Naked. He was naked. He was... oh, my god.*

I fan my flaming cheeks, which proves pointless in the warm, spring midday air. What a hell of a way to meet my neighbor. The vision of him leaning against the stone wall, head resting against his raised arms while the water sluices over his muscled back gives me shivers.

There wasn't an ounce of fat on him. The man is Adonis with a perfectly symmetrical face and proportioned body. *And spectacular ass.* I imagine the same scene in my head but in charcoals or watercolor. I'd call it *Supplication.* The moment was so peaceful and reverent I couldn't refer to it any other way.

As I reach the door to what will be my art studio, I consider smacking my head against it. *What am I thinking?! I've got about a million boxes to unpack and a mailbox to replace, and I want to stop and draw my neighbor?*

"Do yer dinger, Iyla. Get your head on

straight."

Having sufficiently chastised myself, I grab my phone and the business card left by the movers, meaning to correct the wrecked mailbox situation. I'm on hold for a manager when I wander to the back deck to make sure there's no chance I can see into that outdoor shower from here.

I'm mildly disappointed to see that I cannot.

Since I'm still on hold, I drift back into the art room and open the first box. I place the call on speakerphone and set it on the table to free my hands and begin unloading the box's contents. First is a stack of sketchbooks for various media and even some handmade paper for unique pieces.

Two more boxes are unloaded while listening to the boring elevator music, and finally, an agent picks up on the line. I explain to the monotone voice about the mailbox, hoping that'll be it. What I get in return is a lot of red tape speak about pictures, claim forms, estimates, ten business days to review, blah, blah, blah. "An adjuster will call you tomorrow to start the process."

Great. I guess I've done all I can for today. For now, I'll put on some music and put a dent in this unpacking.

Ok, priority one. Bedroom. The movers placed all the furniture so I can put everything away as I unpack the boxes. Finishing this room means my clothes are put away, the bed is made, and the bathroom is readied for use. I *should* go to the kitchen next but end up creeping back into the art room.

By the time I'm finished in the studio, it's getting late. I'm fast running out of daylight and steam but nowhere near done. The third most important thing to get set up before bed is coffee. If I don't get that done, I don't have much hope for a good start tomorrow.

I finish the coffee bar, but by then, I'm dragging, too tired even to pick up a late dinner. Rummaging around in my pantry boxes, I find a snack cake and burrow into my sofa and pillows with a cup of coffee for a short break.

My short break turns into a three-hour nap, and I wake around midnight, still on the sofa. I walk to the kitchen, rinse my cup, turn out the lights, ensure the doors and windows are locked, and shuffle down the hall toward my room.

The light is still on in the art room, and I can't help but walk in, picturing Nolan again. Wide awake now, I'm buzzing with excitement to start over in this new place and sit down in front of the light table. I reach up to flip the light on and off again before running my fingers over my drawing table. I open the drawer, select a perfectly pointed 9B lead, and hover the graphite over a clean sheet of paper.

I cannae help where my mind goes, and the strokes on the page soon take the shape of a scene forever imprinted on my brain. From memory, I've sketched the beautiful form of my neighbor as he stood in his outdoor shower. The only change is that Nolan is pictured leaning against a stone wall beneath a small waterfall in a tropical forest.

The sketch is finished a short time later, and I sit back to study the image. An unexpected feeling flashes bright and hot in my body. I thought it might be attraction for a brief moment, but that's not possible. Shaking my head at the craziness of it, I stand and turn off the light.

I climb into bed and sigh into my pillow. Having exercised that urge to draw, I go back to sleep without any fuss.

The next morning, my phone rings before nine. I reach over to the nightstand to grab it, cursing the birth of whoever's interrupting my Saturday morning sleep-in. Instead of retrieving the phone, my hand comes up empty. *Shit! I forgot!* The plug is far enough away that my cord wouldn't reach the nightstand. I jump out of bed to answer the call and don't recognize the number displayed.

"Aye?" I answer just in time.

"Ms. Dunsmore, my name is Charles. You called about mailbox damage?"

"Aye, I did."

I listen to the same spiel about procedure

and approval from this guy and finally get to the point where the man asks for my email address to send the make-or-break claim form. All I need now is to take pictures and get Nolan to fill out the necessary reimbursement information.

Nolan, I like that name. It suits him.

Today being Saturday means he's likely to be home. *And hopefully, he's dressed.*

I take my time having coffee and a bagel before showering. Afterward, I'm halfway through styling my hair when I stop and wonder what I'm doing. I never put this kind of effort into my appearance on a Saturday.

It's because of the neighbor, my inner bitch voice teases. Wanting, no, needing to prove her wrong, I stop mid-styling and pin up my hair like I do before painting. I do, however, fail to resist making one last check in the mirror before walking out my front door.

The printed claim form wrinkles in my clenched hand as I pace over to Nolan's house. "What's the matter with you, Iyla?" I ask myself.

I've never been shy. Maybe I'm still embarrassed by yesterday's unconventional introduction. Straightening my spine, I start up the front steps and ring the bell before I chicken out. Seconds later, footsteps approach the door, and it swings open. "Iyla, come in."

Nolan is wearing gym shorts and nothing else. He's... wow. My mouth dries up at the sight of him. *So much better than yesterday and yet not.*

His muscled abs and chest are on full display, and my lady parts have taken notice. *What the hell* and *Down girl* are two phrases that come to mind as I step inside the clean house.

Nolan closes the door after me and gestures toward the kitchen. "I was in the middle of making coffee. Care for any?"

"Uh… sure."

I follow him through the living room into a modestly sized but well-appointed kitchen. Nolan points to a stool at the bar and continues to the coffee machine. "What can I do for you?"

His muscled back and arms bulge and flex, stealing my attention. I fight to reclaim it by looking away from him to the sleek, black appliances. "The moving company called about the mailbox. I'm supposed to take pictures and have you fill out this form."

I lay the abused paper on the counter and attempt to smooth out the wrinkles. Nolan regards the document with a sneer. "I'm imagining a scenario where they make it so difficult to see action on a claim or such a long wait for compensation that most people give up in frustration. For the sake of yours and my collective sanities, I'll just go down to the hardware store and pick up a new mailbox."

"I hate for you to have to do that. I want to pay for it at least."

The man smirks at me, raising the temperature in the room a few degrees. *Or maybe it's just my skin heating.* "Why? Did you run it down?"

"No, but neither did you. Could I at least help you put in the new one?"

His answering smile is devastating. "Sure."

Nolan sets down a steaming mug of coffee in front of me and slides a tray of sugar and flavorings over as well. As I stir my coffee, I study the man's face to keep from staring at his bare chest. "How long have you lived here?" I ask.

"I bought the place about seven years ago. I've been in this area for the last nine. What about you? Where was home before this?"

"I was in Asheville for the last four months on a job. Before that, was Miami for several years."

My eyes find his chiseled abs again, and instead of doing the smart thing of excusing myself and walking away, I open my big mouth and stick my foot in it. "So, Nolan, what do you do when you're not showering in the great outdoors?"

Nolan laughs heartily. "On my slow days, I'm a lawyer."

"Slow days? Wow, I'd hate to see what your crunch days look like."

He doesn't clue me in. Nolan smiles coyly and asks more about me. "What was the job that had you in North Carolina for four months?"

"I'm an artist. The Biltmore Estate

commissioned me to do several marketing paintings for them."

"That's... impressive," he says, sounding surprised and intrigued. "And your accent?"

"My parents are Scottish. They moved to America before I was born. Growing up on American TV and in American schools made my accent less pronounced than theirs, but it can get that way if I'm mad enough."

My hands and my panties dampen at the smile that lights his face. "I'd almost like to see that."

NOLAN

Iyla and I talk for a while longer, keeping to safe, we-just-met topics. The musical quality of her voice and accent are soothing. I could listen to her talk all day. Sadly, we both run out of coffee and naturally gravitate toward the front door to continue our separate day's activities.

On the front porch, Iyla turns and offers her hand to me. "It's nice to meet you, Nolan."

With a grin, I take her hand in mine, and we shake. "Same to you, Iyla."

She releases my hand slowly and moves toward the stairs, stopping halfway down to add something else. "I was serious about helping you put in the new mailbox."

"Understood."

Iyla continues down the front walk, and I lean against the door frame and watch her go. *I think I'm going to like this new neighbor.*

Only when Iyla has disappeared around the front corner do I push off the frame and close the door. On my way back to the kitchen, I reach behind the sofa cushion for the t-shirt I took off when I saw her through the peephole.

I'm not usually an exhibitionist like Skin, but I wanted to see if her reaction to me would be the same today as it was yesterday. It most definitely was, even if she was trying her best not to show it.

It's nice to be appreciated.

Standing in the kitchen, I stretch my arms over my head while going over the day's to-do list. *Replacement mailbox, check on the status of my back-ordered patio tiles, and cook-out at Fish's place tonight.*

The mailbox acquisition is easy enough, even if the post barely fits in my car and the bag of cement leaves dust in my trunk. My last stop is to the landscape company, where I learn that my tiles still don't have a delivery date.

That bit of news makes me less than happy. I've got the stash leftover from the initial installation, but that's not enough to replace what was damaged by that al-Shabaab asshole's grenade.

Now that all errands are completed, I make my way back home. I could install the mailbox in just a few minutes, but if Iyla plans to help, I want to take my time on the job. That leaves me with only getting ready for tonight's cookout.

Evening eventually rolls around, and I leave for Fish's house, stopping on the way to pick up several bags of chips. Fish's daughter, Ari, meets me at the door when I arrive, tapping her foot in mock irritation. "Uncle Judge, you're late."

"I know. I forgot your favorite chips and had to go back."

She grabs her chin, scrunches her face, and looks up at the ceiling in thought. After a moment, she smiles and says, "I guess that makes it ok, then."

She takes hold of my free hand and drags me to the back deck. The men are razzing Skin to the women about how he jinxed us, causing the swarm of locusts. He takes the ribbing good-naturedly because what else is he going to do?

The food and company are fantastic as usual, and the team gathers for a private moment to observe our usual post-mission toast ritual. Later, when the women migrate inside to talk and rock babies to sleep, we sit around the firepit nursing longneck beers. The night is cool for late April, and the fire is pleasantly warm. All in all, it turned out to be a great evening.

"Hey, Judge," Skin calls out. "Is that house next to yours still available?"

"Sorry, man. Someone moved in just yesterday. Why do you ask?"

"I'm getting tired of apartment living. I want to start looking for a place of my own."

Devil leans in and says, "Well, well, Fish. It seems Skin is finally growing up."

Skin offers Devil both his middle fingers in response. *Well, maybe not.* "I'm sorry, man. I didn't know anyone had bought the place or that you were looking."

"It's no big deal. Call it a recent development."

Having had a run-in with my crazy neighbor, Bandaid asks, "What are the new neighbors like? Not like devil-woman, are they?"

"Not neighbors, just neighbor. She's cool."

Wrench leans in, intending to press me for more information. "She? Do tell."

"She's got this soft Scottish accent..." I drop my head and laugh, remembering the first time I heard it, *oh shit!*

"What's so funny?" Fish asks.

"We met yesterday morning a few minutes after I got home. I was showering when she walked over to tell me the movers took out my mailbox."

My friends don't understand what's so spectacular about that, so I tell them. "I was in the *outdoor* shower."

As one, the men start howling, imagining the scene. As expected, they start cracking jokes, the worst being from Wrench and involving the phrase half-mast.

Ink taps his beer against my knee and says, "You look like you might want to go for it."

"I won't lie. I'm certainly interested."

Willa walks out of the back door at that moment, carrying a basket of brownies. *That gives me an idea.* A quick glance at my watch says I've got time. I drain the last of my beer and jump out of my seat. "Gentlemen, I've got to run."

I grab a brownie from the basket and kiss Willa's cheek on my way out. "Thanks, Willa!"

"Bye, Nolan," she calls.

On the way home, I stop by Target and grab a basket, cookie mix, cleaning supplies, and some other convenience stuff. As soon as I pull into my carport, I rush inside to assemble the housewarming basket and bake cookies, hoping Iyla doesn't have some weird allergy to sugary sweets.

Sunday morning can't come quickly enough. I'm dressed and pacing the floor, waiting for ten a.m. to roll around before I'll let myself walk over to Iyla's house. Realizing what I'm doing, I laugh at myself for being nervous about making a move on my sexy neighbor.

Iyla answers quickly when I knock on the door, and her eyes widen when she notices the large, full basket. "Welcome to the neighborhood!"

She laughs and moves out of the way so I can step inside. "You didn't have to do that."

"I know, but after our first meeting, I

figured we needed a do-over."

I set the basket on the sofa table and look around the furnished but otherwise bare room. "You know, this is the first time I've ever seen the inside of this house before."

"Really?" she asks, surprised.

"Yeah. The previous owner was the spawn of Satan. I probably wouldn't have come over if the house was on fire."

"Ouch. Remind me not to get on your bad side."

"Don't worry," I say with a chuckle. "If Mrs. Kading is the threshold, you've got nothing to be concerned about."

I spot some big boxes near the wall and decide to offer my services. "You getting settled in all right?"

She bobs her head and shrugs. "Working on it. Moving has been more of a whirlwind process than I'm used to."

Tempted to cross my fingers, I ask, "Could you use a little extra muscle?"

"Who am I to turn down such a generous offer?"

The two of us get to work moving and unpacking, and by evening, we've emptied all but the small containers. "You're rather handy to have around."

"You have no idea."

Iyla gets a funny look at my strange statement. She doesn't know if she's supposed to laugh or ask what I mean. She decides on silence, and I suddenly feel guilty about not telling her what I really am. A heavy weight settles in my stomach like I'm lying to her.

I do my best to shake off the feeling and grab a small box as a means of distraction. When that one is empty, Iyla dusts her hands off and places them on her hips. "That's enough for today. For all your musclebound help, I'd like to offer you dinner as a thank you. However, the best I can offer you is pizza."

"Pizza sounds perfect."

While we wait for delivery, the two of us sit down with a beer, talking and laughing. The woman is so laid back and comfortable with herself that I can't help but be drawn to her. Her crazy mane of brown hair that's precariously tied on top of her head and her big blue eyes don't hurt either.

Iyla may be dusty, messy, and have paint under her short fingernails, but she has the graceful body of a ballerina. The mystifying thing about her is that she doesn't seem to comprehend her effect on people. Or maybe she's used to going unnoticed.

I most definitely see her. And the more time I spend with Iyla, the more I want her.

I'm just about to ask her out when the delivery guy shows up, stealing my chance. The young driver is relieved of his cargo, tipped, and sent on his way, and the two of us sit down with a stack of napkins and two more beers.

Iyla and I scarf down the pizza as if it's the best meal we've ever had. It's refreshing to be with a woman who doesn't carefully calculate every move she makes in front of a man. Iyla is a free spirit on her own path, and in a short time, it's become abundantly clear that the rest of humanity is invited to either come along or stay out of her way.

After the pizza and beer are gone, the atmosphere suddenly changes. Work is done for the day, and Iyla and I sit quietly in the fading light. Actually, Iyla is quiet, and the more time passes, the more tense I notice she's becoming. I wonder what I did wrong to bring about this change in her, but nothing comes to mind.

Worried about upsetting her and not wanting to wear out my welcome, I decide it's time to go before she asks me to leave. "Well, thanks for dinner. I'll bet you're pretty tired and could use some rest. I'll see you later."

Iyla doesn't object to my leaving relatively early. This prompts a deeper evaluation of what I'd done during the evening to upset her. During the short walk home, I go through our conversations to see if I can pinpoint the moment her behavior started to change. Unable to figure it out, I abandon the retrospection for a quick shower and early bedtime.

The next day, PT and SEAL training are typical for a Monday morning, given that we're designated for administrative support roles for the time being. Having just completed a mission, we're out of rotation for a while and will assist with or run training for other SEAL squads and platoons working up for their upcoming deployments.

I'm back home by three and figure it's time to install the new mailbox before the postmaster gets up in arms. Despite her insistence on helping, after last night's awkwardness with Iyla, I start the project on my own.

I've dug out the broken post and have just begun cleaning out the hole with my posthole digger when Iyla walks down wearing work clothes and carrying a thermos and two plastic cups. "Lemonade?"

Unsure of my footing with her, I work to keep my attention on my task without alienating my new neighbor. "Sure."

Iyla works beside me in the dirt with a cool detachment at odds with how she looked at me on her second day here. She's not at all unfriendly, but there haven't been any more prolonged looks, no incidental touches, or unnecessary closeness.

It's obvious that we enjoy each other's company, but today, our interactions are entirely platonic. *So, she's not interested like I thought.* The realization is disappointing. Regardless, Iyla is a pleasant neighbor, and it appears I'll have to be okay with that being the extent of things.

Working as a team, we lower the post into the hole, and Iyla holds it upright while I place the cement. The job is done in no time, and we fist bump to our success before retreating to our respective homes.

Damn.

ESCAPEPROOF

JO CHAMBLISS

CHAPTER 5

CRACK!

The loud sound startles me out of my client research, making me jump and run to the front window. It's Nolan. As I watch, he takes a few more swings at the broken mailbox post to loosen it from the ground. *Well, you promised to help him install the new one.*

I hesitate a moment, thinking about last night. The day spent with Nolan had been so very comfortable. We shared easy banter and friendly teasing, and Nolan began innocently flirting.

That was the problem.

I'm not ready.

Sighing, I glance down at the still-pale sliver of skin on my ring finger and look away just as quickly. *Five months to the day.*

Five months since I was left standing at the altar by a man who couldn't face me to say he didn't want to marry me after all. Five months since I decided to take the Asheville job and made arrangements to leave Miami for good.

I had promised everything to Trevor, and

he didn't want it. Call me gun-shy, but I'm not ready to be in a relationship again, not with my trust issues. Last night, I couldn't reciprocate Nolan's flirting and started pulling away so things wouldn't progress further. *And so I wouldn't lose another friend.* My aloofness ultimately chased him out anyway, and Nolan went home.

Watching him withdraw last night, I almost told him about my past but stopped myself. That's my private humiliation and something I don't wish to be common knowledge.

Still, the memory of Dillan's back as he angrily left the balcony makes me worry that I'll go through the same thing with Nolan. *I won't let that happen.* He's no casual acquaintance; he's my neighbor, and I want to be his friend. I just need to make sure he sees that's all we can be.

The best way to do that is to suck it up and get out there to do as I promised. After changing into some junky clothes, I pour some lemonade into a thermos and set off toward the road.

Nolan is welcoming and friendly, much to my relief, and together, we complete the job without any residual awkwardness from yesterday.

Over the next three weeks, Nolan and I develop a comfortable existence. The two of us hang out occasionally, sometimes having dinner at his place and sometimes at mine. I've pitched in to help him remove some tile in his patio damaged by a fire of some unknown cause, and he's helped me trim some overzealous shrubs around my house.

Having rented one place or another all my adult life, I've got a lot to learn about home and yard maintenance, and Nolan, so far, is a patient teacher.

He hasn't flirted anymore since the pizza dinner, so I've been able to relax and invest in the developing friendship, knowing he won't make a move.

One day, things will change. My heart will no longer be a fragile thing, and I'll be ready to love again. For now, having a safe friend while I heal and put my shattered heart back together is nice.

During all this almost-drama, my work continues as if my location hasn't changed. I paint or draw every day, some for clients, some to sell, and some for myself.

Those I create for myself are mostly of… Nolan, his form, his face. I've never had a better human subject. Ok, he's hot. There's no denying that. Drawing and painting him is no hardship. Besides his beautiful body, his eyes hide a mystery that draws me in like a moth to a flame. My mind begs to solve that mystery and is convinced that Nolan's secret will reveal itself if I sketch and paint him enough. *Or this could just be your outlet since you are attracted to him but fighting it.*

I scoff at the thought. *Not possible. Not so soon after…*

It's time to put that line of thinking to rest, and it's time for breakfast and the day's work. After coffee, I check my site and see that a few of my newer pieces have sold and pack them for shipping. Next, I check the latest message in a thread with my new client, an experimental coffee grower facing high demand. In response to their explosive growth, they're in a rush to develop formal, artistic branding. Negotiations over work and payment have been agreed upon, and they're ready to set up details for my visit.

At least their timing is good. I've settled into my new place, and closing will take place in two days. The plan for the trip is to fly from Virginia to Santa Barbara to photograph and paint the coffee plants growing beneath an avocado grove. Provided they don't use a particular class of pesticides on their plants. I've learned that it's impossible to work while having an asthma attack.

One thing I don't worry about is any deliveries I'm supposed to receive while I'm gone. In all my previous living situations, I'd have to call the post office to pause mail service and adjust regular shipments to avoid losing them to porch pirates. But now that I'm living in a house with an actual mailbox and a good neighbor, I'll ask Nolan to collect my mail for me.

It's just past two, and I'm in the living room setting out pictures when I hear his sedan rolling up the driveway. *He keeps strange hours for a lawyer.* Having awoken early a few mornings since moving in, more than once, I've noticed him leaving home around four-thirty a.m. *With a body like that, he has to be going to the gym.*

I haven't figured out why he sometimes comes home so early. In all the TV law shows I've seen, lawyers are the most workaholic people out there. I should ask Nolan more about his law practice sometime. I don't even know what area of law he practices.

After about an hour or so of Nolan being home, I walk over to his house and ring the bell. Nolan answers the door, and my eyes widen at his battered appearance. "What happened to you?"

He looks like he lost a fight—with more than one guy. A dark bruise covers one cheek, and scratches dot his jaw. "It's nothing. Just some light contact during a sparring match."

"Sparring? Is that part of your workout regimen?"

"More or less," he answers cryptically.

He motions for me to enter and closes the door behind me. "I thought people wore protective gear during training matches so that sort of thing wouldn't happen."

Nolan doesn't answer right away, and I get the idea he's not entirely comfortable with this line of questioning. *What's that about?* "Accidents do happen," he offers.

Seeing his discomfort, I decide the safest thing to do is change the subject. "I have to go out of town for a job on Wednesday. Would you mind collecting my mail until I get back Monday?"

"I can do that."

"Thanks. Now, let's get some ice on that cheek."

NOLAN

Iyla orders me to the sofa while she goes to the kitchen to make up an ice pack. She's offering to care for my bruises while the real explanation for my battered face remains unspoken. Suddenly, the real life I've hidden from her sits like lead in my gut, making me feel guilty as hell for keeping the truth from her.

Hiding my job as a SEAL from Iyla is expected of me, but concealing my career in the Navy doesn't make sense. *Maybe you were more concerned about impressing her than being honest.*

Iyla comes back and leans over me, gently pressing the towel-wrapped ice pack to my head. As she does, I breathe in her scent, a hint of vanilla, something floral, but mostly Iyla. She's close enough that the heat from her skin warms my face. I want her so bad, but I can't let on or even allow my breath to catch, though her nearness threatens to steal it away.

One wrong move, and Iyla will clam up.

I've yet to figure out why, but since the night we hung out after clearing boxes, Iyla's been genuinely friendly but somewhat distant. My thoughts turn bitter as I wonder why it is that I finally find a woman that stirs me, and she's as closed off as Fort Knox.

I suffer through Iyla's gentle care as she inspects the damage, but before long, her tender touches torment me with traces of what I can't have. I clear my throat, and Iyla wakes from her trance and shuffles away from me, embarrassed. "Um… I guess I should leave so you can get some rest. I'll see you when I get back from California."

"Goodbye, Iyla."

She smiles sadly and walks out of my house, taking all the air with her. I watch her through the front windows, and my goodbye sits heavy on my chest. Final. No, she's not moving away, but I'm finally accepting that I won't be making her mine. The realization has my heart breaking a little.

Pulling the ice from my face, I stand and walk to the kitchen to place the bag in the sink. What I need is some physical labor to distract me. Fortunately, my new tile came in yesterday, so I've got plenty to do. I get changed into some work clothes and walk out to get started on the patio repair.

The job takes the rest of the afternoon and the next to complete. During the process, I find several grenade fragments left from that asshole's attempt to kill my team. *I'm so tired of all this shit happening to us at home, to our families.*

Once more, it crosses my mind to transfer back to the JAG office, but again, I push the thought away. If this shit is going to keep happening to my family, I damn well want to be there to fight for them.

I take a moment to admire the restored patio and toss the empty boxes and construction trash in the large bin on the side of the house. Now that this job is done, I walk around the front to check the mail. Things with Iyla may or may not return to the comfortable condition of a few weeks ago, but I'm determined to be someone she can count on.

My box contains only junk mail, as most of my bills and legitimate correspondence come digitally. As I cross our two driveways to Iyla's box, a county sheriff's car rolls slowly up the road. *That's odd.*

I wave at the officer to appear friendly and continue on my mission. The car pulls alongside me and stops. He might have an opinion of me pulling mail from both boxes, but I dismiss the concern as stupid and turn to see what he wants.

"Good afternoon, sir," he offers in greeting.

I tip my chin and answer, "Deputy. Is there something I can do for you?"

The blonde officer smiles. "No, sir. I'm just learning the area. I moved here recently and joined the force. While things are slow, I figure I should become familiar with the territory."

"That's not a bad idea. Welcome. It's pretty quiet around here. All the action usually happens in the Virginia Beach area. We occasionally have our share of drunk and disorderly, but nothing more serious than that."

"Good to know. You lived here long?"

"Seven years."

Looking behind me, he asks, "Which place is yours?"

I point to my house with the stone front. "This is me. There aren't many houses within two miles."

Pointing to Iyla's house, I add, "I've got just one neighbor here, and there's one about two miles behind me on a lake."

"Good people?"

"Good enough. The Matthews are older and live alone as their kids are all grown and gone. The neighbor next door just moved in not a month ago. She's nice."

"What about you? Do you have family with you?"

"Nope. It's just me."

"Why just the two random houses if everything else is so spread out?"

The question is unexpected but not unusual for a cop learning his beat. "The story I was told is that all this land, including the farm behind us, belonged to the Rickshaw family. The two sons hated each other and fought over this area. Mr. Rickshaw died, leaving the big farm to his daughter and split four acres between his sons. They built houses close to the property line to piss each other off. Now, they're both dead, and here we are."

"Men don't like to give up what they see as rightfully theirs, money, land…, or women."

His statement is an odd one, so I don't offer any reply.

"You have a good afternoon, Mr. …."

"Lockmore. Nolan Lockmore."

"Mr. Lockmore."

The deputy drives away without introducing himself, but not before I catch the name on his shiny nametag. *Broderick.* With the odd exchange over, I finish gathering the mail and walk back up my driveway, wondering about the cop. *A policeman doing recon on his beat. I don't know how common it is, but it seems wise.* My curiosity is satisfied, so Iyla's mail gets added to the basket with yesterday's delivery, and I head out back to get a shower.

Dinner that night is a simple shrimp sauté with vegetables and garlic butter. The dish is one of my favorites to prepare, but tonight, it's lacking its usual appeal.

It's because of the quiet.

Iyla and I hadn't spent every evening together, but we'd done it enough that two nights without her company is strange and unsettling. I do my best to put it out of my mind but go to bed early when my attempts to focus elsewhere fail.

"You and the new neighbor still getting along?" Ink asks the following morning.

"Yeah. Why?"

Walking to the gym, he takes a few more steps before answering, "No reason. You haven't spoken about her for a couple of days, that's all."

"She's out of town until Monday for some client meeting in California."

"Oh. Have you talked to her since she left?"

His question halts my steps. "Hey, what is this?" I ask a little more brusquely than necessary.

Ink steps back and puts his hands up. "Whoa, mate. Hostilities are not needed. I won't ask you any more questions." He leans in and whispers, "I just thought the two of you were getting along, and…"

"And what? That it might be my turn? That Iyla and I would fall in love and get married just like that?"

Ink stares at me, baffled by my sudden outburst. "I didn't think anything. I was only happy that you seemed happy with her."

I blow out a harsh breath and run a hand over my head. "I'm sorry, Ink. I *was* happy and was rushing things until she shut me down. The truth is that I don't know what happened. We were friendly and getting close, then bam. She backed off. I've been driving myself crazy trying to figure out what I did wrong."

"Maybe *you* didn't *do* anything. Give it some time. You're smart. You'll figure it out."

"Sure," I answer indolently.

The rest of the day passes in a blur, and I drive home as much in a funk as I was this morning. That all changes when I see Jasper leaning against his bumper in my driveway.

I park and get out, joining my cousin at the back of his ride. Jasper is in his Class A's as if he's just come from court. "You dress up like this for me?"

Jasper shakes his head and my offered hand before pulling me in for a man hug. "Sure thing, princess. You got any good beer?"

I give his back a slap and straighten up again but don't answer his question, my attention having been caught by the patrol car rolling slowly down the street. It looks as if it drove to the dead end and turned around.

"Nolan, beer?"

A finger snaps in front of my face, and I turn back to my cousin. "Uh… beer, yeah."

"You SEAL types check out like that often?"

Rolling my eyes, I answer, "I was watching the cop rolling down the street."

"Is he looking for you or that crazy-ass neighbor you used to have?"

Looking for someone? Iyla? Surely not.

As odd as it is for the police car to be

rolling down our remote and almost empty street, I dismiss Jasper's joke and the fleeting thought I had afterward.

Monday rolls around again after the boring weekend with my team being assigned for work-up. For the first time in a long while, we've finally caught a mission in our designated zone, Europe. We're targeting the same organization that was the focus of our last mission. This time, our target is on the water. It's another boat being used to smuggle weapons, the *Golden Clam.*

Commander O'Reilly is working on obtaining schematics for the specific model boat listed in the intelligence briefing. Like search and seizure missions before this one, he makes sure we have floor plans to study. If this boat is not a custom job, he'll be working on obtaining a vessel of the same model for boarding drills and identifying locations for possible smuggling stashes in the hull.

Once all the current details are discussed, we're dismissed for the day, and the team walks from the briefing room toward the parking lot to go home. Knowing Iyla's coming home today, I sort of rush out of the building, anxious to see her. As fate would have it, I get a text from her as I walk to my car.

I just made it back. If you don't have plans, dinner is on me for helping me out.

If I weren't a glutton for punishment, I'd reply that feeding me isn't necessary for walking an extra thirty feet each day. I won't tell her that, though. The truth is… I've missed her.

The easy way she has, her messy buns, and even her fingernails spattered with all the colors under the sun have become part of my life. With Iyla gone, for the first time since moving into my house, I've felt lonely.

Holding my phone up, I tap out, *Sure thing. Be home in a bit.*

CHAPTER 6

NOLAN

I lean on the gas peddle more than I should, wanting to get home and over to Iyla's house as soon as possible.

As I slow down to turn onto my street, the nose of a police cruiser comes into view. *Again?* The car pulls out onto the highway without any fanfare, so I continue to my driveway. Upon seeing the police car again, I'm haunted by Jasper's jokingly uttered words. *Is he looking for you or your neighbor?* The thought gives me pause, making me wonder about the woman next door.

What do I really know about Iyla? She says she's Scottish, the accent bearing that out. She also said she went from Miami to Asheville for a few months before buying Mrs. Kading's house without even checking the place out in person.

Since Iyla closed on the house just before she left for California, the house hadn't transferred ownership until then. I don't know any of Mrs. Kading's family, so I have no way to ask about the situation. I could call the realtor I'd seen a few times out front, but there's too much of a risk that Iyla could find out I've been checking into her.

Regardless of my desire to make Iyla mine, the gnawing feeling has taken root and won't be silent. What if the woman is in some kind of trouble? What if Iyla *is* some kind of trouble?

Dammit, Nolan, you're not wrong about Iyla. You've never misjudged a character. Even your team relies on your gut instinct when it comes to reading people.

If more is going on here, it has to be that Iyla is running from something or someone. There's no way she's a criminal. *Or it could be that your attraction to her is a crippling bias, and you refuse to consider the possibility.*

To be safe, I take a moment when I get inside to call a professional acquaintance, a Virginia Beach Police Department detective, Evan Bassett. If there's something I need to know, he'll tell me.

I met Detective Evan Bassett first when some stateside asshole tried to kill Devil. At one point, the detective and I were even on opposite sides during an investigation of Wrench, for which he was ultimately acquitted. The seasoned cop's a straight arrow and has the respect of each man on my team, including our commander. All of us even helped find a friend of his that went missing. Now, I need a favor.

"Detective Bassett here."

"Evan, Nolan Lockmore."

The seasoned cop waits for a breath before responding. I can't blame him. Contact with one of us usually means trouble. "Judge. What can I do for you?"

"I have a new neighbor that the local sheriff's office has taken quite an interest in. I'd like to find out if there's anything I should know about her. As a SEAL, any action I'm forced to take in self-defense would put my commander in a tough position."

Yeah, that last part was laying it on pretty thick, but I need answers.

"Name?"

"Iyla Dunsmore, previously of Asheville, North Carolina, Miami, and Colorado."

I rattle off her current address and hear the detective banging away at his keyboard. Thankfully, I've caught him at the precinct.

"That was fast," he declares after only a few seconds.

"What?"

"The lady has no record, aliases, or even an outstanding parking ticket."

"Sounds too clean."

"Normally, I'd agree, but we have records from birth, including one of those kidnap fingerprint kits her parents did when she was a kid. She's either Mother Theresa-clean or the best criminal I've never heard of. And you say County is watching her?"

"It's possible that it's just one deputy. He

says he's new to the area and has been riding around learning the lay of the land, though he's ridden down my two-house street at least three times this week."

"I'll admit that sounds odd, but there isn't anything I can see here that would have anyone looking at Dunsmore. And before you ask, I'd have no justification to inquire about another county's activities. What I can do is alert you if something comes up, provided it's within the law for me to do so."

"Understood, and I appreciate it."

I place the phone on the table, even more puzzled than before. *If it's not Iyla, then what?*

Searching my memory, I can confidently say that I've identified the same policeman driving by our houses two out of three times. The third time, I didn't get a good look at the driver. His overzealous exploration could be nothing more than what he said, unlikely as it now sounds.

Iyla, however, not having a record isn't concrete proof that she isn't or hasn't been into something. It's just as likely that she was involved in something dark and has escaped that life.

There's really only one way to find out. Ask.

I start toward my room to change out of my uniform and realize how ridiculous my plan sounds. Stopping in the hallway, I lean against the wall to think. If Iyla is a criminal, I'd know it by now. On the other hand, if she is running from something, asking point-blank will scare her. The best thing I can do is open up to her about the life I'm hiding to show that I trust her. Maybe then, Iyla will be comfortable enough to do the same.

Looking down at my uniform, I decide that's the best place to start. I grab Iyla's mail and march right out the front door. After reaching her porch, I ring the bell and look across the field on the other side of the street. A moment later, the door opens behind me, and Iyla asks in a small voice, "Can I help you?"

I turn to face her, and Iyla's eyes widen in shock. "Nolan? What... why are you dressed like that?"

I shrug guiltily. "Because this is who I am."

Her eyes travel over the uniform patches before returning to my face. "I don't understand."

"Iyla, could I talk to you?"

Her brows are still knit tightly, but she answers, "Of course. Come in."

I walk through the door, placing the mail on the entry table. Iyla leads the way into her living room and curls up into what I've learned is her favorite chair. With her eyes still wide, she again studies the uniform and quietly waits for me to speak what's on my mind.

"Iyla, I'd like to think we know each other well enough to trust one another."

Nothing in her face screams *retreat*, which surprises me a little for someone who could be in hiding. "I didn't lie to you when I told you I'm a lawyer, but I did leave something out. I'm in the Navy."

"So, you're a Navy lawyer like on TV?"

I shake my head. "No, I used to be. Now, I'm a Navy SEAL."

She stares at me, confused for a moment. "I don't understand."

"Don't understand what?"

"It's just that... I don't know much about SEALs, but I've learned enough from movies to know that being a SEAL isn't something that's openly shared. I fully appreciate the significance of what you're telling me. It means a lot that you would entrust me with something so important. What I don't understand is *why* you're telling me. Or rather, why you're telling me now."

Now, it's my turn to be stunned. Though a good lawyer, I've failed to think through the possible outcomes of this conversation. Iyla's behavior is entirely at odds with what I was expecting. *What did you expect, counselor? That you'd make your grand speech, and she'd spill all her deepest, darkest secrets?*

Damn. I think long and hard about the woman I've gotten to know over the last few weeks. I was wrong. Jasper's flippant comment got into my head and led me somewhere I shouldn't have gone. Iyla isn't running from someone or hiding anything.

So, what the hell is going on here?

Thrown by my complete failure to evaluate the situation correctly, I miss Iyla's first attempts to get my attention. It isn't until she's moved and touches my arm that I finally look up. "Nolan, what is it?"

Staring into her concerned eyes, I mutter, "I just wanted you to know."

She sits down beside me but doesn't break contact. "Ok."

Her eyes urge me to continue, but there isn't much more I can say. "There will be times I disappear for days or weeks without warning. I don't want you to be alarmed."

Iyla picks up my hand and holds it between hers. "Thank you for telling me. I would have worried."

My gaze drops to our joined hands, and Iyla lets go suddenly. The moment turns awkward, and we're both silent.

IYLA

I draw my hands back to my lap, angry that I keep crossing the line with Nolan. Yes, he told me something very important and private to him, but how can I expect someone to respect the boundaries I set if I'm the one who keeps breaking them?

The uncomfortable silence stretches until Nolan stands abruptly. I want to stop and ask him to stay and talk for a while, but the words stick in my throat. I follow wordlessly behind Nolan as he walks out the door. At the bottom of the stairs, he stops and turns around. "I hope you know that you can trust me."

His whispered words sounded almost desperate. Like a vow, I promise, "I do, Nolan."

He turns suddenly and disappears around the house a moment later. For several long minutes, I'm left staring at the space he no longer occupies. *God, I'm making a mess of things here.* I feel too much for Nolan, and it scares me. Because of it, I keep pushing him away after being the one that got too close.

I'm hurting my one friend here by being a coward, and I don't know how to stop it. *Yes, you do. Tell him.* I hang my head for a moment and go back inside to unpack my suitcase, too much of a coward to show Nolan the same courtesy.

After sundown, I step out onto my back deck for some fresh air. From here, I can see the glow of a fire in Nolan's fire pit. Deciding it's time to show some courage, I go back inside and grab supplies to make s'mores, pulling on my boots once I step outside again.

Nolan looks up but doesn't speak as I approach. "You up for some company?" I ask as I hold up the bag of marshmallows.

His smile doesn't reach his eyes when he says, "Sure. Have a seat."

We both jab a couple of white puffs onto the sticks and hold them over the fire, ignoring the crackers and chocolate. After we've each eaten two, Nolan looks at me and smiles. He reaches a finger toward my face, but then his smile drops at the same time his hand does. "You have a little cream on your chin."

I find and wipe away the sticky mallow cream and watch the fire. I'm searching for the courage to speak. Eventually, I put down the grill stick I'm using as a crutch and take a deep breath. "I thought about what you said today. I know I've closed myself off and left you confused. You don't deserve that, and I'm sorry. You've become a treasured friend, and I don't want to ruin that by sending mixed signals and pushing you away.

"Six months ago, I was standing in front of a mirror wearing a beautiful white gown in a little chapel, waiting to get married, when my father came in to tell me that my fiancé wasn't coming. Trevor is an artist like me. We had plenty in common, shared friends, and got along with each other's families. We had known each other for years before dating and had been engaged for nine months before the wedding day. Not once in all that time did he say he had doubts."

"What did he tell you was the reason?"

I snort inelegantly. "He didn't. There was a letter on my doorstep when I went back home. I've never read it, and we haven't spoken. Since then, I've not allowed myself to get close to a man. I can't."

I search Nolan's gaze and silently beg him to understand what I don't want to say. *Please don't ask for what I can't give.*

The heaviness on Nolan's shoulders lifts as though I relieved him of a great burden. His face softens, and he smiles. "Iyla, I'm glad you told me. You are one of the most amazing women I've ever met and a good friend. I wouldn't jeopardize that for any reason."

With the air now clear between us, Nolan places his hand over mine, and I don't feel the urge to pull away. Mesmerized by the warmth he provides, I study his strong, scarred hand until he lifts my chin to focus on his face once again. "One day, you will be whole again and able to give your heart fully to someone. I also believe that you and I have the capacity to be more to each other someday. Just know that until then, or even if that day never comes between us, I like having you in my world however you want to be there."

His words are a salve to my frayed soul, and I place my other hand on top of his. My head comes to rest on his shoulder, and the two of us sit in the dark and watch the flames for a while longer.

When the fire reduces to glowing embers, I decide it's time to return home. Nolan stands, offers me his hand, and pulls me into the best hug since… well, in a long time. "Sweet dreams, Iyla."

"Goodnight, Nolan."

Aided by the landscape lights, I make the short walk back home feeling buoyant and more relaxed than I have in months. I don't have to hide from Nolan anymore. That is a great weight off my shoulders.

Feeling oddly energized after spilling my guts to a friend, I wander to the studio and turn on the lights. Tonight was a beautiful moment, and I want to eternalize it on paper. My long hair goes up, and a fresh sheet of paper is placed on the drawing table. I pour my emotions out on the paper stroke by stroke until Nolan's face appears, smiling by the dancing flames.

It's well into midnight when I put the pencil down and apply fixative to the image. *You will be whole again.* Nolan's voice echoes in my head as I place his portrait with the others I've drawn of him.

ESCAPEPROOF

.

.

JO CHAMBLISS

CHAPTER 7

IYLA

Morning comes early for me and brings an energy and lightness I haven't experienced in a long time. For the first time since moving here, I want to get out and explore my new home. I want to see the beaches of Virginia and feel the cool water of the Atlantic on my toes once again.

Making quick work of packing some drawing gear, lunch, and beach stuff, I set off toward Virginia Beach for the day. After learning about a pair of lighthouses on one of the area military bases there, I travel to the nearest public beach to get a look at them.

The late May air is warm, though the water is way too cold for someone used to living in Miami. Still, it's a beautiful and peaceful place, and I soon find solace in a beach chair listening to the crashing waves.

At home, I always visited the shore with a group, but I think I enjoy the peacefulness of being alone just as much. No one groans when my sketch pad inevitably comes out, and I'm not sucked into an idle chit-chat gossip session.

Looking back, I realize just how out of place I was among what I thought were mine and Trevor's friends. Those people were Trevor's friends that I was grafted into. I never really fit in just being me. It's evident to me now that when we were with them, Trevor even became someone else. I just couldn't see it at the time.

God, I feel so stupid. As cowardly as it was for him to leave me the way he did, Trevor saved us both a lot of misery. Even so, I'll never understand how I could have been so blind. *Ok, Iyla, that's enough wallowing. Knock it off.*

Closing my eyes, I take several slow, deep breaths to calm myself and lean back in my chair.

About an hour into my lounging, a pair of women arrive, each with a child and an infant. I don't pay them much attention at first, spending all my energy watching the water.

The absence of childish laughter coming from their group eventually catches my attention. One good look at the children steals all my focus, and the group becomes all I can see. A black-haired boy about thirteen is fishing at the shoreline with the practiced ease of some of the old pros I used to watch in Miami. Also with the group is a young girl with hair spun from golden silk that can't be any older than six or seven.

Besides the boy's measured movements, his lack of overexcited squeals at catching a fish speaks of a maturity way beyond his years. It's almost sad. Childhood should be a time of exuberance, laughter, and curiosity.

He's a beautiful child, his profile so striking and serene that it begs to be preserved, as he'll soon grow into adulthood. His face will quickly lose its soft contours, becoming sharp and defined with age.

I draw the boy on the deck of a boat, casting out over the open ocean. The sun is at his back, and on his face, I draw the smile that's missing now.

Being even younger, the girl breaks my heart, seeing the absence of childish wonder in her. She seems happy enough playing in the sand, but every once in a while, she looks up to make sure her mother is still where she last saw her. Several times, she gets up, walks over to the sun tent, and talks to one of the infants I assume is a sibling.

There's a heaviness to these children, like they've experienced too much of this world's darkness already. The whole scene makes me wonder about their lives, but it only takes a moment of watching the mothers to know that these children are loved. Treasured.

The blond woman joins her son each time he pulls a fish from the water. The cheering mother photographs every catch, but the boy, while respectful, reacts like it's just business as usual.

The other woman, the brunette, hugs the little girl each time she gets up to check on her brother and even fetches water so the child will always have enough for her castle building.

Now that I'm watching the group collectively, I can see some of the same darkness plaguing the two women. As if it could be in my power to do anything about it, I have this incredible urge to bring some light back to their eyes. An image forms in my head, and the girl's angelic face takes shape on my pad. In the drawing, a power emanates from her eyes to vanquish the darkness that plagues her young life.

Unlike the boy's image, the girl's portrait is full of color, something I perceive is important to bring back to her world. The young girl becomes a warrior, perched on a large stone in the middle of a field of pink, purple, and blue flowers. The sun behind her forms a crown of light on her head, and she wears a flowing gown in various shades of blue. She holds in one hand a scepter and a sword in the other.

I work in some final details to the drawing and drum up the courage to approach the women. One is tending to the two infants in the covered pen while the other reads a book.

"Excuse me," I say gently.

Both women start as if expecting danger, so I immediately show them one of the drawings to demonstrate that I'm not a threat. "I'm an artist and sometimes get struck by an image and have to capture it. Please take these with my compliments. You have possibly the most enchanting children I've ever seen."

The petite blond woman accepts the drawing of the boy and gasps when she looks fully at the portrait. "Oh, my god. This is beautiful."

Her voice cracks when she turns to her friend. "Willa, look at this."

Willa reaches for the paper, and her mouth falls open in obvious surprise. She looks up to where the boy is still fishing and then to me. "You did this? Just now?"

The drawing is returned to the blond, and I say, "Yes. I also did one of the little girl."

I hand the colorful drawing to Willa, whose eyes grow misty as she reverently touches the image. "It's beautiful," she whispers.

"May I show it to her?" I ask.

"Of course," Willa says, still studying the picture in awe. Without lifting her eyes from the page, she calls out, "Ari, come over here. You need to see something."

Willa hands the artwork back to me, and I wait for Ari to arrive from the shoreline. "Yes, Mama."

I kneel in the sand next to mother and daughter. "Hi, Ari. My name's Iyla. I drew a picture that I'd like you to have."

Ari shyly looks to her mother for permission or encouragement. Willa smiles reassuringly at her daughter, who then returns her attention to me. "Okay."

I show her the image, and her deep, brown eyes widen. "Wow. Why do I have a sword?"

"Because when I look at you, I see a warrior."

Her brow tightens doubtfully, so I explain further. "It's true. You look like you've fought some pretty big battles, but you're standing here in front of me. That tells me that no matter the battle you've had to fight, you've always won."

The transformation of her expression and body language is immediate. Little Ari's mind has just been blown.

Whispering, she asks, "What's this sparkly stick?"

"It's a scepter."

"What's that?"

"A scepter is something that shows you to be the queen of your kingdom. You see, Ari, where I'm from, a long time ago, if someone attacked the queen, she led her fierce army to fight back and protect the kingdom. Because the queen and her army were so brave, they won each battle, and their kingdom grew and grew. With each battle you and the army inside you win, your kingdom grows."

Ari continues to marvel at the fanciful image, and I add, "I want this picture always to remind you that if anyone tries to bring you trouble, all you have to do is call up the army within, and you can never be defeated."

The little girl throws her arms around my neck and thanks me for the picture. As she does, gasping sobs come from the two mothers. Ari lets go of my neck and settles in her chair to admire the artwork.

A baby coos in the background, and Willa stands and wipes her eyes. She pulls a wallet from her beach bag, but I hold up a hand to stop her. "Please, no. I didn't do this for money. Besides, her reaction was worth more than any amount you could pay me."

I bid the family goodbye and decide it's time to make my way back home. My things are packed quickly, and I walk to the car wearing a big smile. It's not often that I get to touch someone so profoundly with my work. When I do, it's good medicine for me.

Reaching my back bumper, I stop and look up at my surroundings, turning a full circle. Not just the children and the drawing today, but Virginia, in general, has been good medicine for me. I drive the whole way back toward the quiet streets of my new home with a grin still on my face.

As I reach the outskirts of town proper, a police car pulls in behind me. I check my speed to make sure I'm not in danger of getting a ticket and continue on the path home. After a few moments, I notice that the police car matches my turn for turn. *It's probably because I still have the Dade County, Florida tag.* As I make the final turn onto my street, the policeman continues straight. I guess he wasn't following me after all.

A quick shower at home cleans off the sunscreen and sand, and I sit on the back deck for a while. Now that I'm in a good place, I spend some time catching up with my mom on the new house, work, and life in Virginia.

The biggest takeaway from the conversation is that I am happy here. When I told my mother that, she sagely replied, "You know, I never once heard you say that when you were in Miami."

Sitting alone in the quiet, I can't pinpoint the key factor. I think about it for a while but ultimately decide not to question it and simply embrace my new life.

I spend some time that afternoon answering inquiries and sending out proposals. When evening rolls around, I make up a salad for dinner and get an idea. One thing I miss about Miami is the farmer's market.

While I can't imagine one around here being as big or exotic, it has to be better than nothing. As I munch on a crouton, I pull out my phone and text Nolan. *Is there a good farmer's market around here?*

Of course, I could have looked it up myself, but I felt like asking my friend. With any luck, he'll go with me. No one wants to do everything alone.

He messages back quickly. *Tu and Th*

afternoons. We'll both go. I'll show you the best vendors and the ones to avoid.

NOLAN

Iyla messages back, *Tomorrow?*

I reply, *Sure,* and cross my fingers that my team isn't given the go signal before then.

After PT the following day, the team completes a series of boat seizure exercises aided by other squads. The three VBSS maneuvers are designed to test our responses to ideal circumstances, surprise situations, and completely fucked up conditions. Because O'Reilly's Visit Board Search & Seizure mantra also includes an additional S for Shoot if necessary, we're all armed with lasers for the exercise.

To set the scene as realistically as possible, the commander employs Jock's squad, our dirtiest rival team, to the FUBAR run of the drill, knowing they'll do all they can to knock us on our ass.

This last of the drills goes off with every hitch possible, but my team still takes the boat. For good measure, we leave Jock hog-tied on the deck for the referees to deal with afterward. We might pay for it later, but it felt good today.

Once we're dressed again, it's time for an update meeting with the commander. "We've gotten a tip that the boat is on its way to pick up a shipment of munitions and explosives. The USS Roosevelt is being sent in preparation for our takedown. Once we get word to go, you'll be flown out to *The Big Stick and* ferried in a smaller vessel to intercept the smugglers. For now, we're in a holding pattern. You know your roles. Dismissed."

You all know your roles. Yeah, all except me. All SEALs are trained to be capable medics, top marksmen, confident demolitions handlers, and multilingual, but the guys on my team take things to another level.

For years, I've watched my team do the impossible because of the remarkable traits these men display. Fish is the finest leader in all of Team Two. Bandaid puts sailors back together while gunfire sounds overhead. Wrench either orchestrates failproof explosions or saves our asses from bombs intended to destroy us. We have world-renowned snipers in Devil and Hawk. There isn't a mountain Skin can't climb, and even Ink is a cultural customs encyclopedia. I'm an excellent navigator, but so are most other SEALs.

Beyond being capable, I don't know what I add to the team.

What I do know is that I'd be a damn good JAG attorney. Maybe Jasper was right. Perhaps it's time to make the change. I don't want to leave the team, my brothers, but what if someone out there could bring more to the table?

While I'm lost in my head, my team members clear the room faster than they used to, most of them now having someone waiting for them at home. When I'm still there as Commander O'Reilly gathers his papers, he sits back down and crosses his arms. "Something on your mind, Lockmore?"

"Nothing, sir. I'm just trying to understand my specific role for this mission."

"Same as always."

"Always, sir?"

The commander snickers. "After all this time, you still haven't figured it out?"

"Beyond navigation, which isn't always needed, I have no idea. I know I'm just as good as any other SEAL, but I fail to see what I contribute that the other men don't."

Commander O'Reilly shakes his head and uncrosses his arms, tossing a pen on the table. "I take personal offense to that. I like to think that in your team, I've curated the finest squad of men this man's navy has ever seen. The other Wendigos have obvious tangible skills, sure, but—you really don't know?"

"I wouldn't still be here if I did."

O'Reilly steeples his fingers and leans back in his chair. "Which member of your team is to be present any time a combatant is being questioned in the field?"

He takes my silence to mean I understand. "You have a sixth sense about people. I don't know how you do it, but you read people better than any interrogator I've ever known. And more than once, that intuition of yours has saved asses by seeing something none of the others picked up on. So, your particular skill may not be needed on every mission, but neither are the others. That doesn't make you any less valuable to this team. Now, get out of here. I've got work to do."

I stand and come to attention, then turn for the door. *Curated.* O'Reilly said he curated this team. We were hand-picked for our abilities and never knew.

Sorry, Jasper. It looks like you'll be waiting a while longer.

The drive home is made in somewhat of a daze. I go inside to change and walk over to knock on Iyla's door. She answers, wearing a loose, button-up top in white and large-print floral shorts. Her long, brown hair falls in beachy waves down her back.

I've never seen her dressed up like this, and she takes my breath away. I have to clear my throat a time or two just to be able to speak. "It's a little early, but the best vendors set up before all the others. Are you ready to go?"

"Absolutely."

We walk to my car and start toward the farmer's market. Once there, the two of us wander around, shopping and sampling, and I introduce her to some of the people I've gotten to know over the years. I laugh as Iyla tries some local honey and ends up with the sticky syrup all over her chin. She falls in love with Amish cheese, declaring it to be the best she's ever had.

Watching her closely, I notice a new effervescence she didn't have before. It's a stab and a balm to my heart simultaneously, making me wonder if I'll always want this woman. And if I'll ever have her.

At the next booth, I wait in a short line for my guilty pleasure, green tomatoes, as Iyla flits off to a vendor displaying colorful scarves caught in the wind. Just as I finish paying for my selection, I look up to find Iyla and watch a man approach and lay a hand on her shoulder. Iyla lets out a surprised yelp at the unexpected contact, and all my protective instincts kick into gear.

I move with purpose in her direction, not recognizing the man until his head turns so that I can see his profile. *Dammit, it's the cop dressed in civilian clothes.*

The hair on the back of my neck stands on end, and I hoof it, all but sprinting to reach them before things escalate. When I'm fifteen feet away, Iyla, shrill with shock, says, "Dillan?"

Dillan?! She knows this guy?

The casually dressed man grins huge. "Iyla, what are you doing here?"

Curious and wary, I slow my approach and listen to their exchange. "I live here. What are *you* doing here, Dillan?"

"I like to come up here when I have a few days off."

The man's easy lie stops me cold, and all kinds of red flags go up. Why would the cop lie? Feeling even more uneasy about the man, I close the distance between us and slide an arm around Iyla's shoulders.

The man's face darkens as he scans upward from Iyla's face to mine, and instant hatred flashes in his eyes when he recognizes me. "Who's your friend?" I ask Iyla.

Since the man damn well knows who I am, or at least that I'm Iyla's neighbor, I bite my tongue to see what happens when she answers. "This is Dillan Broderick. He's a friend from North Carolina."

Her voice still carries a trace of bewilderment at the man's sudden appearance, which doesn't relax my battle-ready tension. Broderick doesn't let on to Iyla that we've met, but the look on his face clearly communicates that he's not pleased with my presence. This is especially obvious in how his gaze travels slowly over Iyla's body and stops to focus on my arm wrapped possessively around her.

Unaware of the intense stare-down, Iyla continues with the introductions. "Dillan, this is my neighbor, Nolan."

"Deputy," I say tightly.

Without acknowledging me, Dillan focuses all his attention on Iyla once again. "Since

I'm in town for a few days, we ought to get together for dinner and drinks."

Iyla opens her mouth to respond, but I interrupt. "Sure, I have yet to show Iyla all the best places. I'd be glad to set up something for the three of us."

Broderick's shoulders stiffen, but his face remains passive. "You have my number, Iyla."

The asshole pushes his luck and leans in to press a kiss on Iyla's cheek. Broderick is intentionally defiant, blatantly disregarding me, and attempting to stake his own claim on Iyla.

I want nothing more than to rip the arm off the lying bastard, but Iyla looks freaked out enough. Besides her shock at seeing him here, she's utterly oblivious to the undercurrent of hostility between us two men.

The cop leaves the area, and Iyla watches with furrowed brows. She also finally notices our slightly intimate position and ducks out from under my arm. She's not upset. Iyla looks like she's been caught off-guard again.

"Iyla, are you ok? You look like you've just seen a ghost. Is that guy a problem?"

"No." She shakes her head as if to cast off the spell she was under and explains. "Dillan and I met when I took that commission at the Biltmore. We were friends, but he wanted more. I said no, and we haven't spoken since."

"And he's here on vacation?"

"I guess. That's what he said."

I consider telling her what I know but decide this isn't the time or place to do so. "Did you get all you came for?" I ask instead.

"Yeah. Let's go."

Iyla is quiet during the walk to the car and the whole trip home. I assume it's due to the unexpected run-in with a rejected lover. Out of concern, I park in her driveway and walk Iyla to her front door. At any moment, I expect her to verbalize some of the questions I have about the sudden appearance of the jilted man.

What comes out of her mouth instead knocks me for a loop. Somewhat accusingly, she asks, "What was with the caveman routine? I thought you understood my boundaries."

Shit.

CHAPTER 8

IYLA

Nolan's jaw drops, completely thrown off guard by my question. I didn't have the presence of mind to work it out earlier due to the shock of seeing Dillan, but going over the situation on the way home, the memory of his arm sliding around me came to the forefront of my mind. The move was uninvited and disappointing after the talk we had by his firepit.

Nolan gawks a moment, surprised by my irritation, then collects himself. "Whoa. I realize how it looked, but trust me, I wouldn't have done it if I didn't think it absolutely necessary."

"What are you talking about?"

"Iyla, I need you to trust me. Can we talk inside?"

Staring at my friend, I realize I do trust him, and the anger melts away. "Of course, I trust you. Ok. Let's talk."

I lead the way inside and sit on my favorite chair. Nolan follows suit but perches on the sofa's edge, looking uneasy.

"Iyla, Broderick lied to you."

My head, which was leaning on my fists, lifts slowly. "Wait. Back up. I'm lost."

"I know. Give me a minute, and I'll explain everything. First, I need to know if you told Broderick you were moving here."

"No. The last time I saw Dillan, I hadn't even decided between my top two locations yet. I'm pretty sure I didn't even mention to him that I had a top two."

"Ok. Now, how well do you know this guy?"

"Nolan, what's this all about?"

"Please, Iyla, answer the question."

I'm not one to be pushed around, but Nolan seems so rattled. I've never seen him this way, and it worries me. "We met by chance at a park in Asheville. Food trucks gather in a certain spot by a pond for evening diners. I started going there and would catch him on his shift break. We started talking and hit it off. That was early on in my time there, so we spent more than three months getting to know each other."

"Yes, but how *well* do you know him?"

"Better than you," I bite out.

Nolan looks downward, and I feel like shit for lashing out. "I'm sorry, Nolan. I just don't understand what's going on here."

"I get that. Just stay with me. What kind of a relationship did the two of you have?"

"We were just friends, Nolan. Dillan asked me out once, and I told him no. The last time I saw him, he kissed me, but I pushed him away and explained that I didn't want to start anything with him or anyone else."

"How did he take the rejection?"

I roll my eyes, and my voice raises in frustration. "It wasn't rejection. I wasn't ready to jump into another relationship after recently being left at the altar. Are you going to get to the point?"

Nolan drags a hand through his hair and sighs. "The point is that Broderick might not have seen things your way. Does he know about your ex-fiancé?"

"I never told him. You're the only person I've ever told. I still don't understand what all this has to do with anything."

Nolan takes a deep breath, and the hesitation on his face has my stomach clenching. "Iyla, I've seen Broderick on our street three times in the last ten days."

I gasp in air and bring my hand to my mouth. Through my fingers, I breathe, "What?"

"He was in a patrol car. A local sheriff's car. He's not on vacation."

"But…" my mind is reeling, so I can't even finish the thought. "Why?"

Nolan shrugs in a move meant to come off as nonchalant. It's an epic failure. "It could be a big but odd coincidence."

"But you don't believe that. Do you?"

He doesn't respond, which answers my

question loud and clear. "You put your arm around me."

The man nods. "I heard him lie to you. That automatically put him in the asshole category and brought out my protective side."

I bring both hands to my head, pressing my fingers into throbbing temples. "Wait a minute. We're making a big deal about something that could be nothing. I should just call and ask him outright. Dillan's a policeman, for god's sake. Not some drug dealer or mafia hitman."

Nolan taps his fingers on the sofa table, unconvinced. I imagine it's an occupational hazard for someone used to dealing with the worst of humanity. I'm sure this is a big misunderstanding and that there's a reasonable explanation for this whole mess.

When my friend remains silent, I try to get him to reengage. "Nolan?"

Scarred knuckles rap on the wood surface, and Nolan stands. "Iyla, I want you to know I'm here if you need me… for anything."

He walks out the front door, leaving me at a loss for what to think. He didn't wear his usual smile as he left, and as I watch him through the window, I begin to wonder if I should be more concerned.

Dillan is here? He lied? Why?

What do I do now? Should I do anything? Nolan held me against him, assuming I needed protection from Dillan. Do I?

Nolan said that Dillan had been on our street more than once, yet he acted like seeing me was a surprise. I still believe it has to be a coincidence. The alternative is too impossible even to consider.

The only thing I know right now is that wondering and worrying about what may or may not be going on is a waste of energy. I should just call Dillan to straighten this out.

But I'll wait till tomorrow. The situation has shaken me, and I want to call when I have a level head. For now, what I need is a paintbrush in my hand. That'll clear my head and calm my nerves.

I take the time to change out of my nice clothes and pin my hair up. I have one final image to create for the coffee company. They liked the watercolor but were fifty-fifty on wanting color on their final image. Since the color piece didn't sell them instantly, I've been asked to do a shade drawing of the same perspective and print the same base outline on Bristol paper.

The paper is taped down, and all my pencils are laid out to get started.

Four hours later, I'm sitting in the studio waiting for the fixative to dry. I set out another blank Bristol sheet and start drawing again. This time, Nolan's concerned face appears from the pencil strokes, his jaw hard, teeth clenched, eyes boring into mine, pleading.

Pleading for what? What are you worried

about, Nolan?

I smudge the area around his eyes and think about how he reacted, how his first instinct was to protect me. My fingers linger on his lips, recalling his study, reassuring grip holding me against him. I think I liked it—a lot.

Withdrawing my hand from his illustrated face, I angrily wipe my graphite-covered fingers on my apron and push away from the table. *Dammit, Iyla. It hasn't even been six months since you were left waiting for a man who decided he didn't want you. And this was after knowing him for years. You can't be falling for Nolan barely a month after meeting him.*

The face of my next-door neighbor stares back at me from the art table, daring me to deny what's in my heart.

The image staring back at me is beautiful. My skill as an artist, I mean. It isn't Nolan's perfect face with its sexy stubble, and definitely not his wise, kind eyes.

Damn. Who am I kidding? Nolan gave me the space I asked for, becoming the friend I needed even though I could tell he didn't want to. He made me laugh and gave me the courage to bare my soul and start healing instead of perpetually denying the grief of a lost relationship.

Someone like that needs a woman who is whole and without trust issues. At this point, I wouldn't be able to let him in. Nolan deserves better than that, better than having to wait on a woman who might never be ready to love without holding back.

Continuing my study of the image, I strengthen my resolve to remain Nolan's friend and not wreck his chance at happiness. My phone rings, pulling me from my reverie, and I'm grateful for the break from my bleak thoughts.

The name on the screen sends chills down my spine, but I decide to meet this head-on and answer the call. "Dillan?"

"Iyla, it's good to hear your voice. I still can't believe I ran into you today. So, Chesapeake. How do you like the area?"

I'm at a loss for how to proceed. If Nolan wasn't mistaken and Dillan was driving around here, it means he has at least an idea where I live. I don't understand why he's putting on like he doesn't know.

"Iyla?"

"Sorry. It's nice. Quiet. Not beautiful like the estate grounds, but I guess there isn't much that would stack up to the Biltmore."

"No, I suppose not. Are you up for a visit? I'd love to see your new place."

"I live pretty far out of town. Why don't I meet you? There's a park downtown, a little like the one we visited in Asheville."

"All right. I'll grab us some coffee. Should I bring three coffees or just two?"

I'm tempted to ask Nolan to go along, but

I won't get any answers out of Dillan if he's there. "Just one. I'll pass on the coffee being as late as it is."

Not even bothering to change out of my work clothes, I drive toward City Hall. I park across the street at the walking track that has a creek meandering around its border. This is my first time at the park, but I've noticed it several times while doing business at the shops in town.

I don't see Dillan yet, so I sit on the bench closest to the parking lot and face the babbling creek. For the life of me, I can't even guess how this conversation will go. All I know is that I'm nervous.

A figure slides into the space beside me, and I turn to face Dillan. He gives me his signature grin, the one that made women in Asheville, young and old, flush when graced with its appearance.

His casual smile makes me mad for some reason, and I decide it's time to let my Scottish out and throw tact out the window. "You're not on vacation. You took a job here, didn't you?"

"Did your boyfriend tell you that?"

"Neighbor, not boyfriend. Answer the question."

The smile fades away, Dillan drops to rest his elbows on his knees, and he sighs. "After you left, Asheville just didn't hold the same interest for me. It was empty without you."

"So, you followed me here? How did you

even know where to find me?"

He chuckles, but I'm not laughing. "I'm a cop, remember?"

His casually delivered explanation floors me, and I visibly flinch. "Dillan, that's just plain wrong and unlawful, I'm sure. How could you sneak around my back like that?"

"Oh, come on, Iyla. It's not like you wouldn't have posted the hell out of that information online anyway. I didn't even use police resources. These days, a third-grader can find an address for someone."

His cavalier view of my privacy infuriates me, but that's not a battle I'll win today.

"Are you happy here? What's it like living next door to that gorilla that can't keep his hands to himself?"

"Don't call him that. Nolan is a nice guy." Not to be steered off-topic, I forge ahead on my inquisition. "Why are you here? The last time I saw you, you stormed off, angry at me."

"I missed you, Iyla. We had fun together. I want that back. Come to dinner with me."

Dillan reaches for my hand, but I stand and pace the ground in front of the bench. "I don't think it's a good idea."

"Why not?"

"You want more than I can give. I tried to tell you twice, but you wouldn't listen. I told you I wasn't ready to be in a relationship, but you kept pushing."

"Why? Tell me why, Iyla."

I stop pacing and turn to face him. After a sigh, I say, "One month before moving to Asheville, I was abandoned on my wedding day. Now, do you understand?"

"Shit. I thought you were playing hard to get. I'm sorry. I wish I'd have known."

Dammit. Did I cause all this trouble by trying to hold onto my pride? Could all this have been avoided?

"I don't tell people because it's pathetic and embarrassing."

"Don't be embarrassed. I'm the one that should be ashamed. Will you forgive me?"

I nearly roll my eyes again. "Yes, I forgive you. Now, I've got to get back home. I have some deadlines to meet."

"I'll see you around, Iyla."

"Ok, Dillan."

I'm in my car and driving home less than a minute later. Back in my driveway, I kill the engine but don't immediately go inside. *That wasn't so bad, so why do I feel so guilty as though I was lying to him? And what reason would I have to feel guilty in the first place?*

CHAPTER 9

NOLAN

I've just opened my door to walk back to Iyla's house when I hear her car's engine start. She pulls down her driveway, and I go back inside and pace the floor. *She's gone to meet that bastard; I know it.*

The woman was so sure that Broderick's deceit isn't a symptom of a greater problem. She's blind. *Or maybe you're just jealous.*

"FUCK!"

I need a distraction. Snatching my keys from the console table, I storm out the door while calling Skin. I pull into the parking lot at Dune a short while later and take the empty seat next to my teammate and friend. "Rough day?" he asks without looking my way.

"You could say that."

The bartender tips his chin toward me, and I gesture toward Skin's drink.

"I hear you're thinking about retiring."

His words hit me like a slap to the face, but I try not to show it. "Nope. Where'd you get that?"

"I have my sources. So, it's not true?"

He turns his seat to look at me head-on. Unblinking, I confess, "It was a transfer, not retirement."

Skin's armor drops to reveal a rare moment of vulnerability. "We've been through a lot over the last two years. Losing one of you guys would be worse than losing an arm. That may be selfish to say, but there it is."

"Ramsay, I could no more leave you guys than I could willingly give up breathing."

He nods and returns his gaze to the worn bar top. "But you've thought about it."

A tumbler slides in front of me, and I take a sip. "Yes, I have. I want more."

"I know you do," he whispers.

I take another slow sip. "I almost had her."

"What happened?"

I drain the rest of my drink. "Someone hurt her. Now, she won't let anyone else get close."

Skin pats me on the back. "I'm sorry, man."

"Yeah. Me too."

We finish our drinks and relocate to the pier out back to watch the fishing boats come in.

Iyla's car is parked safely in her driveway when I return home around eleven. As much as I'd like to check on her, all the lights are off at her place. Tomorrow will have to be soon enough.

I sleep until eight since my team isn't scheduled to report to base today. Instead of checking in on Iyla after breakfast, I drive toward Virginia Beach's seventh precinct. The receptionist is the same dusty, old woman who greeted me warmly when I was here to defend Wrench against murder charges. "I'm here to see Detective Bassett."

"Is he expecting you?"

"Probably. My name is Nolan Lockmore."

"Have a seat," she orders.

Five minutes pass before the bullpen doors open. "Lockmore, what are you doing here?"

"I need to talk to you."

Basset glances at the ancient receptionist and gestures for me to follow him to the back. Prior to the hallway opening up to the bullpen, Bassett directs me to a conference room on the right.

I take a seat, and Bassett opts to perch on the table's edge. "Is this about your neighbor?"

"In a roundabout way. I was wrong to suspect her of anything. The problem is a cop."

This gets the seasoned detective's attention. He walks around the table and drops into the seat opposite me. "I'm listening."

I tell Bassett everything from the repeated drive-bys to the lies Broderick spilled during the chance meeting.

"I agree this stinks, but I don't know what you're asking here. I have no authority outside of VB city limits."

My frustration boils over, and I jump up

and start pacing. "I know that, dammit. I only want to know if this guy is a ticking time bomb."

Bassett leans back in his seat, his casual demeanor at odds with the tight lines around his mouth. "I know what you want, but I can't help you. The fact that the guy has a badge and is a recent hire tells me he doesn't have a record. That doesn't guarantee that he's clean, but whatever he has or hasn't done in his career hasn't resulted in him losing his job. Even if I were to look and find something, you know I couldn't share that information with you. You're a lawyer. I shouldn't have to tell you this because you already know it."

He's right. Coming here was a waste of time. I shove out of the chair and reach for the door handle. "Lockmore, wait. I haven't forgotten what happened to Delano and Wray. If this guy even looks like he might be heading down that same road, you go to the sheriff. Being a cop, if he fucks up, his head would roll a lot sooner than a civilian's would."

Bassett rises from his seat and joins me at the door. "You also need to hear this. Rural sheriffs have a hard time keeping deputies who'd rather be in a big city where all the excitement is. If your sheriff is like that, he won't cut your guy loose until he does something that would bring bad press to the department."

That introduces an element I hadn't thought of. "Thanks, Evan."

"There's no need to thank me. Your team saved the life of a good friend of mine. I'm happy to do the same."

"Hopefully, that won't be necessary."

I walk back out into the sun, feeling no more at ease than I did walking in. With nothing else I can do and loaded down with nervous energy, I head back home to do some work in the garden.

Half an hour later, I'm dressed in gym shorts, a ratty tee, and old runners. I retrieve my string trimmer from the tool shed and gas it up. I'm about to yank on the starter cord when I hear swearing coming from Iyla's backyard.

My heart pounds as I sprint across the lawn, but I force my feet to still so I can evaluate the situation. It doesn't take long to realize that Iyla's not being threatened; she's complaining.

At the property line, I stop to watch Iyla sitting on the ground, stabbing at the dirt with a garden trowel. "Problems?" I ask with more than a hint of humor.

Iyla looks up at the sound. She's splattered in mud from head to toe from working in the dirt after the heavy rain that moved in overnight.

"This is not as easy as they make it seem in commercials," she rants.

I fight to keep the laughter from my voice when I say, "Though the rain does a good job of softening the soil, having the right tool helps."

I jog back to my garden shed and pull out

a digging shovel. Upon returning, I place the pointed tip at the edge of the spot that Iyla was mutilating. I brace my foot on the left side and force the blade deep into the earth. "See? Much easier."

Iyla grumbles what I'm sure is a cute Scottish curse. "Only because you have all those muscles."

I lift my arm and flex my bicep. Iyla rolls her eyes, stoops to place a colorful Nandina plant in the hole, and shoves the dirt back over the roots. "Well, that's one."

She stands back up and turns around, and I chuckle. She must have wiped her muddy hand across her cheek, leaving a dirty streak from chin to ear.

"What's so funny?"

"You got a little…" I point to my own cheek, and Iyla reaches up to swipe at whatever's on her face. The problem is that her hand is still muddy, and she only succeeds in making matters worse. Now, I'm howling in laughter.

Iyla realizes what she's done and groans. I'm still laughing when she narrows her eyes in my direction. "Think that's funny, do you?"

Fast as lightning, she reaches up and smears her muddy fingers across my chin. Her lips lift into a self-satisfied smile as she retreats. I lift my brows in mock censure, and her eyes sparkle in challenge. Ever so deliberately, I reach down, dipping my hand in the muck, raise back up, and spread a handful of mud down her right arm.

She nods defiantly and bends to grab the trowel she'd been using. With much fanfare, Iyla extracts the mud stuck to the small shovel and, with an evil glint in her eye, steps forward and rubs the dirt on my chest.

"Hmm," I say, tilting my head to the side. Mirroring her actions, I scrape the mud off my digging shovel and throw it in her direction, scoring a direct hit square on her belly. Iyla methodically pulls the glob of mud from her shirt and then launches at me.

Muddy hands go all over my face and hair, and I make no attempt to fight her off. Instead, I duck down and lift her to my shoulder, carrying her to a specific part of my backyard.

Iyla laughs and pounds on my back, going as far as shoving a handful of mud inside my shirt. "You're gonna pay for that," I warn playfully.

I don't stop until I reach the dirt area behind the fire pit. Because it drains poorly, it's the one place I haven't sodded yet, thankfully.

I set Iyla's ass down in the sloshy mud, which turns out to be a miscalculation on my part. Iyla grabs handful after handful of mud and launches them in my direction. As I'm dodging blows, the little minx takes advantage of my distraction and grabs my ankles.

Her wicked plan works, and I lose the fight

with gravity and slippery ground. I splash down in the muddy puddle beside Iyla but refuse to give up. Rolling over, I go on the attack, grinding mud onto every area of Iyla's exposed skin.

In doing so, I learn that Iyla is very, very ticklish. She laughs until she can't breathe, calling out, "Uncle! Uncle!"

I still my hand, and my chest heaves in silent laughter. In her attempt to escape being tickled, Iyla has burrowed herself about two inches deep into the mud. We're both covered from head to toe in muck, and Iyla is wearing the happiest, most contented smile I've ever seen.

Lying in the mud, hovering over this beautiful swamp creature, I become lost in her eyes, and my laughter dries up. There's a heat in her gaze that I haven't seen there before.

Hope and desire fill my chest, and I pluck a twig from Iyla's hair to keep from doing something we both might regret. I peel a leaf from her forehead next, but then shock blasts through me when Iyla lifts a hand to brush dirt from my forehead.

Her eyes track downward, catching on my lips, making me want her more than my next breath. My entire body is on fire, but I'm too scared to move, to breathe. My greatest fear is that Iyla might see me in the same light as that bastard cop, who doesn't understand the word no.

The moment stretches on for an eternity, and I feel like I'm dying. I start to pull away but freeze when Iyla whispers my name. In a completely surreal moment, the little mud nymph lifts herself out of the muck and presses her lips to mine.

My eyes close in silent prayer that I hadn't just imagined the kiss. When they open again, Iyla's eyes are wild, and her breath is coming faster. She moves her mouth that's still under mine, and I have all the evidence I need.

Lowering my body, I push her back down and respond with a kiss of my own. I start out gentle at first, exploring Iyla's soft lips. I'm amazed and content with Iyla giving me this, but she lets me know she wants more when her tongue pops out and begins teasing. *She's about to break me.*

Groaning with the strain of holding back, I lay my body on hers, pressing us deeper into the mud and sinking deeper into her eager mouth. The taste of her vanilla lip balm is sweet on my tongue, but I'm soon overwhelmed by the passion that Iyla has kept pent up all these weeks.

Muddy fingers work their way around my neck, pulling me closer, and the two of us get lost in each other.

Having tasted her mouth and found it to be like fine wine, I'm dying to see if her skin's as sweet as her lips. I pull back to see if any part of Iyla is not muddied by our antics, but I don't find a clear place to touch her.

Reading my mind, Iyla pulls her hands

from my neck and reaches for the hem of her shirt. The damp and dirty fabric is pulled over her head, revealing a ruined white cotton bra and perfect skin. I don't waste any time, blazing a trail over her collarbone to her shoulder.

Iyla's desperate whimpers spur me on, as does her grabbing me by the ass to pull me back to her hungry mouth. She's shifted, so I'm now wedged between her thighs, and I know she can feel the hard tip of my erection pressing against her soft center. Iyla rocks her hips upward once and pulls her lips from mine. "Nolan," she begs breathlessly. "I want you."

The fierce determination in her eyes is nearly my undoing, but still, I hesitate. "I don't want you to regret me."

"Nolan, I've felt this way since day one but have been fighting it. I was scared to try again, but I'm not anymore."

Look at her, Judge. What do you see? Conviction. Boldness. Desire.

Rocking back to my knees, I lift Iyla from the mud and wrap her legs around my waist. Holding tightly to her, I stand and take determined strides toward my outdoor shower, not stopping until we're standing underneath the oversized rainhead.

The water is cold at first but heats up as quickly as we do. Iyla's arms are cemented around my neck, and I claim her mouth in a scorching kiss. The clean spray quickly soaks through our clothes and begins to wash away some of the mud. I'm so wrapped up in Iyla's sweet mouth that I don't even notice.

Wanting to see and feel all of her, I pin Iyla against the smooth stone wall and drag her bra straps down her arms. The cotton lingerie falls away when I flip open the front closure. Voice roughened by desire, I ask, "Do you have any idea how beautiful you are?"

With mud streaking down over her pale breasts and bits of leaves and twigs stuck in her hair, Iyla is still the most beautiful thing I've ever seen. The water continues to rain down as I pin Iyla's hands against the stone above her head and lean in to whisper in her ear. "I've wanted you since you walked up on me in this very shower."

She shivers at my words, and I tease my way down her neck with teeth and tongue. I release Iyla's hands and slide mine down her arms and body until I cover her soft breasts. The pads of my thumbs pass over her nipples, hardening them into stiff peaks.

Iyla arches off the wall and hisses in response. Then she's loosening her legs around my waist and lowering her feet to the floor. She reaches for my shirt, encouraging me to peel off the wet fabric. Her hands go to my chest, feeling over the dips and bulges of my abs, and I pull the pick holding up her messy hair.

Aided by the water, the long, brown waves cascade down her body and release the mud stuck in the strands. Iyla reaches for the waist of my shorts at the same time I grasp her hips. We both kick out of our soaked shoes, and I let her push my shorts to the floor for me to step out of.

With shaking hands, I take a knee before her, pull off our socks, and reach for the band of her leggings and panties. I peel the garments from her legs and toss them over the rail.

I rise again slowly, taking a steadying breath as my eyes rake over her beautiful body. Towering over Iyla again, I look deep into her eyes as the water pours over us. Her mouth is open, and she's breathing hard. "Are you on—"

"Yes," she interrupts.

I reach around her neck to cradle her head in my hand and pull her hard against me. My lips crash down onto hers, and I dip my tongue into her sweet mouth. My other hand lowers to her slick folds to test her readiness. Iyla is soaked, but not from the water raining down on us. I circle her clit two, three times, and Iyla moans into my mouth.

Releasing her head, I grip her hips, lifting her level with my straining erection. Iyla presses forward, begging me with her body to fill her. Spreading her wide, I press forward slowly, sinking into her tight, wet heat as Iyla moans. Her arms go around my neck again as she throws her head back. *God, she's fucking tight.*

I pull out and press in again slowly to get her used to me. In no time, Iyla whimpers, encouraging me to go faster. I give her what she wants, picking up the pace and tilting my lower body to hit Iyla where she needs it most.

Soon, Iyla tenses and goes limp, breathlessly calling out my name while she comes. Her powerful inner muscles spasm around me, setting off my own intense release. Iyla's tight sheath continues to constrict and relax, drawing out my pleasure.

With my hands braced on the wall behind her, my forehead drops to rest on Iyla's shoulder. This woman has just turned me inside out. Iyla has pierced my soul, and I never want the wound to heal.

The pounding water splashes off my back while I fight to regain my equilibrium after such a powerful experience. My muscles eventually stop quivering, and I reluctantly lower Iyla's feet to the floor. I reach over to turn off the water and immediately pick up my woman and take her inside. Not caring that we're soaked and not completely clean, I lay her on my bed and take her again, slowly this time.

Iyla whispers my name as I move within her, raking her fingers over my scalp. I pull out and glide the tip of my cock over her clit until she falls apart in my arms. Then I plunge back into her tight, wet heat until I lose myself in her.

Later, we're lying on the damp sheets, trembling from another orgasm. Iyla is draped across my chest, and my hand is splayed over her lower back. Not wanting to risk shattering this moment but needing to know, I cautiously ask, "Iyla, why did you change your mind?" *About me, about taking a chance with us.*

She lifts her sleepy head and smiles. "I didn't change my mind. You did. Each time I got too close and pushed you away, you let me. I knew how you felt, but you put my issues and need for space before your own desires. No one has ever done that for me before. You make me laugh and don't let my grief control my every waking. You're different. It was you, Nolan. You changed my mind."

I kiss her temple. "Maybe I am different, but I can't be the friends-with-benefits type. If you want this, want me, I'm all in. If not, you need to tell me now."

CHAPTER 10

IYLA

Propping my head on my hand, I look Nolan in the eye. "I don't want one and done or a friend with benefits either. I want your respect for boundaries, your sense of responsibility, and your protective streak. I want you, Nolan."

I look back down at the faint scars littering his skin. "I will need your patience, though. My wounds are new and tender. You and I have shared something great, but my scarred heart might take a little time to warm up to the idea of becoming vulnerable again."

He tips my chin up. "Hey, I won't rush you. I've already said that I like having you in my world however you want to be there, but I wasn't kidding when I said I was all in. I'm too old to play around. And now that I've had you, I belong to you completely and will wait as long as it takes for you to feel the same."

"Thank you," I say with sincerity. Then, to lighten the mood, I ask, "Just how old are you?"

"I'm thirty-four."

I roll my eyes. "You're not old. I'll be

thirty-one next month."

In a sad Scottish accent, he says, "Aye, you're just a wee lass."

I slap at his chest and pick at some dried mud still in Nolan's hair. "We need proper showers and food. Why don't you give me a shirt and take a shower? Then we'll go to my place for me to shower and cook some dinner."

Still in his pitiful Scottish accent, he says, "Well, who am I to refuse such a generous offer?"

Nolan climbs from the bed and walks naked to a dresser to retrieve a t-shirt for me. The sight of his solid body makes me swoon. *He's beautiful from any angle,* I muse.

After what had to be the fastest shower in history, we're walking through our back yards to my screened-in deck.

"How are you with a knife?" I ask Nolan.

He cuts his eyes to me and lifts a brow.

"SEAL, right. Ok. You cut up the vegetables while I shower, and we'll have shrimp and veggie stir fry over fried rice."

"Yes, ma'am," he replies after snapping to attention.

Later, when I'm clean and all the cooking has been done, we take our plates out onto the deck with glasses of wine.

The entire evening is spent talking, kissing, and touching on the lounger as fireflies light up the night sky.

"What made you want to be a SEAL if you

were already in the Navy as a lawyer?"

Nolan brings my hand to his mouth and kisses my fingertips. "When I first joined the Office of Judge Advocate General, I was assigned to work under an asshole Major who was the equivalent of a state's attorney. The man had an impressive conviction rate that he was immensely proud of.

"One day, I was assigned a case in which a SEAL killed a local operative who freaked out when faced with an extraordinarily dangerous situation. Instead of listening to the SEAL team leader's instructions, the man was determined to abandon his post and make a break for safety, though it would expose the position of the entire SEAL team and others working with them.

"You can imagine what the consequences of that would have been. To protect the lives of his men and the rest of the local operatives, the SEAL team leader killed the hysterical man before the whole mission could be blown. The team completed their objective successfully, but the leader was charged with a crime to appease the foreign government's leaders.

"I was assigned this man's case and read over all the files, SEAL team members' statements, and even the special operative manuals for the Navy, Marines, and Army for guidance on this type of hypothetical situation.

"Of course, nothing like that is addressed in any military training curriculum for apparent reasons. In my best efforts of due diligence, I also interviewed several high-ranking military officials for their off-the-record evaluation of what *should* happen in that situation. They all agreed they would have likely taken a similar course of action but stated that rendering the man unconscious would have been preferable. Three of the generals I interviewed acknowledged that unless the man were within arm's reach, killing him would have been the only option.

"I took all that information to the Major. His only words to me were, "Our job is to fry them, son. If you want to get him off, you should go work for the other side. That was it. He wouldn't even hear me out. A cousin of mine also worked as a JAG but as a defense attorney on another base. I met with him to get his take since he'd been a JAG lawyer for two years already.

"Jasper told me about many similar cases that he lost because military justice often saved face by using servicemen as scapegoats. I didn't last too much longer after that. I spent every free minute studying the law of war and volunteered for SEAL training.

"Now, I have first-hand knowledge of what these men and women go through when a fraction of a second is all you have to make a decision that may or may not be supported by military brass. I use that knowledge to work with organizations that provide legal advice and services to wrongly accused and convicted servicemen and women."

I stare at Nolan in awe. He gave up a more leisurely, if not prestigious, career and put his life on the line so that he could fight for the people who fight for my freedom. That's unbelievable.

"You're the hero's hero," I say in admiration of him.

Nolan blushes at the praise and steers the conversation back to me. "When did you know you were destined to be an artist?"

I roll my eyes. "You expect me to follow your story with one about how I've painted all my life?"

His lips briefly touch mine. "Yes. I want to know all about you."

"Ok. I've painted and drawn all my life. That's all I ever wanted to do. Fortunately, I'm good at it."

I lay my head back down on his chest. "Nolan, what you do... that's the most amazing thing I've ever heard. You're a good man."

Nolan pats me on the ass and stands, bringing me with him. "I know tomorrow's Saturday, but I've got training in the morning since we didn't have it today. We meet at five, so I better get some sleep."

He pulls me against him and lowers his mouth to mine. His kiss is just as intoxicating as it was earlier, and I'm disappointed when he pulls back. "Iyla, today has been a dream come true. I'm already looking forward to the next time."

Nolan gives my ass a squeeze, and then he's walking down the back stairs. I follow him as far as the open deck and lean over the rail. "Hey, Nolan. Do you have a military nickname?"

He turns and walks backward while he answers, "It's Judge."

"Judge? That definitely fits. Goodnight, Judge."

"Goodnight, Picasso."

NOLAN

PT is pretty typical for us, and afterward, the team meets with Commander O'Reilly for a last walk-through of our mission strategies and backup plans ahead of our impending deployment.

Our entry will be identical to our VBSS on the Vlastvuy, a smuggling vessel trading diamonds for enriched uranium. I don't expect this time to go as easy as the Vlastvuy's takedown, though. This time, we're dealing with gun runners, and this time, the ship's captain isn't just a skipper looking the other way.

I'm driving home by noon, and just as I reach the outskirts of the small town near home, flashing lights in my rearview have me pulling over next to one of the many area strawberry fields.

Familiar blond hair emerges from the patrol car, and I know my day has just gone to shit. I roll down the window and place both hands on the steering wheel, not wanting to give this guy a reason to pull anything.

"Sir, do you know how fast you were driving?"

"Yes, I do, officer. I was driving fifty-five, which is the limit on this road."

Broderick nods and makes a show of inspecting my uniform and car. "This is quite a nice car for a pissant sailor. It doesn't appear that you're an officer. Kind of makes you wonder what else you might be into to have such a nice ride. Could it be gambling? Drugs?"

"I don't believe my vocation has any relevancy to whatever traffic violation I may or may not have committed."

"You smug son of a bitch. Step out of the car."

Fucking hell. So, he's not even going to pretend that this is legit.

This whole stop is bullshit, and I have no desire to play along except that screwing up like Broderick wants me to will leave my team a man short. Their safety is not worth whatever shit this asshole is trying to start.

Moving slowly, I leave my right hand on the wheel and use my left to open the door. At all times, I make sure both my hands are splayed open and visible to the asshole behind the badge.

As soon as I'm standing, I'm jerked to the front of the car, spun around, and slammed to the hood. My hands are wrenched behind my back, and cuffs are placed on my wrists. "I didn't know you were some Navy bitch. Let's see what else there is to know about you."

He kicks at my ankles, spreads my legs, and frisks me. Broderick doesn't have cause, but pointing that out won't accomplish anything.

My wallet is pulled from my pocket, and he rummages through all the cards, continuing to make snide comments until he comes across my business card. His voice doesn't carry the same bravado when he reads, "Nolan Lockmore, Attorney at Law."

That's right, asshole. You've pissed off your worst nightmare, and that doesn't even include the part about me being a SEAL.

"So, you're a squid and a hotshot lawyer."

I lift my chest from the hood of my car and turn to face the cop who's just started a war. "Yes, I'm a lawyer. A lawyer that knows you have no cause for detaining me. Either arrest me or stop this bullshit and get these chains off."

Broderick steps in close and throws a punch to my stomach. I don't react the way he expects, so he warns, "Stay away from Iyla. She's mine."

Staring daggers at the bastard, I say, "Iyla belongs to no one, and I don't take orders from you."

My wallet and its contents are dropped and scattered at my feet, and the jackass deputy unlocks the cuffs.

"I'll tell you this one more time. Stay away from Iyla."

The cop walks away and gets back in his car. The engine starts, and he floors the accelerator, bringing his car way too close to mine. Close enough that I have to dive over my hood or get hit.

"Stupid mother fucker!" I scream as I pick myself up from the patch of strawberries I just rolled into. I dust dirt and a white powder off my uniform and walk around to pick up my stuff from where that idiot dropped it on the ground. In the next breath, I get angry at myself. The one damn time, stateside that I needed my body cam, I wasn't wearing it.

I consider going to the sheriff about what just happened, but he doesn't know me, and it would be a case of Broderick's word against mine. Based on Bassett's explanation of small-town police forces, I imagine the sheriff would be more inclined to believe his deputy without proof of some sort. And Broderick knows it.

That means my hands are tied… this time. I'll be sure to keep my camera on me for when, not if, this happens again.

During the rest of the ride home, my mind is on Iyla. This guy is/was a friend of hers. A friend who lied to her about being here. I think she went out to meet him after that encounter at the farmer's market, but I haven't asked. After what just happened, I feel a great need to do so now.

I pull into my driveway and jog over to her front door. I ring the bell and knock, and Iyla answers a few seconds later. Overwhelmed by a sudden need to feel her against me, I take Iyla in my arms, pressing her head to my chest.

Almost immediately, Iyla starts coughing, then coughing and wheezing. I glimpse her panicked face just before she runs from me to the living room. I chase after her and pass through the archway just in time to watch her up end her purse, spilling all the contents out onto the floor. From the chaos, she picks up an inhaler and draws two puffs. *Asthma.*

"Iyla?!"

She throws up a hand to keep me back. "Stop. Please. Something… your clothes."

My clothes? My… Oh shit. The white powder. I take off running toward the back door, nearly tripping down the stairs in my rush to get the danger away from her. As fast as I can, I strip out of my boots and uniform down to my boxers. Next, I grab the garden hose and rinse off from head to toe.

Hoping I've gotten rid of the irritant, I rush back into the house to check on Iyla.

She's still on her hands and knees in the living room, but her breathing seems to be a little easier. I drop to the floor beside her and pull her into my lap. "Iyla? Iyla, look at me."

She does but is otherwise still. "I don't know much about asthma. Do you need an ambulance?"

Her eyes close again, but she shakes her head.

I hold on to her with all I've got, for I don't know how long, never taking my eyes off her face or chest.

Little by little, her breathing quietens and evens out. "Iyla, open your eyes."

She does, thank god, and I wipe the sweat from her forehead. "Are you ok?"

"Yes," she whispers. "Sorry to scare you."

My thumping heart begins to calm down, and I press my lips to the top of her head. "Don't apologize. I'm sorry I did this to you."

"No, it's my fault. I should have told you."

"Ok, that's enough. Stop talking and just breathe."

Her eyes close again, and she rests her head against my shoulder.

Sometime later, I feel the slightest touch of Iyla's fingertips on my chest. "How do you feel?"

"Better. Sore in the chest, but ok."

I gather her in my arms and stand to find a more comfortable place to sit. When we're settled on the couch, I ask, "How often does this happen?"

"Not very. I can think of only five times in the last twelve years."

Iyla pushes up to a sitting position, and her

brows knit together as she's thinking through something. "What was on your uniform?"

Now isn't the time to tell her what happened with that asshole Broderick, so I keep the details to a minimum. "I was at a strawberry farm before coming here. I got some white powder on my shirt but didn't think any more about it after I dusted it off."

"Oh. I learned the hard way that there are a few pesticides that I react to. When I have agricultural clients, I have to get a list of what they use on their crops before committing to a visit. It just doesn't come up very often."

"Are you sure you're okay?"

"I'm fine, Nolan. I promise. I'm hungry, actually."

"Let's get you up, and I'll see what I can do about that."

CHAPTER 11

IYLA

My chest is sore like an elephant sat on me, but I keep that information to myself for Nolan's sake. We relocate to the kitchen, where Nolan looks through my fridge and cabinets, wearing only damp boxer shorts. "What can I make for you?"

"I think just some scrambled eggs."

Nolan cooks enough for both of us, and we eat the simple dinner at the bar. Though Nolan protests, I insist on handling the dishes when we're finished. I'm just closing the door to the dishwasher when his phone rings. "Lockmore."

Not wanting to eavesdrop, I grab a disinfecting wipe and scrub down the clean counter.

"Zero eight hundred."

That's all Nolan says, and then he places his phone on the table. Turning to lean against the counter, I ask, "Is everything all right?"

"Yes. I have a meeting on base in the morning."

Nolan stands and looks toward the

backyard. "I guess I need to gather my clothes from your lawn and put on some clean ones. I know you're feeling better, but it would save me a lot of worry if I could stay and look out for you tonight."

"Of course, you can stay."

"Thank you. I'll run home, take care of things, and be right back."

I wait until Nolan is out of sight and go for my inhaler. I'm breathing much better, but there's still room for improvement. I take a puff and adjourn to the living room, where I stretch out on the sofa.

Nolan is back in less than ten minutes, and I make room for him on the cushions. The room is quiet with the TV off, but neither of us seems to mind. "Tell me about being a SEAL."

Nolan picks my feet up and places them in his lap. As he speaks, his fingers begin a slow massage of my soles. "There isn't much I can tell you. I've been with this same group of men for seven years now. The eight of us were hand-picked by our commander to form a squad, which is half of a platoon. Our leader, Fish, is the only naval officer in the group. He's been a SEAL the longest. Two of our guys are snipers. We have an actual MD on the team. That's Bandaid. Ink is a tattoo artist and has a Ph.D. in anthropology. Wrench is a mechanic and even owns his own shop. Skin, the youngest of us and so named for being a bit of an exhibitionist, is a munitions expert."

"Do you get along well?"

He chuckles, making me think maybe not. "You don't?"

"We're like brothers. I think we're as close as any group of people can get. We're all uncles to each other's children and best friends off the battlefield."

Must be nice. The friends I thought I had in Miami were quick to disappear after… well, after.

The delicious work on my feet stops, bringing my eyes to Nolan. "Iyla, my team is on alert. I'm going to have to leave soon. I know you travel for work as well, the difference being that I won't always have much warning and will never be able to tell you where I'm going or for how long."

"I understand. I'll probably worry about you. Think you can handle that?"

That elicits a small smile. "When we get back, I'll introduce you to my friends and their families. The women are great and used to dealing with the worry. Hell, they pile up on someone's couch to drink wine and watch movies while we're gone."

"That sounds great," I say through a yawn.

"How about we talk about that more later? It looks like you could use some sleep."

I don't argue with him. After an asthma attack, I've been known to sleep eighteen hours. Right now, my body says that I'm overdue for pillow time. The two of us climb into my queen-sized bed, and I fall asleep with Nolan's arm draped across my hip.

Nolan is gone when I wake up at ten the next morning. I drag myself out of bed and into a shower, feeling much more human than I did last night. After dealing with my long hair, I wander into the kitchen, wanting a big glass of orange juice. I've only taken one sip when my phone rings. *Dillan.*

I don't really have the energy to hold a conversation, but I hope a conversation will finally clue him in. "Hello."

"Good morning, Iyla."

"Good morning, Dillan."

"What's wrong? You don't sound very good."

"I had an asthma attack last night. It's left me a little fatigued."

"Damn. I didn't know you had asthma."

"It's not a big deal. What's up?"

"I wanted to see if you had plans tonight. There's an art walk in Virginia Beach. I'd like to take you there and to dinner afterward."

Ugh. The obvious answer is no. I could say it's due to the asthma. Not a lie. The problem with that excuse is that it leaves an open door for him to ask again later. I also don't want to tell him that I'm seeing Nolan, given that I'd only recently explained to Dillan why I'd refused to date him.

It's none of his business. You don't owe him

anything, I remind myself.

"I'm going to pass, Dillan."

"Pass?"

"Yes, Dillan. Pass."

The call goes silent, and then I hear him laugh darkly. "I don't believe it."

"What don't you believe? I told you months ago that I didn't want to date. Maybe I could have told you why, but I don't like advertising my sad story."

"You could have, yes. That's not the unbelievable part. Even though you wouldn't let me in, I knew we were building something special. I missed you when you left Asheville — missed you enough that I quit my life there and moved to Virginia. You may not believe this, but you'll want to try again with someone one day. I don't want to miss my chance when you're ready."

Some might find his words romantic, but his statement makes my blood boil. "Miss *your* chance when *I'm* ready? That's rather presumptuous, don't you think? You listen to me, Dillan. I can't help whatever rash decisions you made on your own. Especially after what happened the last time we were together. And as far as you being the one to wake Sleeping Beauty, let me tell you something. If and when I decide to be in a relationship again, I will be the one to decide who it will be with. Not you or anyone else. Got that?"

Dillan doesn't respond for a long time, so I think he's hung up. "Dillan?"

"I'll see you soon, Iyla."

The call ends, and I stare at the phone, Stupified. *What just happened?*

NOLAN

Standing over Iyla's bed, I button my uniform and watch her sleep. We've been friends for more than a month now. We've been… something else for less than forty-eight hours. It's way too soon for me to have the thoughts that I'm having. *Loving this woman could be easy.*

I'm not afraid of falling too fast. I'm old enough to know what I want in a partner, and Iyla is it. She's carefree and always ready with an easy smile. A smile that usually comes with a streak of paint or smudge of pencil dust from the art she so masterfully creates. There's not a superficial bone in her body, yet she's one of the most beautiful creatures I've ever seen on this earth.

The only thing that scares me is the thought that I might scare Iyla. Pushing her, even unintentionally, is the fastest way to lose her friendship. Nothing would be worse in my mind than to be compared with that asshole cop. *And she doesn't even know how much of an asshole he is.*

I get parked on base and walk inside to find out where this intelligence briefing is being held. Fish stands in the hallway when I walk past reception and waves me into the situation room.

"You look different today," he says.

"No, I don't. You're imagining things."

"Bull shit," he mumbles.

O'Reilly storms into the room and takes his usual seat. "Listen up. We've got information on our smugglers. We now have a good location and trajectory for the vessel. We also have the go-ahead to take the ship, but there's a problem."

"Of course, there's a problem," Wrench grumbles.

"You were going to deploy today, but the *Roosevelt* has had to answer a distress call from a cargo vessel attacked by pirates. The delay means they'll be late to the rendezvous point to receive you, which obviously shreds our timeline. We have to get these guys while they're still in international waters, or we risk backlash from foreign governments sympathetic to terrorist activities. The US is sending a ship to relieve the *Roosevelt,* and you will be deploying at zero-five hundred. Not to cut it too close, but by the Pentagon's calculations, the carrier should arrive at our staging coordinates about ten minutes before you."

"Shi-it." From Fish.

"Shit is right," O'Reilly agrees. "Whatever we have to do, we cannot miss this boat. Now, get out of here and get some rest."

Unlike our last meeting, I'm the first one out the door today. From behind me in the hallway, I hear Ink and Skin whispering to one another. "Did he get a haircut or something? He looks different."

Ink's soft Aussie accent jokes, "I don't think it's a new haircut, but he looks like he got *something.*"

I ignore them both, but a grin breaks out on my face as I push through the door.

Before going to check on Iyla, I run home and change out of my uniform, and she calls for me to come in when I knock on her back door. "I'm in the studio."

I follow the sound of her voice to find her leaning over a table that has a light underneath a white drawing surface. She's tracing an outline from one sheet of paper to another using a black square stick. "What's that?"

"This?" She holds up the stick. "It's compressed charcoal."

"Oh, of course it is."

Iyla rolls her eyes. "Ok, smartass. It's one of my three favorite mediums to use in art. It creates shade drawings like pencils do but with greater depth. And it's completely matte instead of having the sheen of graphite."

Her words go over my head completely, and my face must show it. Iyla laughs and crosses the room to open a drawer. From it, she pulls out an impossibly beautiful piece, considering it's all the gray color of everyday pencils.

From another drawer, she pulls out a very different kind of drawing. Like she said, the color of this piece is infinitely black. I would have never thought about it, but I can imagine that if either drawing were done using the other medium, as she calls them, neither one would have turned out the masterpieces they are.

"I see what you're talking about."

She replaces the pencil drawing and opens the drawer to return the charcoal piece. Something in the drawer catches my eye. "Wait a minute. What's that?"

Iyla's cheeks flame red, and she stammers while trying to close the drawer. I take hold of her hips and move her away from the drawer handle. "Oh geez. Do you have to look?"

I pull the flat storage drawer all the way out and find not one or two but numerous pages of charcoal pieces with me on them. Though looking at my face and... naked body does nothing for me, Iyla obviously poured her heart and soul into these works.

Iyla is still trying to stumble through an explanation, but I don't need one. I round on her and wind a hand behind her neck. In the next heartbeat, I'm pulling her against me and owning her mouth. The page she was holding flutters to the floor as I back her out of the room toward her bed.

She's now shed her embarrassment at being caught ogling me and is now clawing at my clothes. I stop pushing at the edge of her bed and pull her shirt over her head. The bra comes off next, and then I take a knee in front of her. Pants and panties are pulled slowly down her legs, and then I press my nose against the sweet spot at the juncture of her thighs.

I can smell her arousal, and it spurs me to action. The first swipe of my tongue is a direct assault against her clit, and Iyla yelps and fists her hands in my hair. *Good, but not good enough.*

For better access, I wrap my arm around the back of her knee and lift upward, opening her up to me even more. I'm merciless in attacking her most sensitive spot, but want Iyla to shatter in my arms. I need her pleasure before I can take my own.

I don't tease or circle to prolong her wait. I make continued passes over her clitoris, not stopping until she cries out and tries to jerk away from my hold. When she's weak from orgasm, I hold her in place and keep stroking over her now-swollen bundle of nerves. Iyla's whimpers soften to moans of ecstasy, the sound going straight to my dick.

Even at this slower pace, she's soon tensing up again and hoarsely shouts my name as a second orgasm hits. With a satisfied smile, I press my lips to her mons and gently lift and place her on the bed.

Iyla lies boneless and watches me strip off my clothes. Now naked, I climb up and hover over my sated woman. She lifts a limp hand to cup my cheek and guide me down onto her. I press inside her slick heat as she pulls me to her mouth.

Her body is still spasming with the aftershocks of her release, and I feel every little squeeze. This, Iyla, is every dream I've ever had, and she's mine.

That revelation pushes me over the edge, and I slam into her repeatedly, causing the bed to shake. Through gritted teeth, I demand, "Come on, baby. Give it to me one more time."

I pull out, fitting my mouth over her pulsing clit, sucking hard. Iyla screams through another orgasm, and I climb back up her body, spearing her with my cock. Her body arches off the bed, and I finally let go, freezing above her, as an explosive climax thunders through my body.

I collapse beside her, thoroughly wrung out. The two of us lie in bed, wrapped up in each other as we bask in the afterglow of the best sex I've ever had.

"Nolan, would you have dinner with me tonight?" Iyla asks breathlessly.

I could joke and laugh off her question as we've shared dinner many times now. However, this time, I know she's asking something different. "Iyla, I'd love to have dinner with you."

While she traces lazy circles on my middle, I list the places we could go, starting with the closest. We decide on a local bar and grill that should be easy to get into on a Sunday night.

Now comes the part that I haven't been

looking forward to. "Iyla, I have to leave in the morning."

Her hand stills for a moment, and then she resumes her circles. "Oh. Just make sure you come back."

I don't miss the fear in her voice. I'm sure at least some of her apprehension is due to knowing I have a dangerous job. The rest is Iyla realizing she's put herself out there again and that there's a possibility that she might lose me because of my work.

"Iyla, I know it'll be hard, not knowing where I am or if I'm even alive, but I've finally found what I've been looking for. And I'll be damned if I'm going to fuck that up by not coming home."

Iyla squeezes me tight, and we lie together in silence for a long while.

Later in the day, I go home to get changed and drive to her door to collect her properly. Iyla is gorgeous in a casual blue and white striped halter dress. Her long, brown hair floats about her shoulders in soft waves, and she's wearing a little makeup around her eyes.

For the first time in my life, I'm having trouble speaking. So I don't flub this up, I keep my mouth shut and offer her my arm. It takes until we reach the passenger door before I find my tongue. "You look beautiful tonight."

Her answering smile knocks me for a loop. I need to remember to thank my lucky stars tonight that she's mine.

The drive to the restaurant, the Stateside, takes us past the strawberry field that Dillan's near-miss had me diving into. It reminds me that I still haven't talked to Iyla about her possible meeting with him a few days ago. *Not tonight, Lockmore. You're not letting a conversation about that dick ruin your first date with Iyla.*

We pull into the parking lot of Stateside, which is pretty sparse, being a Sunday night. I've just exited the car when a police cruiser pulls into the lot and stops behind me. *I swear to god. I don't need this shit tonight.*

Ignoring the asshole cop, I walk around and open Iyla's door. Her mouth gapes open when she notices Broderick leaning against the hood of his cruiser. "Dillan, what are you doing here?"

He ignores her question, instead focusing on me. "This car has been reported stolen. You'll need to go to the station to straighten it out. I'll take Iyla home."

"Like hell, you will. This is bull shit. I haven't reported anything stolen, and nobody is taking Iyla anywhere unless she says so."

"This is your last warning, Neighbor."

He continues to stare me down, and Iyla jumps between us, thinking Broderick is still talking about the car.

"Look, Dillan, Nolan is the owner of this car. He didn't report it stolen. Someone in your office has made a mistake, or somebody is playing a prank here."

My instincts are screaming at me to do something I'd rather not, which is to have it out with the cop right here in front of Iyla, ending this once and for all.

Do or die, Lockmore. This fucker isn't backing down. Shit. "He's not talking about the car, Iyla. Your friend Dillan is threatening me… again. He wants me to stay away from you."

A rush of emotions flashes over Iyla's face, as numerous as the colors she paints with. Anger, betrayal, disbelief, and disgust all make an appearance. "How dare you? How dare you?! First, you disregard my wishes twice in Asheville, then you show up here and insist that you'll be the man I move on with."

He fucking did what?!

"Now, I find out that you've been trying to isolate me from my only friend in this town."

"I thought he was only your neighbor."

Iyla's eyebrows shoot up, and her hands go to her hips. "It's none of your damn business what he is, but since you're trying to make it your business, I'll tell you."

The more Iyla talks and the more worked-up she becomes, the more her Scottish brogue comes through. "Nolan isn't just a neighbor or friend. Nolan is my choice. I'm moving on, and I'm moving on with him."

Broderick pushes off his car, and I step

protectively in front of Iyla. "You heard her. She's not interested, so it's time for you to walk away."

"Ok, Neighbor."

The man walks back to his car, climbs in, and drives off. Behind me, Iyla trembles, but not in fear. She's angry. Very angry.

"I cannae believe that man. He's a right fud."

I watch the cop's taillights fade as Iyla continues her tirade behind me. It's as impressive as it is amusing. At one point, I can't help the bark of laughter at the Scottish cursing going on back there. Iyla huffs and stomps her way around to glare at me. "Are you aff yer heid?"

"I have no idea what any of that meant, but I loved it."

The anger slowly melts from her face until she's laughing with me. "Come on. He's gone. Let's go inside," I tell her.

"The fecking bawbag."

"Bawbag?"

"No, you're not saying it right."

I bite back a laugh and ask, "Just what is it that I'm trying to say?"

"Scrotum."

"Wait, no. You're going to have to teach me something else to call him. I can't walk around saying scrotum all the time. Even if it's in Scottish."

Iyla's laughter fades, and her tone turns serious. "What just happened? And why didn't you tell me he had threatened you?"

Bringing her hand to my mouth, I kiss her palm and press it to my cheek. "First of all, with all that I've faced as a SEAL, I'm not intimidated by one asshole. Secondly, his threats mean nothing. Only cowards make threats. Real men don't need to."

CHAPTER 12

IYLA

"Thirdly, you chose me."

My eyes fall to his lips, and my tongue darts out to wet my own. "Yes, I chose you, but you already knew that."

"And now he does, too. If the man has any pride, he'll walk away."

His hand holding mine drops but doesn't let go as he leads us to the restaurant's entrance. *If he has any pride at all...* I stop walking. "And what if he doesn't?"

My grip on Nolan's hand halts him, and he turns toward me. His jaw is tight, and his eyes are narrowed and intense. Overall, it's an incredibly intimidating sight. I'm convinced I've just met the SEAL side of Nolan. "He'd better."

His menacing promise gives me shivers, and I wonder what all has happened between the two men that I don't know about.

Inside, Nolan and I are led to a booth near the back, away from the bar. I take a moment to peruse the menu and lean back to watch this powerhouse of a man who exploded into my life.

"What's that look for?" he asks.

"I'm just glad to know that my instincts aren't completely defective."

At Nolan's puzzled look, I explain, "I've suffered a bit of self-doubt since Trevor left."

"It looks to me like you're making the most of your talent."

I snort inelegantly. "That's the easy part. Me growing up to be an artist was a foregone conclusion."

"How so?"

"My father grew up the apprentice of a pipe carver. When he moved my mother, sister, and me to the US, he took a manufacturing job but continued to carve and sell his pipes for extra money. My mother painted them sometimes. Hell, I was born with paint under my fingernails. My whole life, if anyone asked what I wanted to be, the answer was always an artist. When I graduated high school, I had multiple scholarships to choose from and got my art degree from The U in Miami. Art wasn't anything I had to choose or chase. It was just always there."

"None of that sounds regrettable."

"Maybe not, but that's where things go wrong. I stayed in Miami after graduation because one of my professors offered me a job in his company. We did what I would describe as large-scale graphic design but with physical media instead of computers. Trevor worked in the company as well. We became friends and started dating, becoming engaged two years after that.

"Long story short, I'd grown accustomed to life just happening without struggle, and I accepted it without question, Trevor included. Assuming love came as easily as art, I was too cavalier in how I approached relationships. Trevor made that all too clear, and I was devastated when he left.

"After Trevor, I realized that, besides art, I had no idea what I wanted out of life. I took the Biltmore job to get out of Miami and built walls to protect myself so I'd have time to heal and figure myself out.

"Since then, I've met two men. The first one was not a problem for me as there was no attraction, even though every other woman I saw seemed to drool over him. Again, I wondered if something in me was broken because I just couldn't see it.

"Fast forward four months, and I meet you. From then on, every day, I had to remind myself that I was not ready for a relationship. Even after a month, how could I know my lack of judgment wasn't leading me into another bad situation?"

"And now?"

"And now, I know for a fact that my instincts were right about Dillan… and you."

Nolan lifts his glass in toast. "To your instincts."

The rest of our first date goes much smoother than its beginning, and we walk out to get Nolan home before his early morning deployment. He holds the door for me, and as I walk out, I have a moment of panic. "Nolan, your car's not here."

He rushes out to the landing to see what I don't see. "That bastard."

I pull my phone from my bag to call Dillan. *After this, I'm deleting you from my phone.* The phone rings and rings before going to voicemail. I try and fail two more times and then text him.

Nolan calls the sheriff's office and swears loudly. "Their office is closed for non-emergencies. They won't open until eight am tomorrow, and I'll be long gone by then."

He tries another number but doesn't appear to get an answer. A third call nets a live person, and I listen to Nolan's half of the conversation. "Skin, I need your help. Are you busy?"

"I need a ride and to stay at your place tonight."

"It will be, just not today. Remember that restaurant you guys came to in Chesapeake, the Stateside?"

"I owe you."

Nolan slides his phone back into his pocket. "We've got a ride coming. Since there's nothing I can do about my car until I get back, I'll ride back to Virginia Beach with Skin tonight to have a way on base in the morning."

Placing his hand on my lower back, Nolan guides me back inside the bar to wait for his friend. It takes half an hour, but eventually, Nolan gets a text to come outside. I, on the other hand, haven't heard a word from Dillan.

A newer model silver Mustang is pulled up to the sidewalk when we step outside. The driver's door opens, and a muscled man in a tight, white t-shirt steps out. He jogs over to greet us, wearing a big grin. "Hi. I'm Leo, though if this guy's talked about me, he probably called me Skin. You must be someone very special."

"That's up for debate. I'm Iyla."

He laughs and shakes my hand. "Let's get you home so this guy..."

Skin stops midsentence as if he's not sure what he can say, so Nolan jumps in to set the record straight. "She knows what we are."

"Right. Let's move, and maybe somebody will tell me what the hell happened to your car."

Nolan groans and leans the seat forward, allowing me to climb in the back. The powerful sports car pulls out onto the road, and it hasn't been thirty seconds before Skin asks, "So, which one of you wants to go first?"

"I'll pass if you don't mind," I answer.

"Damn. I was hoping to hear more of your accent."

"Down boy," Nolan warns. "And I'm not calm enough to talk about it yet."

A silent communication passes between the two men, and Skin nods somberly.

The Mustang soon pulls into my driveway, and Nolan exits to let me out of the back seat.

"Iyla, I'm glad I got to meet you."

"Thanks for the ride, Leo."

"Anytime."

Nolan and I go inside my house, and I'm immediately spun into his strong arms. "I'm sorry that asshole ruined our first date."

"We can always try again."

My sexy SEAL captures my lips in a panty-dropping kiss, and in my head, I'm cursing Dillan for making it so that Nolan has to leave for the night. Before things get too heated, I pull back and lick my lips. "You stay safe. I want you to... come back."

I hate that my voice cracked and gave away my greatest fear.

Nolan cradles my face in his hands, and his forehead lowers to mine. "I'm coming back."

Gripping his wrists, I muster every bit of Scottish indignation I have in my blood. "You do that, Nolan Lockmore. You do that."

An hour later, I'm lying in a hot bath, fighting off a swarm of dark thoughts. *He'll come back. You're not wrong about him.*

It's a groggy start for me the next morning. Being around eight a.m., I assume Nolan is already in the air, on his way to face down something that would give most people nightmares.

Just thinking about it is enough to drive me mad. Speaking of mad, it's time I tried Dillan again. I'm going to try to get Nolan's car back.

Climbing out of bed, I have a simple oatmeal breakfast and shower before sitting at my desk to get some invoicing and website updating work done. By noon, I've finished what I needed and decided it was time to deal with Dillan.

Surprisingly, he answers on the first ring. "Hello, Iyla."

"Bring the car back, Dillan."

"Hey, I told Lockmore what he needed to do. He ignored the advice of a sheriff's deputy."

"That's a load of crap."

"Let me ask you something. Why is it you're fighting your boyfriend's battles? Is he not much of a man?"

"He would probably already be filing a complaint with the sheriff if he hadn't deployed this morning."

"Ouch. That'll result in a hefty storage fee at the impound lot."

"No, it's not because you're going to fix this."

"I am?"

"Yes, you are."

The silence on the other end makes me shift in my seat and feel like I've backed myself into a corner. *Too late now. Hold your ground no matter what comes out of his mouth.*

"I'll do it on one condition. I come over, and we talk."

"Absolutely not. Not after the stunt you pulled last night. That was a petty asshole thing you did. You have his car in his driveway with keys in my hand by five p.m. today, or I will report this to your superiors."

"Hmm. You drive a hard bargain. The sailor's car will be returned."

"And Dillan, there had better not be a scratch on it."

He hangs up on me then, and I start to worry. That was way, way too easy. Unable to focus on anything besides my nerves after the call to Dillan, I pace the floor all afternoon, only stopping to peek out the front window occasionally.

Right about four-forty, I hear an approaching vehicle and glance outside to see a roll-back tow truck backing up Nolan's driveway. I step out onto the front deck to oversee the operation, keeping my fingers crossed that no damage is being done to Nolan's car. *So far, so good.* The guy manning the machine appears to be doing a careful job, just like you'd expect from a professional outfit. I didn't expect to see Dillan climbing down from the cab of the roll-back truck.

What the hell is he doing here? Dillan saunters over to my front steps as though he's not the asshole that caused all this trouble to begin with. "Nice place. Quiet. Secluded."

I don't engage, standing silently with my arms crossed over my chest. Dillan smiles, unaffected by my attitude. "What? Not even a thank you? I don't think that's very nice."

"You don't want to hear what I think."

I've barely gotten the words out of my mouth when the tow truck drives away without Dillan. "Hey! Wait!" I call out, but it's too late.

"Oops," Dillan says without a trace of remorse. "You wouldn't mind giving me a ride back into town, would you?"

"You're kidding."

"Come on, Iyla. I'm stranded here."

"Not my problem."

"It's a hell of a long walk."

"After what you've done, why should I care?"

Dillan sighs, shoves his hands in his pockets, and looks down at the ground. "Because I made a mistake yesterday. I was jealous and did something stupid that hurt a friend of mine. So, please? Will you give a friend a ride into town?"

At first, my only reaction is a massive eye roll, but the genuine sadness emanating from Dillan has me giving in. "Fine, but if you say one word about Nolan, I'm kicking your ass out."

I turn to walk inside to retrieve my bag and keys, and Dillan tries to follow. I stop him with a finger jab to his sternum. "No, you stay out here."

With an inward curse, I dash inside, grab

my keys, purse, and phone, and lock my front door. I stomp insolently to my car and drop into the driver's seat. Dillan moves to follow unhurriedly as if he hasn't a care in the world. "Which way are we going?" I ask as we come to the end of my street.

"Take a left."

This county road is about a ten-minute stretch of farmland before reaching the outskirts of the little town. Just inside the town proper, Dillan gives me directions for a series of turns in and around the backstreets behind Main. I'm quickly losing my patience, and he drapes his arm across the back of my seat.

"Move your arm."

"Sorry. Stretching out feels good. I like to feel good when I ride."

I've no doubt he meant those words as dirty as they sounded. "I'm giving you about ten seconds to stop giving me bullshit directions before I stop this car and put you out on the street."

"Fine. Go about a mile and turn right on Chesterfield."

I'm unfamiliar with the area roads, but I won't admit that to Dillan. Less than two minutes later, finally, I'm directed to pull into the driveway of a small, one-story house.

Dillan doesn't immediately move to get out of the car, so I drop a not-so-subtle hint. "You're home. You can get out now."

"You know, Iyla, I think I've figured you out. You got dumped by some limp-dick artist, come to Asheville, where you become intimidated being around a real man, and end up in Virginia with the sissy-boy lawyer. I think you don't know what you want and need a strong hand to set you straight."

In the next instant, he leans over the console, wraps a hand around my left thigh, pinning my left hand, and pulls my face to his with his other hand around my neck. My right arm is pinned between us, making it impossible for me to fight him off. Dillan shoves his tongue into my mouth, and my eyes well up with tears.

Just as I get the idea to bite down on his tongue, Dillan retreats enough to whisper in my ear. "You may hate it now, but you'll learn to like it, and then you'll crave it."

Then, as if he hadn't just assaulted me, Dillan calmly exits the car and walks into his house. His door closes, leaving me alone in his driveway. I'm in over what happened and sit frozen for what feels like an eternity.

Coming to my senses, I lift a shaking hand to put the car in gear. *I have to… I have to go to the police.*

It still takes another few seconds to make my body obey, but it eventually does. I slam the car in reverse, squealing the tires as I back out of his driveway. I come to the end of the street and turn left, but then I don't know where to go next.

My eyes are blurry with tears, and we made so many turns. At least I have my phone.

Calling up maps, I search for the local police station and find that there isn't one for a town this small. My only option is to go to one of the branch offices of the Chesapeake County sheriff's department. The listing for the closest one says it closes for non-emergency business at five. I let out a choked cry and then another. It's five fifteen. Entering my own address, I rely on the GPS to get me back home, where I collapse onto the sofa sobbing.

The next morning, around eleven, I wake on the sofa, fully dressed in yesterday's clothes. I peel myself from the cushions and shuffle to the bathroom. My eyes are puffy, and my skin is blotchy from crying.

I'm not crying anymore. Now, I'm angry.

Without waiting another second, I hop back in the car and drive straight to the sheriff's office. I walk into the building looking like ten kinds of crazy, or at least feeling like it. With a bored half-smile, the receptionist asks, "How can I help you?"

"I'd like to lodge a complaint about one of your deputies."

The woman blanches as if I've shocked the life out of her. After a blank moment, she recovers somewhat and picks up her phone. Soon after, I'm whisked to a back office and closed in with a surly-looking senior deputy. "What can I do for you, miss?"

"I'd like to file a complaint against one of your deputies for absolutely abhorrent behavior."

"Who is this complaint about?"

"Dillan Broderick."

"You wouldn't happen to be the party with the stolen car snafu, would you?"

"Stolen car snafu?" *Yeah. Right.*

"Yes. Deputy Broderick came to me yesterday in a bit of a panic. He'd identified a stolen car by its plate and general description from a car-jacking that put the owner in a coma. The witness couldn't give the make and model as he didn't recognize the type and couldn't read the badging. The deputy located the stolen car by its plates and matching description, only to realize the original written report had two of the tag numbers transposed. He verified this by the VIN number. After discovering this error in the original report, Deputy Broderick acted quickly and returned the impounded car to its owner. Our office has also arranged to cover all fees associated with the vehicle's recovery and return."

"Sir, I'm not here about the car. My complaint concerns the deputy's behavior before and after the car was taken."

"Ma'am, I can understand how frustrating the situation must have been, but I can assure you that Deputy Broderick was the first to point out his honest and understandable mistake and personally saw to it that the situation was rectified on his off time."

"SIR, I dinnae come here to talk about a damn snafu. Your deputy assaulted me in my car yesterday evening."

The man goes white as a sheet. *Now I've got his attention.* He clears his throat and asks, "Would you please describe for me what happened?"

"He kissed me. Forcibly."

"He kissed you. Where did this take place?"

"In my car, sitting in his driveway."

The man's forehead wrinkles in concentration, and he appears to have difficulty understanding what I've said. "Let me get this straight. You're not complaining about his acting on a flawed stolen vehicle report or that there was damage to the vehicle upon its return to you or an associate of yours. You're alleging that you gave this same deputy a ride to his home after he corrected the mistake and that he kissed you."

Shit. Brilliant move, Dillan. Sadistic but brilliant.

"I realize how it sounds."

"No. Ma'am, I don't think you do. Cops aren't perfect. This particular one came here from a big city with all the technology in the world. He may be feeling his way around our archaic systems and will have a hiccup here and there, but when a man not only owns up to his mistakes but works to correct mistakes that others made that he didn't catch, I give the man the benefit of the doubt. What I won't put up with is someone in the community retaliating against an officer doing his job. I'll show clemency this time, but I'll warn you not to try your extortion scheme in this department again."

The deputy sheriff stands and opens his office door, indicating the conversation is over.

ESCAPEPROOF

JO CHAMBLISS

CHAPTER 13

NOLAN

"So, are you going to tell me what happened or what?"

Skin's question was so loud it caught the attention of everyone on the team. I wouldn't talk about it last night or on the way to base this morning. Now, I'm wishing I had.

"What's wrong, Judge?" Fish asks. "I noticed you rode in with Skin."

I sucker punch Skin in the arm without looking away from Fish's curious stare. Keeping names out of it because I know how these guys are, I explain everything that's happened since my first encounter with Broderick.

"A cop?!" Ink declares.

"Makes things interesting," Wrench adds unhelpfully.

Fish shuts them up and asks, "Do you think she's in danger?"

I shrug at his question, not in indifference but uncertainty. "So far, he's all mouth except for the shit with my car."

"And the gut punch," Skin points out.

"Does she have someone she can call? Other than local LEOs, I mean?" Devil asks.

"Shit. I should have thought of that. I should have thought to give her Bassett's info. He doesn't answer to a sheriff and is in a different county anyway."

Skin places a hand on my shoulder and squeezes. "We could always get the commander to talk to Bassett. Get him to ride out and check on her."

"No. Not unless I could warn her first. And another unknown voice on the phone assuring her that the detective is safe wouldn't be enough. I just have to hope that I haven't underestimated the bastard and that she'll be fine for a few days. With any luck, she'll go out of town for business and be completely out of his reach."

"I'm sorry all this shit's hitting at the same time, but we're going to need your head clear." Fish looks around at the group. "Settle in. Get some extra rest. We don't know what the other end of this ride is going to look like."

Damn, but was he right. An hour from the rendezvous coordinates, the plane receives a message from the Roosevelt. They're running late. *Of fucking course.* The aircraft enters a holding pattern, and the countdown begins. The plane can hold as long as the *Roosevelt* arrives before it reaches a certain fuel level. At that point, it has to leave, mission be damned.

With fifteen minutes to spare, Fish makes a bold decision. "If this bird has to leave, it's leaving without us. Now would be a good time to pray that the sailors on The Big Stick are decent fishermen."

One of the crewmen comes to the back of the plane ten minutes later. He shakes his head. "They're close, but the captain says we've got to go."

"Open the launch ramp."

"Sir... the cloud deck is too low. We don't know—"

"I said open the fucking ramp!"

The crewman's eyes go wide. "Ye... yes, sir."

He sprints to the ramp controls and picks up a phone to speak with the cockpit. When he turns his head back around and gives a thumbs up, he slams his hand on the ramp release.

Over the noise, Fish yells, "Open 'em early. Make this ride as slow as you can."

The eight of us jump into the cloud, which completely blocks visibility to the water. There's still plenty of light, given that it's six p.m. local time, so we'll have a visible target once we break through the cloud base. Hopefully, it won't be just water.

Because of the cloud's density, we can't see each other, so all of us will ensure that our descent is straight down. No one wants to glide into someone else and send them plummeting to their death.

No more than three seconds pass before I break through the mist. The instant I do, I bank right and cross my fingers that I'll land on the deck of the carrier racing in our direction instead of smacking into the front of it.

The three-hundred-yard-long flat top makes it underneath Fish just in time for his toe to touch down on the leading edge of the deck. Each man after has a little more clearance but still has to make the landing at a full run to keep from falling over and getting chewed up by the rough landing surface. *Damn, that was close.*

A shocked crew runs out to meet us as we remove our chutes. We salute the officer of the group, who returns the greeting with a chuckle. "You guys must be dangling some big brass ones to attempt a jump like that. I'm Commander Masterson, the XO. Your pilot radioed us to say they couldn't wait for us any longer and then a minute later to say that you were now our responsibility. I'm pretty sure they think you're shark bait right now. We've got a line set up to reach your SEAL commander, so if you haven't shit yourselves, we'll get you briefed and ready to go. My crew will see to your jump gear."

"Thank you, Commander."

We follow the XO off the flight deck into a wardroom where command central has been assembled for this mission. The ship's captain is already there and speaking with a familiar voice over a conference speaker. "Here're your boys now."

"Lieutenant Hill," Commander O'Reilly begins. "The boat is no longer following the projected course. It's now anchored thirty miles off the coast of Morocco, just west of due north of Casablanca. Captain Swisher's crew has been provided the coordinates."

The captain stands and points to a chart of the area. "Even though we've been delayed, I've had a crew dedicated to monitoring this bug. Since dropping anchor forty minutes ago, there haven't been any vessels to come near your target. Or at least not yet."

Strange. I'm sure we all have questions, but we let our lieutenant take the lead. "Crew activity?"

"Quiet," Commander O'Reilly reports. "We only count four men instead of the ten typically on board. Except for the periodic patrol, you'd think these guys were pleasure cruising. You're going to set out as planned from the *Roosevelt* at dusk. With our attack coming so early in the night, the crew will all be awake, so taking out their radar is off the table. You'll have to stage outside the *Golden Clam's* radar range and dive to cover the remaining distance. If the *Clam* gets underway before then, we'll reset, and the *Roosevelt* will stand by while we regroup."

I tune out the logistical chatter to digest the new information. *Why would they pick up a shipment and leave most of their men onshore? That's a hell of a security risk. If a break in the ranks caused the split, these guys on the boat wouldn't want to stick around for anyone to catch up to them.* "Excuse me, sir."

"Go ahead, Lockmore."

"Can you run down the port activity or contact for the *Golden Clam* over the last forty-eight hours?"

"Only the last eighteen. Before that, the Clam spent a lot of time in congested waters. Anything could have happened at that point. We can confirm that the boat docked in Morocco for five hours. That's when the crew disembarked. The remaining crew did receive a shipment, but based on its size, it does not appear to be weaponry. What's on your mind, Judge?"

"Assuming they picked up their main shipment before Morocco, the missing crew may be in Casablanca to negotiate with a buyer. That could explain why they'd want the boat out of the dock and safe from a doublecross."

"It's a good possibility."

The leather of Captain Swisher's chair creaks as he leans forward and props his elbows on the desk. Speaking to O'Reilly, he says, "Tim, if your boys take the boat, they could stake out on board until the rest of the players call for the boat's return. That would give the CIA a chance to get the dealers and the buyers."

"That's our plan then."

"All right, boys. Let's get you set up."

My team is given a place to rest for the next two hours or so before we gear up. At dusk, the primary boat officer leads us down to the launch deck.

A crane extends and rotates downward, dangling a rigid hull inflatable boat beside the launch deck. We've ridden a boat down this way many times, but I've never been a fan. As I stare at the ancient but effective rope and pulley system, a single crewman approaches our group. "Jackson Piquette. I'm the coxswain on your mission. The sea state is at a four, so your ride won't be too rough."

All nine of us step down into the RHIB, and the linemen start to lower the boat into the ocean below.

The instant we're released, the boat speeds over the whitecaps, barely visible in the darkness on its way to our destination six miles away. The coxswain keeps in constant contact with the boat officer of the *Roosevelt* and steers the inflatable masterfully in the dark.

"Good luck, Lieutenant," Piquette says when the boat stops.

Fish acknowledges the coxswain, and we fall out, remaining at the surface until we're about a hundred yards away from the Clam. At this point, we dive and spread out to board the Clam at specific points. Skin, Hawk, and I are in one group and will board on the port side, which has an opening in the rigid handrail.

We remove our fins and tanks, placing them in a mesh bag that's secured to the hull below the waterline.

Skin reaches up to cut the ropes stretching across the rail opening and lifts himself onto the deck. I follow behind him, with Hawk covering us from below. When I clear the rail, Skin and I cover the deck fore and aft while Hawk boards and gets in position. Once he signals that he's ready, we leave him to advance along the ship's port side and start toward the companionway to the lower deck.

Fish and Ink will take the two guys on the bridge while Devil keeps watch on the starboard side. Wrench and Bandaid are going below with us but entering through the starboard side hatch.

This boat isn't all that big and appears to have seen better days, the complete opposite of the last smuggling ship we dealt with. New, old, none of that shit matters. All we care about is securing the two men below deck.

Wrench is the first of us to reach the bottom. Coming down the companionway, I can just see a pair of feet belonging to the man my teammate is creeping up behind. The crewman is standing in the galley scraping the scales off a fish.

The rasping noise covers our approach, so he has no clue we're coming. Wrench grabs the guy, covering his mouth with a gloved hand to keep him from alerting anyone else. The knife in his hand starts swinging, but Bandaid catches that hand and jabs a needle into the man's neck.

Skin and I give way as they carry the unconscious man toward the hatch, and then we recommence clearing the area. The other smuggler isn't in the bunks or the head. All that's left is the engine room since this boat doesn't have a lazaretto like similar models.

I get a little niggle at the back of my neck and motion for Skin to stop his advance. Scanning the beat-up salon, I check for red flags. Nothing jumps out at me, and we still need to secure the boat. I make the decision to take point and gesture for Skin to get behind me.

I drop to a knee at the engine room door and listen for sounds beneath the hatch. The ship's engine is silent, so I should hear our guy moving around. I don't.

Standing as far to the left as I can, I open the door and use the barrel of my rifle to widen the opening. "Please don't kill me. I have information," a heavily accented voice says.

The request is unexpected, and something about the way he said it sets off warning bells in my head. I level my rifle with the man's head and step into the doorway. He has one arm in the air, and one is resting in a makeshift sling. I can't see that hand.

Something's wrong here. My insides are screaming. The man's hand shifts inside the thin fabric of the sling just as a corner of his mouth turns upward.

Fuck no! "Get out of here, Skin!"

I send a round into the man's forehead and turn to meet the shocked face of my friend. "MOVE! MOVE! MOVE!"

The whole way out, I'm yelling to the rest of the team, hoping that they hear me or at least heard the shot. Skin races toward the companionway with me on his ass. He reaches the first step, but that's as far as we get before the port side bulkhead explodes, shooting napalm and shrapnel at the two of us. Skin's left side bursts into flames, and I take several blows from the improvised shrapnel.

He screams and tries to extinguish the fire, but I know we're quickly running out of time. I pick up my friend, race up the stairs, and throw him over the rail into the ocean while still screaming for the rest of my team to abandon ship.

As I climb over the rail, another explosion shakes the boat. Something strikes the back of my head, and I don't even feel the impact of the water.

A splitting headache wakes me from a nightmare sometime later, and I squeeze my eyes shut even tighter against the too-bright lights in the room. My entire upper body is throbbing, and I think I'm about to…

Someone shoves something against my

mouth to catch the puke so it doesn't end up all over me and whatever bed I'm lying in. *God, my chest hurts.* Without looking to see who's in the room with me, I start asking about Skin. "Where's Ramsay?"

"He's on his way to Germany." *Devil.*

"Did everybody make it out?"

"Yes. Thanks to you."

I try opening my eyes, but the sickening pain won't allow it. Someone flips a switch, throwing the room into blessed darkness. My eyes finally open to see five of my teammates sitting and standing in the dim light. As I suspected, I'm in a ship's medical ward. "Where's Bandaid?"

"He's taking care of Skin. Before they left, Skin told us that you carried him after he was hit with the napalm. He couldn't put the fire out, but you got him into the water."

His pain-filled screams fill my head, and I speak up to change the subject. "You guys are okay?"

"We're fine. When we heard the shot and then you screaming for us to abort, no one hesitated. You were the last one off the boat."

"I think I had help. I wasn't even conscious when I hit the water."

"We know," Wrench says. "You nearly drowned. It took three of us to find you under the surface and nearly forty seconds of CPR to bring you back."

"Where are we now?"

"Back on the carrier headed for the naval base in Rota." Fish answers. To the rest of the team, he says, "Now that Judge is awake, I want the rest of you to get cleaned up, get some food, and find a place to sleep."

"What about you," I ask our leader.

"I'll do the same as soon as I've updated the commander again."

The men start to file out, and I close my eyes. Whether I sleep or not, I don't know. My mind is playing on a loop the images of the flames licking up Skin's body to the soundtrack of his screams. Those screams get louder and louder until I hear, "Whoa there, son."

I open my eyes to see Captain Swisher standing next to my bed. Fish is at the foot. "What happened?"

"I think you were back on that boat again." He turns around and looks for something, holding it out to me when he finds it. "Here. Drink this."

Sitting up is difficult, but I won't show it. I lift a bare left arm to accept the cup and stop reaching when I notice all the bloody bandages. "How long have I been out this time?"

"About five hours," Fish answers.

Still counting wounds, I ask, "Am I still going to have a job after this?"

"It's not as bad as it looks. You're being given IV antibiotics just in case, but you'll be back."

"What's the word on Skin?"

Captain Swisher clears his throat. "Chief Petty Officer Ramsay suffered second and third-degree burns on his left arm, shoulder, neck, and cheek. The doctors report that the third-degree burns are not widespread, partly due to the fact that his uniform was still damp. What they say really saved him was the speed at which he was thrown into the cold water of the Atlantic. They also say that the quick dunk means that, for the most part, he won't lose elasticity in his skin except for a few small places. And because I know you're going to ask, he'll most likely be able to return to active duty as well... if his mind can handle it. He'll have significant scarring, mentally and physically."

Significant scarring. And I'm the one that moved him behind me. If I had left Skin on point, he would still be behind me and wouldn't have gotten burned. *But I would have burned, and the whole team likely would have been killed in the ensuing explosion.*

Knowing there's no end to the *what-if* second-guessing, I shut off that line of thinking. Turning to Fish, I ask, "What now?"

"We'll be in Rota in another six hours. Then, O'Reilly wants us on a plane home."

"What about Ramsay?"

Fish shakes his head. "He'll be at Landstuhl for at least two weeks."

ESCAPEPROOF

JO CHAMBLISS

CHAPTER 14

IYLA

My walk to the car is made entirely in a daze. Dillan knew or at least suspected that I'd go to the police after he attacked me. I did and played right into his hands. He set me up so that no man with a badge will listen to anything I have to say, no matter what happens.

Dillan can do whatever the hell he wants.

Despite the warm temperature, I feel a sudden chill and rush to get as far away from the station as possible. I end up on a bench by the creek at the city park.

"You may hate it now, but you'll learn to like it, and then you'll crave it."

The need to get away overwhelms me, and I spring up from my seat after just a few seconds. Running to the car like the hounds of hell are after me, I jump inside and toss gravel in my rush to get out of there. I run inside my house after the short drive, lock the door, and throw my stuff on the floor.

My first stop is my office. I open my email to look up the contact information for a DC architecture firm looking for someone to do a colossal watercolor rendering of a model they've constructed for a new hospital. I'm scheduled to meet with them on Thursday, but I'm hoping they'll be okay with me meeting earlier.

I've got to get out of this town.

My email goes through, and I rush to my room, haphazardly throwing clothes and things into a bag. My art supplies get packed with much more care, and I check my email one last time before turning out the studio light.

Ms. Dunsmore,

An earlier meeting time is not a problem. I'll see you at nine am tomorrow.

Archi Hoover, AIA
Principal Architect
Hoover Raymond Architecture Studio

"Oh, thank god."

All my things are thrown into the car, and I start the four-hour drive to DC, not taking an easy breath until I've reached Norfolk. I arrive in Alexandria midway through the afternoon, check into a hotel, and finally release the tension in my shoulders when I'm behind that locked door.

Dillan's words have been playing on repeat inside my head throughout the entire drive up here, and I've been worrying myself to death about what he means to do. My thoughts get me nowhere, and I pass out curled up on the bed long before the sun goes down.

By morning, I'm a little less high-strung

and grateful to lose myself in work, a safe distance from Dillan. The entire morning is spent in a modern glass and concrete building with the hospital project's chief and landscape architects.

The scale model they've constructed is four feet wide, three feet long, and two feet tall. Though void of color and texture, the all-white model is a beautiful mockup of their design. The chief architect gives me a tour of the model, and a good hour is spent going over building materials and plant species to be used around the structure. Once their presentation is finished, I take dozens of pictures of the model in front of a green screen.

I experiment with several angles, points of view, lighting orientation, and manual focus. Given the layout of the hospital campus, finding one view that adequately represents the project's full capability and aesthetic will be a challenge.

Looking through the shots that I took, I linger a little longer than necessary before retiring to my hotel room to start work on the rendering.

My easel is set up with a fresh sheet of paper, and my mini-projector is perched on the desk behind me. The model image I've selected is then projected onto the watercolor paper so I can pen the image to paint.

I work the rest of the day and the next, bringing the image to life. After rinsing out my brushes, I email Mr. Hoover to let him know I'm finished. He responds right away despite the late hour, and we set up a meeting for nine in the morning to present the finished work.

All stakeholders are present for the unveiling, and everyone seems pleased with the final product. The rendering is to be used in all promotions of the coming state-of-the-art medical facility as well as being hung in the main lobby after construction.

I leave the meeting and the city, satisfied with another job well done but still nervous about returning home. Sure, this trip gave me a temporary escape, but I knew it wouldn't help in the long run. I keep wondering how long Nolan will be gone and hoping for a miracle that he'll be there when I get back.

The drive back to Chesapeake is made much slower than the trip out. I wish I could take a different route than the main road through town, but that would mean driving through someone's field. All I can do is keep my eyes on the road and hope I don't spot Dillan patrolling in the area.

Traffic seems to be light in town, and the only car I see between town and home is a pickup with dark tinted windows that passes me for driving too slowly.

I breathe a sigh of relief when I pull off the county highway onto my street. I stop the car long enough to collect mine and Nolan's mail and park in my usual place. Now, all I can think about is a large glass of wine and a long soak to settle my nerves that have ratcheted up since arriving back in Chesapeake County.

My key has just slid into the deadbolt lock when Dillan's voice sounds behind me. "Where have you been?"

I scream, mail goes flying, and I spin around, holding my keys in front of me like a weapon. "Get away from me!"

He shakes his head slowly as he stalks forward. I swipe out at him with my car key to stop his advance. The move is pitifully ineffective, and Dillan rips the keys from my hand and spins me around, pressing my chest against the door. "That wasn't very nice. I asked you a question. Where have you been?"

"None of your damn business!"

My arm held behind my back is wrenched higher, causing me to cry out in pain and lift to my toes to relieve the ache in my shoulder.

"Try again," he murmurs against my ear.

Sobbing, I tell him the truth. "I had a job in DC. A new client needed a watercolor rendering."

"That's a good girl. See, you're learning already."

His painful grip on me loosens, and I turn back around, slamming my back against the door.

"Kiss me, Iyla."

Tears begin streaming down my face as I shake my head no. Dillan laughs. Actually laughs. "If you're afraid of your neighbor seeing us together, it's a little late for that and something he's just going to have to get used to."

I pull in a sharp breath. "What did you do?"

He shrugs a shoulder. "I wouldn't worry about that. I'd start thinking about how you can start behaving like a good girl while you have my patience. I'd hate to have to take out my frustrations on the weak and prissy lawyer. I'm sure by now that you know what I can do."

"You leave him alone!"

"You want something? You'll have to earn it. Kiss me, Iyla."

I remain frozen in my spot, and Dillan steps toward the stairs. "Wait!"

Stiff legs shuffle across the porch, and Dillan looks at me expectantly. "Kiss me like you kiss him or no deal."

My tears flow harder, and I feel like I'm giving away a piece of my soul as I touch my lips to his. The kiss is wooden, and Dillan grunts and starts to pull away. Desperate to protect Nolan, I slip my tongue between the bastard's lips, which he accepts greedily.

Even as his hands slide over my body, I keep mine firmly against my sides. I'm giving all I can and hope that's enough to stave off Dillan's threat. *God, please don't let Nolan drive up and see this.*

Dillan takes his fill and pulls back. "Mmm. Do you like it yet?"

"I hate you," I whisper.

He chuckles darkly. "Needy little girls always do at first. Before long, I'll be in your blood, and you won't be able to imagine living without me."

"Never," I whisper.

Dillan is on me in a second. He crushes me against the wall and reaches beneath my shorts to cup me over my panties. "Oh, baby. I could take you right now. Fuck the memory of the neighbor right out of you. He touched what's mine. Swayed your pretty little head."

Unwelcome fingers draw little circles over my center. I struggle against Dillan's hold, but the man is too strong. "If you keep fighting me, I might have to kill him."

I squeeze my eyes shut and try to block out Dillan's touch. I'm paralyzed. As much as he repulses me, I have to know. "Why me?"

"I told you. I like beautiful things. You aren't only beautiful; you create beauty with just the stroke of your wrist. All you need is a little discipline. I'll give you that, and you'll be perfect."

His words. So dark. How did we get here? Dillan releases me so suddenly that I collapse to the landing. When I open my eyes again, he's gone. I curl into a ball, unable to move for a long time. As sunset sends the shadows crawling across my yard, I start to worry about Dillan coming back.

I can't be here when he does, but

somehow, he'll know if I try to escape through town. There's only one fecking road. I crawl inside and rise on shaky legs, racing to my room to grab a blanket, pillow, and some clothes. I collect a bottle of water and my biggest knife from the kitchen and cross my backyard into Nolan's. He has a lounge chair on his back deck where I can spend the night.

NOLAN

No more updates come in about Skin during our final hours on the carrier. The rest of the team seems to be as off-kilter as I am, with one of us missing. Considering my jacked-up head and multiple holes, they divvy up my gear to carry to the waiting transport. I'm walking fine, but every move I make pulls the dozens of stitches I received.

From the flat top, we're trucked directly to a waiting plane. Bandaid stands beside it, looking haggard and worn despite his clean uniform.

He walks up to me as I gingerly climb down from the truck bed. "How are you doing?"

"I'm alive. And people tell me I still have a job."

"No medical discharge for you. I don't think O'Reilly would allow it."

"How's Ramsay?"

"Lucky. Your quick actions saved his... well, his skin. For the most part, the long-term damage is limited to scarring."

I drop my head, overwhelmed and emotional with relief. Bandaid places a hand on my shoulder in support. One by one, the rest of the team does the same. I blink away the dampness in my eyes and take a deep breath. "Let's go home."

The eight-hour flight passes slowly, and I turn my phone on as soon as we touch down at Oceana. It's after ten p.m., and my phone sounds with a security alert from three hours ago. I start the footage and see Iyla carrying a blanket, pillow, and bag to my back deck.

She settles on my chaise, and the video soon ends from lack of motion. *What the hell is she doing that for?*

Pulling up the system app, I scroll through the log to see if there have been any other strange occurrences. Monday night, the carport camera shows my car sitting in its place, making me wonder how it got back there to begin with. The video continues, and I see the interior light come on as if someone's just opened one of the doors. I don't see anyone, and the light turns off several seconds later. That video ends.

The following entries are several notifications from earlier that same day, timed around a quarter to five. A roll-back truck can be seen backing up my driveway carrying my Genesis. The driver jumps down from the cab and starts unloading.

The video continues, and my blood runs

ice cold. Broderick steps out of the passenger side of the tow truck and walks toward Iyla's house. The worst part is watching the tow truck leave – without Broderick.

I've got to get home. Right the hell now. Knowing my teammates have loved ones waiting at home, I don't ask any of them for help. I send a text to Jasper instead. *Wherever you are, whatever you're doing, stop and get your ass to the Little Creek helipad.*

It's late, but I know that won't be a problem. Thankfully, Jasper answers quickly. *Sure thing, Sweetheart.*

By the time the Seahawk taxi ferries us from Oceana to Little Creek, Commander O'Reilly and Jasper are both waiting next to the landing pad. The two men in navy field uniforms approach the plane and open the door. Jasper's eyes widen when he takes in my appearance and offers his arm to help me down.

When we're clear, the helo lifts off, and O'Reilly squares off to say what he came to say. "Ramsay's burns will require minimal grafting. He's scheduled for the procedure tomorrow morning and has not so politely requested that I line him up a ride home. You men get out of here. I don't want to see any of you on base until Monday."

We split off in our separate directions, and Jasper carries all my shit. During our walk to the parking area, I try calling Iyla, but the call goes straight to voicemail. Jasper looks like he wants to talk but holds his tongue until we're seated in his car. "Are you all right?"

"I'm ok. Listen. I need to get home fast. Something's wrong."

"I'll step on it."

The drive is still agonizingly long, even with Jasper risking a reckless driving citation. Before the car stops, I push open the door and run toward my house, much to my sliced-up body's protest.

I shove the front door hard enough to bounce off the wall, turn off the alarm, and head straight for the back deck, where the video showed Iyla. I open the deck door quietly to keep from scaring her. She's still there, asleep, wrapped in her blanket.

Carefully dropping to a knee, I bite my tongue against the grunt of pain again so I don't scare Iyla. I can sense that Jasper has followed me out onto the porch, but thankfully, he remains quiet as well.

I reach up and brush the hair off her face. "Iyla. Wake up, baby."

She stirs and then lets out a terrified scream as she scrambles away from me. "Iyla! Iyla, it's me. Nolan."

Her body goes limp, and she lets out this deep, sorrowful sob. "Nolan!"

Ignoring the pulling and popping of my stitches, I gather her to my chest. I sway a little as

I stand and carry Iyla inside. Jasper moves out of the way and watches the happenings with a worried frown pulling on his features.

As soon as we're in the kitchen, I set Iyla on the counter and take hold of her face. "What happened? Tell me what's wrong."

She squeezes her eyes shut, and I know what she's hiding is bad. "Iyla, sweetheart, please look at me."

The soft hiccups of her crying continue, but she does slowly open her eyes. Her beautiful blue orbs take me in and widen to saucers as she notices my injuries. "Oh god, Nolan. What happened to you?"

She jumps from the counter, running her hands over my face and bending to inspect my left arm. "You're hurt. How bad is it?"

I grab her hands and stand her back up. "Iyla, I'm fine. Why were you sleeping on my back deck?"

She looks away and to the floor. My own eyes drift closed as I guess what must have happened. "Broderick."

Iyla nods without looking up. I pull her against me and look up at Jasper. He reads my expression and pulls out his phone to begin recording. "Iyla, I need you to tell me exactly what happened. I know he was here. He showed up on my security feed."

"Dillan was waiting when I got home. He…"

Hard sobs rack her body. I bottle my rage, taking slow, measured breaths, and Iyla continues. "I made him bring your car back. He pinned me and kissed me. I went to the police to report him, but Dillan had set things up so that I would look like someone retaliating against him for doing his job. No one would believe me. His boss even threatened me. That meant Dillan could do anything he wanted. I came home and packed to go to DC for a few days. When I came back, he knew and was here waiting. He said... He made me..."

Iyla falls apart in my arms, and it's all I can do not to pass her off to Jasper and go kill that son of a bitch. "Iyla, I need to know. Did he rape you?"

"No. He told me to kiss him like I kiss you and do it willingly. He said he'd hurt you if I didn't. I didn't want to! I'm sorry, Nolan. I didn't want to. And then he touched me. Oh god, Nolan. He touched me all over. I'm sorry. I'm sorry."

"Shh." I wrap my arms around her again and stroke her long hair. "I'm not mad at you, baby. Never at you. When did this happen?"

"Today. After Dillan left, I ran over here and hid here in case he came back."

"You're safe now. I won't let him hurt you."

I pick her up and carry her to my bed, settling her beneath the covers. "Rest now. You're safe. I'll be back."

Iyla reaches for me with panic in her eyes. "Please don't go."

"I'm not going anywhere. I need to talk to someone in the kitchen. I'll be back in less than ten minutes."

I touch my lips to her temple and back out of the room, closing the door softly. Standing in the hall, I take a few deep breaths and return to the kitchen.

"Wow," Jasper says. "How about you clue me in to what the fuck is going on?"

Eyeing him warily, I ask, "Is this as my lawyer or as family?"

He crosses his arms. "How about as someone who wants to keep you from spending the rest of your life in prison for the murder I see in your eyes."

With a shaking hand, I gesture to the dining room table. "Have a seat. I'm about to blow your fucking mind."

CHAPTER 15

NOLAN

Jasper whistles long and low at my story and leans back in his chair. "There's more to this. More that she didn't say."

"I know, but I didn't want to push her anymore tonight." I rub my hand over my head and down my face in frustration.

"Look, it's nearly midnight, and none of us will be able to do shit tonight. Why don't you get some sleep? I'm sure she'll do better if you're with her anyway. I'll check in with you after work tomorrow, but you call if anything comes up before then."

"Thanks, Jasper."

Since the man has his own key, he lets himself out, and I return to Iyla. A lamp glows softly beside the bed, and Iyla's eyes are open when I enter the room. Keeping my eyes on hers, I walk to the bed and strip off my uniform.

Her eyes leave mine to scan down the length of my body, her face growing increasingly troubled the more she sees. "What happened to you?"

"I was in a small explosion. Fortunately, my injuries were not severe."

Iyla gasps. "Was anyone else hurt?"

Skin's tortured screams sound in my head, making me cringe. "Skin. He took the worst of it."

"Nolan, I'm sorry. Will he be ok?"

"I'm told he'll be fine. I haven't seen him since the explosion. He's at a hospital in Germany."

I climb into bed beside Iyla and pull her to me. "Are you all right?"

She shudders, remembering what happened. "I'm scared to death, and I've never been afraid before."

"Iyla, I want you to understand something. I know you and most other people see me as a gentle soul, and I guess, for the most part, I am. But I will kill this man if I get the chance. I won't hesitate, I won't show any mercy, and I won't feel remorse."

I barely hear her whispered reply, "Good."

Wrapped in Iyla's warmth, I fade quickly and wake in what seems like moments later, feeling groggy. My phone indicates someone is at the front door, and I blink a few times to clear my vision to check the screen.

Six SEALs are standing on my front porch. Pulling my arm out from underneath Iyla's head, I stand and pull on some track pants from the closet. I'm a little stiff this morning, but tight muscles loosen up as I move toward the front door.

I open up and signal the guys to keep quiet when they come in. Each man gives me an odd look as he passes, confused by the order. "Does your head still hurt that bad?" Bandaid asks.

"No, I don't want you to wake—"

"Nolan?" Iyla's startled voice sounds from the hall.

I turn in that direction and walk over to grab her hand. I touch her cheek and study her face. "How are you feeling this morning?"

Iyla glances over my shoulder and back at me. "I'm okay. Who are they?"

"My team. If you feel up to it, I'd like you to meet them."

Her chin lifts, trying to hide her trepidation. "I'm fine."

Despite her claim, Iyla walks hesitantly with me toward the group of intimidating men.

"Iyla, this is Wrench Delano, Fish Hill, Hawk Morgan, Ink Fischer, Bandaid Myers, and Devil Murphy. Guys, this is Iyla."

Fish and Devil perk up and share a look. "Iyla? That's an unusual name."

"Aye. It's Scottish."

The two men glance at one another again, and I feel completely out of the loop on something.

"Are you, by chance, an artist?"

"Aye."

Fish grins and reaches for his phone. He

scrolls for a moment and then holds the device out to Iyla. She leans over, sees a picture of Ari and little Chris, and gasps. "She's yours?!"

"She is."

What is going on?

Devil does the same, showing her a picture of Colton.

"I don't believe it."

"Don't believe what?" I ask.

"I've met these kids. On the beach my first week here."

Fish shakes his head. "Your lady drew them and gave the sketches to Willa and Rory."

He turns to Iyla and says, "You may not know this, Iyla, but that picture means a lot to my little girl."

Iyla nods despondently, making Fish's brow furrow. "Are the two of you all right? We didn't mean to intrude. I don't think any of us realized you were seeing someone," my leader says.

I shake my head. "Iyla moved in next door just over a month ago. We've been together for about a week. And no, we're not all right. We've got a problem. A big problem."

"Whatever it is, you know we've got your backs."

I turn Iyla to face me and say, "These guys are solid and smart, and any one of them would fight to the death for you just as I would. If you're up to it, I'd like to read them into what's been happening."

Iyla's bottom lip trembles slightly, but she nods. "Ok. If you trust them, I trust them."

We all take seats in the living room, and I walk the team through everything that happened up to our deployment. And then comes the hard part. I ask Iyla to recount in detail what happened after I left Monday morning. Knowing this is going to be difficult for her to say and for me to hear again, I pull her into my lap. She struggles through the telling of it just as I'm struggling to keep calm listening to it.

Along with the bastard's sick ideas about owning Iyla against her wishes, I'm struck by how meticulous Broderick's planning was to set things up as he did. The guy is patient and calculating. That's the most dangerous type of enemy you can have. They don't act in haste, and they don't make mistakes.

The entire group is silent when Iyla finishes talking. Like me, they're all at a loss for what to do. Devil is the first to speak. "Since the guy found and followed you here, I doubt leaving would do you much good."

Wrench leans forward and says, "Cameras. Put invisible cameras fucking every damn where. Catch this guy on video and put him away."

"No," this from Hawk. "He'd expect you to do that. Not that cameras are a bad idea, but he's going to attack in areas where she has no control. He *wants* her to become a prisoner in her home. Isolate her. Make her crazy."

"But she won't be alone, and he knows that," I counter.

"Yeah, and he will keep baiting you until you slip up. Then he's going to haul your ass off to jail. And based on what we all just heard, he'll have his boss's support," Hawk says.

"So, where does that leave us? Me turning the other cheek while he terrorizes Iyla?"

"Calm down, Judge." Fish says. "That's not what we're suggesting. We're just talking through all the angles like we always do."

"We need to let this guy think he's winning and set up a trap for him."

"What kind of a trap, Ink? This asshole is operating like he's got an IQ higher than yours. He's thought of everything. One step out of the norm, and he'll sniff it out."

"Simple. Iyla is going to have to be bait."

I jump out of my seat, barely keeping Iyla from tumbling to the floor. "What the hell did you just say?"

"I'm not suggesting we tie her to a tree in the woods and leave her, dumbass."

"Please. Stop!"

All eyes turn at Iyla's trembling voice. She's hidden her eyes, but the tears escape from beneath her hands. "I'm not a coward, but I can't…"

"You're not bait," I finish for her. I won't

allow it. Not when this guy has been able to anticipate every move we've made thus far.

Bandaid speaks up for the first time since walking in. "So, what do we do then?"

Again, there's a crippling silence among the group. No one has a single damned clue.

ESCAPEPROOF

JO CHAMBLISS

CHAPTER 16

IYLA

My faith falters when no one speaks up. If these men whose lives revolve around surviving danger don't have any ideas, I'm in much more trouble than I thought.

I start babbling, grasping at straws. "You have good security here. What if we make it look like I've left? We can take my car and hide it somewhere, and I can stay here. Dillan will come to look for me at my house. With any luck, he'll try to break in, and you'll get him on camera."

Ink shakes his head. "That could work, but what if the guy fakes receiving a report of a break-in at your place and shows up to investigate? Anything he did would be passed off as having been done by the perpetrator."

"But not if someone *is* at the house."

"What do you mean," Fish asks Nolan.

"Someone could move into Iyla's house. Someone that would be there if and when Broderick came sniffing around."

"Maybe, but not yet. For now, let's go with what Iyla suggested. We'll blank out her house and have one of us drive her car away from here."

"That'll be me," Wrench offers. "I can hide her ride in my shop. I'll even pretend to work on it in case the douche gets curious."

"Ok. Wrench, you go ahead and take the car."

I get up and walk to Nolan's bedroom to get my keys, pausing at the door before walking back out. I allow a two-breath moment to pull myself together and rejoin the men in Nolan's living room.

I remove the fob to my CRV and pass it to Wrench. Something must strike Nolan because he blurts out, "Iyla, did you go into my car for any reason Monday night?"

"No. Why?"

"My security feed picked up the interior light coming on for a few seconds sometime around ten p.m."

Hearing this, Fish jumps up and runs out the door. "Wrench, wait!"

Fish walks outside, likely to check out Nolan's car in light of the new revelation.

For the next few minutes, I'm reviewing what has been said and listening to what's still being discussed about my life's nightmare.

I want to scream. This is insane. Bait, guards, bombs planted in cars. I fight to keep a cool head and actually help, but it's a struggle.

Deep breath, Iyla. They're talking about covering all openings in my house to keep someone from being able to see inside. The front windows have thick curtains, but the back ones are bare. What can you offer to help them help you?

"I've got plenty of canvases and large, thick papers that can be used to cover the windows," I announce to the crew. "They're in the side-by-side flat file boxes. I can show you which ones would be the most opaque."

Nolan sends the remaining guys to check through my house before he'll allow me to step foot inside. While waiting for them to send us, Fish and Wrench come back in from the carport. Fish holds something behind his back and motions Nolan over.

Judging by the looks on their faces, I don't want to see what it is that they've found. Based on the expression on Nolan's face when he sees what Fish's hiding, I *know* I don't want to see what they've found. Nolan crushes what looks to be a handwritten note in his fist and lifts his eyes to mine.

"Easy, Judge." Fish warns.

"What? What did the note say?" I press.

Nolan's voice is strained when he answers, "He says you made a deal with him to return my car. And that it was worth it."

Dillan's provoking Nolan. "I made no deal. I did threaten to report him if the car wasn't returned by the end of the day on Monday."

Nolan's face relaxes until Fish hands him another paper. This one has the veins in his neck

ESCAPEPROOF

popping out.

"I did drive him home after the car was delivered."

"You what?! Why would you do that?" Nolan asks in disbelief.

"Watch it, Judge," Wrench warns.

I blanche, unused to seeing Nolan angry, and divert my eyes, directing my answer to Fish. "The tow truck left him here, and it's a long walk back to town. Dillan asked that I take him home. To that point, his actions had merely been petty, and he was, before all this, a good friend. He seemed genuinely apologetic. I didn't know what he'd done to Nolan."

Wrench approaches me, holding two time-stamped images. He doesn't ask me anything or offer comment on what's pictured. One has that grainy look of a surveillance camera. It's of Dillan and me in my car stopped in front of a business. His arm is draped across my shoulder. Pointing to the picture, I explain, "That was just before I threatened to put him out if he touched me again."

The next image is from his driveway. Dillan is leaning over the console. I'm pinned in my seat, and he's kissing me. Only, in the picture, there doesn't appear to be any struggle.

I shudder at the memory of feeling helpless and look back up to the three men. Their faces are blank of any emotion—all of them.

The rest of the guys walk in Nolan's front

door then. Even they sense the tension in the room and stop their advance.

"You think I'm lying. You think that I'm working with Dillan and set all this up."

I start backing up into the kitchen, trying to reach the back door. Realizing I'm running away, Nolan swears and chases after me. "Iyla, no one thinks that."

He catches me on the back deck and spins me around. "Yes, they do. It's all over their faces."

"Well, I don't believe it, and that's all that matters."

Looking off toward my backyard, I ask, "I assume they've checked out my house and deemed it clear?"

"Yes."

"Then I'm going home." I pull out of his grip and walk to my back door, locking it once I'm inside.

An hour or so later, I'm halfway through covering my windows when I hear my car pulling out of my driveway. A short time after that, there's a knock at my back door. Nolan.

I open it and back out of his way without a word. He marches in with determined strides, wraps a hand firmly around my neck, presses me to the wall, and shoves his knee between my thighs. His lips crash down on mine in a demanding kiss, dominating my entire existence until I forget how to breathe.

I want to fight him at first, still burning

from the humiliation of the other men's doubt. Ultimately, I cannot resist, the pull toward him being too strong. His erection grows and presses against my middle, and Nolan pulls his mouth away to touch his lips to my forehead.

Through the pounding of blood in my ears, I hear him whisper, "We've all seen fear enough to know when it's real. Not one of my team doubts you. What we're not used to, what's got us worried, is dealing with an enemy that can manipulate a situation as masterly as this asshole can. We'll figure out how to proceed — together. For now, let's finish covering these windows and get you out of here."

After an exasperated sigh, I concede and resolve to relax a little. Nolan and I get started again on the windows, and the job is done quickly with the two of us working together.

Every window is covered, leaving my new house dark and shrouded in shadow. The result is tomb-like and unwelcoming. It's horrible. Like a flower, an artist needs light, and we've just finished choking it out of this place.

Urgently wanting to escape, I hastily pack some clothes and walk into my studio. I don't gather any supplies since it's Friday, but I grab my laptop to answer any inquiries from potential clients.

It's past noon when Nolan and I return to his house. He confirms all the doors are locked up tight and takes the bag from my hand. His large, ropey arms wrap around me for a hug I desperately need, and I notice a spot of dried blood on his sleeve. *His stitches!*

My mind goes back to the last eighteen hours and all Nolan has done despite his injuries. *Last night, he picked me up and carried me more than once. Today, he was stretching, securing covers on my back windows.*

Shaking my head, I carefully peel back his sleeve to evaluate the damage. Seeing the dried, bloody bandage, I push out of his arms and take his hand, pulling him down the hall to his bedroom.

"What are you doing?" he asks, a bit puzzled.

"Taking you to fix up your wounds. You've been busy taking care of me when you're the one full of holes."

Nolan doesn't argue. He just smiles mysteriously as I pull his shirt over his head. I remove his shoes and pants when the wounds continue down his waist and then plant him on the tile ledge of the tub surround. "You ought to get a skelping for not taking better care of yourself."

I begin peeling off the old bandages covering his stitches to replace them with fresh ones. Nolan chuckles at my quasi-threat. "A skelping?"

"An ass-kicking. Where do you keep your first aid supplies?"

Nolan points to the linen closet, and I walk over to find what I need. Holding a basket of gauze and tape, I return to Nolan and stand between his knees to dress the wounds on his left shoulder.

I start on the wound with the most stitches. While I'm taping the gauze, Nolan's right arm snakes its way around my back, and his hand slides under my shirt. He leans forward until his forehead rests between my breasts, and I finish bandaging the wounds in his bicep.

He tugs at the hem of my shirt before I can relocate to reach his forearm. Nolan pulls off the tank and removes my bra without me trying to stop him. His arms tighten around me, holding me close enough to swirl his tongue around a nipple. The act sends heat straight to my core, and I feel myself growing slick. My other breast receives the same treatment, but then I pull out of his grip. "Behave. I need to finish changing your bandages."

Without bothering with my shirt, I grab the basket of supplies and Nolan's right hand and lead him to his bed. I divest him of his boxers and push him down onto the mattress. Then, sitting between his knees, I dress the wounds on his legs scattered from mid-calf to just below his hip.

Every once in a while, I glance up to see his eyes intensely focused on me. Not at my hands performing first aid but on my face and bare chest.

I also can't miss his steadily growing erection.

When I'm finished with all the bandaging, I move the supplies to the bedside table and return to my place between his legs. The heat in his eyes challenges me, and I lower my head to kiss the tip of his penis.

My tongue darts out to give Nolan's hardened member the same treatment my nipples received, and then I take him inside my mouth.

I take him as deep as possible before pulling off to work my lips and tongue just on the head. I do it again and again until Nolan moans and his body tenses. "Iyla, stop. I need to be inside you."

A quick glance at his wounds reveals that I should be able to do this without touching any stitches. I slide off the bed and shove my shorts and panties down. When I settle above Nolan's hips, I slowly sink until he's filled me up. Damn, but he feels so good. Thoughts of Dillan's fingers on my intimate places threaten to derail our moment, but I open my eyes and focus on Nolan's face. He's touching me now, and the set to his jaw says that Dillan will never touch me again.

NOLAN

Iyla rides me hard. She feels so damned good that I don't even feel the stitches and soreness. Her full breasts bounce above me, but the look in her eyes is what holds my attention.

227

Iyla holds my gaze like a lifeline, an anchor to keep her from being swept away by a storm. I hold up my hands, and her eyes squeeze shut briefly. "I'm touching you, Iyla—only me. I'm massaging these beautiful breasts."

A hand trails down her trim stomach to touch the place we connect. And then I find her clit. "I'm the one driving into you, touching your pussy. Now, come for me."

Iyla cries out when I pinch her clit, and her rhythm hitches as an orgasm rocks through her. She doesn't stop, though. Her tight heat chokes my cock until I climax equally hard.

Falling forward with her hands on either side of my head, Iyla holds herself off my chest. She's breathing fast, and I'm struggling to breathe at all. I keep my groans to myself because every bit of the pain was worth it.

I'm still inside Iyla as her hair cascades down my side, tickling slightly as it slides over sensitive skin. I drag my fingers up and down her arms while her delicate inner muscles contract around my softening dick.

I would lie like this all day without complaint, but my stomach picks this moment to start growling. Right after mine starts, Iyla's does the same.

Turning my head slightly, I read my bedside clock. *Just past thirteen hundred.* With the early arrival of my team, neither of us had breakfast, and we hadn't stopped for lunch either.

"Would you like something to eat?"

Iyla mumbles against my neck, "Not before a shower. I'm a mess."

Running my fingers through her silky strands, I offer, "I'll do lunch while you shower. Deal?"

"I won't argue."

We grudgingly get up and go our separate ways. Since Iyla's nerves are shot, I'm working on something light for lunch. I'm nearly finished when I get a text from Wrench. *All tucked in. No one followed me.*

That's good news. *Thanks, man.*

I put my phone back on the counter and reach for a couple of small plates. The breakfast table is set, and Iyla comes out a while later, looking fresh as a spring morning — except for her weary eyes.

I pull out a chair for her to sit down. "Thanks," she says, looking at the simple spread appreciatively. "I'm not used to being served. This is nice."

"You're very welcome."

Iyla is quiet as she nibbles on the simple lunch of tuna salad and crackers. She's not here, lost in her head, concentrating on something. The *what* remains a mystery until she blurts out, "I need to get a gun or something."

I don't respond right away, being a little surprised by her statement. It's not that I don't think she's level-headed enough to handle a weapon; I just hate the thought of Iyla carrying the weight of taking a life, should it come to that.

Being careful not to dismiss her idea, I concur... to a certain degree. "You should have access to something you can confidently and comfortably use to defend yourself. A gun will take time to acquire because of the required training course, and knife training takes even longer to master. Would you be open to something non-lethal and less training-heavy as long as it was an effective self-defense tool?"

"I guess. What do you have in mind?"

"Several things. After lunch, I'll make a few phone calls to see if I can get delivery this weekend."

"Thank you."

The two of us finish the meal and clear away the mess. Iyla goes for her laptop, so I set her up to work in my office while I go out back to do what I can to restore Iyla's sense of safety and control.

My first call is to Ink. "Hey, mate," he answers on the second ring.

"I hate to ask anything since you guys just left a while ago, but I need a favor."

"Anything. You know that."

"I do, and I appreciate it. I need tasers for Iyla, one projectile and one for up close."

"Ah. The lady wants a weapon."

"She does."

"It's a good sign that she's still got her

head on straight, especially since she's willing to use non-lethals. When do you need them?"

"Before I have to leave for base on Monday."

"You'll have them."

"Thanks."

My next call is to Bassett. I'm calling him to get his input on the development of the Broderick situation. I know he can do nothing to help in an official capacity, but he'll listen and give sound advice.

The receptionist patches me through to his number, and his gruff voice comes on the line. "Bassett here."

"Detective, it's Nolan Lockmore."

"Lockmore. This makes two calls in as many weeks. Am I to assume this is a continuation of our last conversation?"

"Yes. Things have escalated, and it turns out that our problem is highly intelligent and a talented manipulator. The man sexually assaulted Iyla twice but has worked the system so that any attempt to report him to his superiors looks like retaliation by a disgruntled civilian."

"What are we talking about here?"

I lay out for him the threats, the stolen car incident, and the two attacks on Iyla.

Bassett is quiet for a moment, then says, "Lockmore, you already know what I'm going to say. You need surveillance cameras. Your only hope to stop this guy is to catch his crimes on video."

"Yeah, my only problem is that, so far, he's even been able to use body positioning on CCTV footage to his advantage."

I describe the two pictures left in my car as evidence to support my claim.

"In that case, my next suggestion would be to avoid him when possible. And because it won't always be possible, you and Iyla need to start wearing auto-upload body cams that he can't access or manipulate."

"I don't like that plan for one reason. While *I* don't mind the risk, I don't want Iyla being raped just so that we'll have proof that Broderick is a predator."

I snap my mouth shut after realizing I yelled that last part. Bassett's voice is calmer when he replies, "I wouldn't want that either. You need to have *her* wear an obnoxiously big Bluetooth camera and announce to the asshole that she's recording should he come around her again. He won't risk doing something on real-time, uploading video that he can't destroy."

"That sounds better, but he'd assume I'd also be wearing. The problem then becomes that we'll never obtain evidence to use against him."

Bassett scoffs. "You know better than that. Even the most patient criminals screw up eventually, especially when they feel untouchable. You have to be equally patient and smart. Make him blink first."

"You're right. Thanks, Evan."

"Good luck, and keep me informed."

The call ends, and the hand holding the phone drops by my side. A waiting game. That's what this has just become. Fucking fantastic.

ESCAPEPROOF

JO CHAMBLISS

CHAPTER 17

NOLAN

The rest of the day passes quietly, with Iyla working and me going through my body camera equipment to find a good one for her to wear. We share a frozen pizza and salad for dinner and head to bed early after the stressful night before.

I follow Iyla to my bedroom, where she strips out of her clothes and climbs beneath the covers as I watch from the doorway. "Aren't you coming?" she asks.

God, she's beautiful, so natural and wholesome. I'll do anything to keep her safe and in my life. Right now, I need her in my arms.

I push off the frame and join her in bed. Ten minutes after turning off the light, Iyla is still tense. "Iyla, are you all right?"

She's slow to respond but eventually says, "I got a text this afternoon from an unknown number. It was Dillan."

I *want* to know what it said, and I *don't* want to know what it said. Deciding it isn't important at the moment, I figure it won't do either of us any good to discuss it now. "You can show me in the morning. For now, I want you to try and relax."

A few minutes later, Iyla lies on her stomach with her arms folded under her pillow. She hasn't relaxed a fraction. I roll to my side, facing her, and stretch my left hand over her upper back. Gently at first, I work my fingers over Iyla's tight muscles.

Up her arms, across her shoulders, her neck, and down her back, I move, working out kinks and trying to get her mind off the Broderick shit. Shortly after I apply the same treatment to her scalp, she eventually loosens up. Iyla's breathing deepens, and she finally falls asleep. I take great pride in being able to help her relax and close my eyes to get some sleep myself.

The next time I open my eyes, the sun is peeking through the gaps in the closed blinds, indicating I've slept later than usual. Iyla's side of the bed is empty, which shocks the hell out of me for not waking up when she left.

I jump out of bed to look for Iyla but stop when I turn the corner of the hallway. She's sitting at the table drawing as coffee brews and something that smells great bakes in the oven.

Knowing she's okay, or at least safe, I return to my room and remove my bandages for a shower. The hot water stings, but I lean into the feeling. My slight discomfort is nothing compared to Skin's pain or Iyla's fear.

Forgoing new bandages, I dress in a T-shirt, track pants, and running shoes and reenter the kitchen as Iyla pulls a pan of biscuits from the oven. She hears me coming and looks up, wearing a smile on her face. "I found a box of sausage in your freezer. I hope this is all right."

"More than," I tell her.

We sit with our coffee and build breakfast sandwiches with the sausage, eggs, and cheese she prepared. I've eaten two of the soft biscuits before broaching the subject that had her so uptight last night. "You want to tell me what the message said now?"

Iyla shakes her head but slides the phone across the table to me. Picking up the unlocked device, I open the text app and read the message from the sender Unknown.

Your lips are so much sweeter when you beg me to taste them. I wonder if it'll be the same with the rest of your body. I bet your pussy tastes as sweet as it smells.

If this weren't Iyla's phone, I would have already destroyed it. This shit has got to end. It's time to test Bassett's theory. "I'm going out."

Iyla's face pales at my announcement. "You're going out there? What if he comes after you again?"

"I'll rig up a dashcam facing my window. Broderick won't try anything then because he'll know I'll have proof that he's dirty."

Iyla fidgets with her napkin, unconvinced. "Are you sure it's a good idea?"

"Sure enough. Keep out of sight and don't answer the door for anyone. I'll be back soon."

It only takes a minute to set up the dashcam in my car and connect it to my phone. If Bassett's right, it'll act as a shield, ensuring safe passage.

The trip into town is uneventful. I visit the grocery store to stock up and start back home. I could have waited another day to make the journey, but the truth is, I wanted to try out the camera idea long before allowing Iyla to leave the safety of my house.

I'm not surprised when lights flash in my rearview mirror during the drive home. *It's showtime*. That bastard, Broderick, steps from his patrol car and pulls on his cap unhurriedly. I itch to take his hands and break every finger before cutting them off. I'll never forget the sorrow on Iyla's tormented face when she told me of the bastard forcing his touch on her.

I'm only able to resist the urge because I'm betting that's what he wants me to do, especially while he's in uniform. Broderick finally approaches my car, and I hit the record button on the camera. The recording starts, and the video plays in real-time on my phone screen, currently in its dash mount. There's no way he'll be able to miss seeing himself at a half-second delay on the large screen.

"Good morning, sir," Broderick says with a sinister grin. He studies the inside of my car from behind reflective aviator glasses. I almost smile when Broderick stalls on the phone screen bearing his image. The bastard's smile fades, and his jaw clenches when he realizes he can't touch me.

Pretending to be unaffected, he looks up and over the roof of my car and says, "Be sure to stay in your lane, sir. You don't want to become a casualty."

I recognize the thinly veiled threat for what it is and answer in kind. "Neither do you," I growl.

Broderick has nothing to add, so I put the car in gear and drive off, leaving his worthless ass standing on the side of the road.

My car is parked in my carport before I turn off the camera and blow out a deep breath. The camera worked. Bassett was right, but I'm still concerned that tactic will only delay Broderick making his move. I'm not afraid of that asshat, but after seeing what he's done so far, I am concerned about what he can do from behind his badge.

Since I left instructions for Iyla to stay out of view from the front of the house, she won't know it's my car that pulled up, so I hurry inside to let her see I'm back. Iyla drops her pencil and rushes over to help when I walk through the door holding several grocery bags. "Did anything happen?"

I'm a little less than completely honest in

my answer. "Not a thing."

We're busy putting the food away and hear Iyla's phone chime with a new message. Iyla flinches at the sound and pulls the device from her pocket without looking at it. "My parents don't text. It has to be him." She presses her finger to the pad, unlocking the screen, and hands it to me.

Iyla, where are you? I see Neighbor didn't get the message I left for him. Did you find it and throw it away? I should tell him how you begged me to stay and put my mouth on you. Did you tell him I'm addicted to your taste? Does he know how well your cunt fits in my hand?

The phone is gently laid on the counter face down, and I take a few deep breaths. I know what Broderick is trying to do, but I won't deny being pissed enough to kill.

Iyla glances at the phone like she's considering reaching for it. I cover the device with my hand and shake my head. She clears her throat and whispers, "I still have his contact info programmed into my phone, but he sends these messages from another number. I should block it and delete them."

"No, it's important to keep all the messages for when Broderick finally fucks up. Until then, we have to lay low and be patient. Just… don't read anymore that come in."

"When he fucks up…" Iyla shakes her head as if she doesn't believe this will ever end. "When will that be? When I've lost my business, my house, my mind? I'm not ready to let that happen. I may have been spoiled with a smooth ride in life so far, but I have earned my place. I finally know who I am and what I want, and I'll be damned if I let some arsehole take it from me!"

She jams her phone back in her pocket and adds, "I'll stay here with you because you offered and because I... because it's safe, but I am not going to be frightened into giving up my career and my first house."

Jumping out of my seat, I firmly grasp her shoulders. I lower my eyes to hers and promise, "That's not going to happen. Broderick thinks he's covered all the bases, but he's already messed up. He didn't anticipate us fighting back."

I pull Iyla with me as I sit at the table and position her between my legs. "I didn't tell you this, but he pulled me over on my way home just now. He didn't try anything because he spotted the camera on the dash."

Iyla lifts a brow cynically and frees herself from my arms to put the milk and juice in the fridge. "So, all it's going to take to make the big, bad wolf leave me alone is a little bitty camera?"

She's clearly not convinced, and I don't blame her. It's a flimsy plan for short-term application, and I don't try to make her believe otherwise. "Right now, the only thing I'm sure of is that running isn't an option. Ink's right.

Broderick found you here. He can find you anywhere."

I pull Iyla to me again. "Broderick has shown his hand. He won't make a move with me in the picture. That's why he planted the pictures and has been baiting me. He's waiting for me to make a wrong move so he can arrest me and leave you vulnerable. I'm fucking terrified because he won't have to wait long. I can be called away on short notice. What happens then?"

Iyla softens after I voice my greatest fear. She wraps her arms around my head, pulling me to her breast. "I'm sorry, Nolan. I am scared, but even more, I hate that you've been caught up in this. I don't want you hurt."

"The only way Broderick can hurt me is to take you."

"It sounds like I need a full-time bodyguard."

You're not too far off. "I wouldn't rule it out."

IYLA

I was only half kidding, but I lean back to study Nolan's face and find that he was as serious as a heart attack. That's *it. I've met my tipping point.* "I want to paint," I announce abruptly.

Nolan's lips thin, but he nods, understanding that I need this. "May I come with you?" he asks gently. "I've got some case files I can work on quietly while you do your thing."

"Be my guest," I answer with a wave of my hand.

Nolan gathers his laptop, and we lock up before crossing our backyards to my kitchen door. While Nolan sets up on the kitchen table, I walk into my studio and realize I made a gross calculation. The dark room resembles a dungeon, and artificial light is a lousy substitute for the sun.

Spinning in the doorway, I ask, "Do you think we could uncover these windows for a while since they face the woods?"

The tightness around his eyes says Nolan isn't thrilled with the idea, but he capitulates. "As long as we're out of here before dark. Otherwise, this side of the house will glow like a beacon."

"Ok. I won't turn on any lights. When it's too dark to work, it'll be time to go."

"Agreed."

I almost prance to the window to take the mat board down. Next, I open the media drawer and run my fingers over all the various tools. Ultimately, I grab my Conte sticks, select a toothy paper, and sit at the drawing table. Drawing soothes me, and I look forward to working out my tension with each stroke of my hand.

My base image begins with dark gray and black. Up and down, I scratch the stick over the paper in a series of short and long strokes, seeing a forest of mangled trees take shape. Though dark and lifeless, the grove of trees is beautiful in mourning the loss of its magnificent crown of summer leaves.

Pulling a light gray from its slot in the box of color sticks, I focus on the left side of the image. A pale figure emerges from the edge of the forest, working her way through the woods. What she touches glows with her light even after she passes, making her easy to track.

Eventually, the figure comes to a place where the trees are growing too closely together to go any further. She's caught in the branches and cannae escape.

Picking up a black-red stick, I lift my hand to draw a dark figure in the far remnant of her light but stop myself just in time. *What am I doing?*

I put down the stick and stand up to stretch as the first streaks of color in the sky indicate the setting of the sun. Nolan walks up behind me and splays his hands on my belly, pulling me against his chest. "How is it going?"

"Dark. It's not me."

He looks at the piece over my shoulder. "Hmm. It's enchanting, but you're right. It's not you."

"It feels like I've drawn a nightmare. My nightmare."

Nolan starts to sway then, and I lean into him, laying my head back against his muscular chest. He hums in my ear, and nimble fingers lift to cup my breast.

His soft humming gradually shifts to singing, and I quickly recognize one of my favorite love songs. Nolan has a beautiful voice, and before long, I'm lost in the music he's making in my ear and on my body.

One hand is still massaging my breast, and his other drifts downward and steals beneath the waistband of my palazzo pants. Warm fingers ease their way into my panties, and the first touch to my clit has me lifting on my toes. After that, I settle into Nolan's swaying rhythm as he continues singing to me.

His thick digits glide through my slickness with no teasing, hitting the right spot with each pass. An orgasm slams into me unexpectedly fast, and I don't hold back my loud cry from its intensity.

Nolan slows his fingers to ease me down but then soon starts again. The second orgasm hits even harder, with me calling out his name this time.

The singing stops, as does the swaying. "I love you."

Nolan's whispered words set my soul to flight. His hands come to rest on my waist, and I turn around in his arms. "I love you, Nolan."

My hands wrap around his neck, and Nolan takes my lips in a kiss meant to steal my breath. He can have my breath, my heart, my soul, everything.

Nolan releases me and tucks a stray hair behind my ear. "We've stayed here too long. We should go."

I know he's right, but all I want to do is crawl into my bed with Nolan and have him tell me he loves me again. I guess I'll have to settle for crawling into his bed a few minutes from now. My legs are still jelly from my two orgasms and can barely carry me. I cover the windows again as Nolan packs up his computer, and we leave my house for the return trip to his.

The rest of the night is blessedly calm, and for the first time in my adult life, when I go to bed, I do so, knowing for certain that I'm exactly where I'm supposed to be.

CHAPTER 18

NOLAN

It's just before daybreak, and Iyla is sleeping next to me with her head on my chest.

I told her that I love her.

I've never said those words to a woman before. As a kid, sure, but never as an adult that understood their meaning. The declaration wasn't blurted out in the heat of the moment. It's been there for weeks, simmering beneath the surface. The way Iyla called my name in ecstasy just destroyed my ability to hold back the words any longer.

Iyla begins to stir as the sun rises, the light pouring through the transom windows casting a pink glow in the room. I push up onto an elbow to watch Iyla sleep. The sheet sits at her waist, leaving the expanse of her smooth back on display. Unable to resist the temptation, I lean forward and drag my lips over her bare shoulder, whispering. "I meant what I said. I love you, Iyla."

A few minutes later, eyes still closed, Iyla lifts her head and smiles sleepily. "I want to draw you today."

"You've drawn me several times."

"I want to draw us together."

My answering grin is devilish. "Is it something we act out? Will this be X-rated?"

Iyla opens and then rolls her eyes. "I wouldn't hang it in a church. Our faces won't be recognizable, but I'll know it's us. You'll understand when you see it."

"Can't wait. Breakfast first?"

An hour later, we return to Iyla's back deck for another session in her studio. There has been no further contact from Broderick, and no sightings have been made. I don't imagine the respite will last, but as long as it's safe, I'll give Iyla all the art therapy I can. Once inside the house, she heads straight for her studio and stops at the open door.

I rush forward at Iyla's anguished scream and shove her behind me. Gun up, I scan the room, swearing under my breath. Our respite is over. Shredded artwork litters the floor, and all Iyla's drawings of me have been stuck to the wall with knives.

Iyla wails, and her whole body trembles against my back. From what I can see, no equipment has been destroyed—only the finished art. That bastard wanted to hurt her. He fucking succeeded.

I shuffle Iyla away from the room before she sees the message Broderick left for me. *You've fucked my woman for the last time.* He scratched it in red across one of the drawings.

Guiding the incoherent Iyla, I don't stop moving until we've grabbed her purse, bags, and laptop from my house and reached my car. Iyla is no longer crying. She's numb, motionless, and silent as I back my car down the drive.

We make it out of Chesapeake without being pulled over by Broderick. Only after crossing the county line do I put my gun away. I keep driving toward Virginia Beach to an art store I'd looked up a few days ago. Before I should have, I considered turning one of my spare bedrooms into an art studio. I'm glad now I did.

I don't know why I go there instead of Little Creek, except that I need a place to make some private calls and hope the smell of paint will snap Iyla out of this terrified stupor.

Iyla is still unresponsive when I lead her into the combination store/studio space. "Baby, I've got to make some calls. Will you be all right for a few minutes?"

"I'll be fine," she answers tonelessly.

She doesn't look fine. "Are you sure?"

Iyla groans and grabs a brush from a large display of tools. *Well, that's at least something.*

Leaving Iyla to her dispassionate browsing, I walk to the opposite side of the space to a row of private rooms. After stepping into one and closing the door, I pull out my phone, somewhat nervous about my first call. I hate disturbing him on a Sunday, but this can't wait. Fish answers after the first ring. "Hill."

"Fish, I need to take a few days' leave."

"Dammit. Judge, I know shit is jacked up right now, so I hate to tell you this. You're not going to get it. All leave for Team Two has been canceled, and all SEALs have been recalled. The men we captured from the boat gave the CIA big threads to follow. Our smugglers probably knew these assholes were a liability, which is why they were assigned the suicide mission in the first place.

"The lid on this is about to blow, and every man is needed. I'll still talk to O'Reilly about what's going on, but it doesn't look good. Give me a few minutes to check in with the commander, and I'll call you back."

The call ends, and I peek out the door to check on Iyla. She hasn't moved. My phone rings, and I sigh, seeing the commander's number on the screen. Closing the door behind me again, I answer the call. "Lockmore, here."

"I'm sorry, Lockmore, I'm afraid the best I can do is have you put her in the safehouse cabin on base for a while. If you should deploy, I'll personally guarantee that Ms. Dunsmore will have whatever she needs and won't leave base without an armed escort. Is that good enough?"

"Good enough. Thank you, Sir."

Now, to update Jasper. That call serves to ensure I remain on the legal side of things. My cousin listens carefully without comment and then goes on a three-minute rant laced with a little of what he'd like to do to Broderick and a lot of what I should do to protect Iyla and me.

With Jasper's advice tucked away in my head and his promise to be available to Iyla, I put my phone away and leave the changing room. The only problem is I don't see Iyla anywhere.

I check every aisle, each of the studio rooms, and even the bathrooms. She's not here. The clerk doesn't have a clue, and Iyla's not out front by the car when I check. Cursing my stupidity, I take off, running toward the back of the store.

IYLA

Nolan walks toward the wall of small rooms on the opposite side of the art house, and I mindlessly peruse art supplies I have no intention of buying. I can appreciate why he brought me here, but shopping is the last thing on my mind. Everything here only reminds me of the destroyed art scattered over my studio floor.

I pick up a random book, half-heartedly flipping through its pages. About halfway through the book, my gaze catches on the image of a stormy ocean scene. I can relate. A familiar chill settles over me when a shadow crosses the book.

"Don't say a word."

The softly spoken command draws a tear

from my eye as my heart seizes. *How…?*

I drop the book I'm holding. The clattering noise it should have made would have attracted the store employee's attention, but Dillan catches it before it can land and make a sound.

"Out the back. Let's go, Iyla,"

Voice shaking, I say, "I'm not going anywhere with you."

Dillan runs his nose up my cheek to my ear. From a distance, it probably looks like a lover whispering dirty promises to his mistress. "You'd better. I planted three grams of meth in Lockmore's car the day I returned it. If you don't come with me, I'll call it in. His military career will be over. He'll lose his law license and go to jail."

Hoping to stall until Nolan comes out, I ask, "How did you even find us?"

"Uh uh. Move now, or I'll report drugs anyway for him touching you. Before you get any ideas, you'd never find the stash without a drug-sniffing dog. And Neighbor will be arrested before you even get the chance to look, so don't test me."

My insides quake as I plead with the universe to open the door hiding Nolan from view. Dillan places a phone next to my ear, and I hear ringing and a voice answering, "Chesapeake Dispatch."

Nolan doesn't deserve this, Iyla. I pull in a shaky breath and turn toward the rear of the store. Dillan ends the call and shoves me hard when I don't move fast enough.

I know if I make it out that door, there's a chance Nolan will never find me, so I hold my purse close to my chest. Carefully as I can, I unclip a fuzzy purple puffball from the outside and drop it on the floor.

Hopefully, Nolan will recognize it and figure out what must have happened. I also slip my hand inside my bag and grip the small hammer I decided to start carrying. I had no other weapons, and the hammer seemed better than nothing.

"Hurry it up," Dillan orders.

We walk through the back door, and I don't hear Nolan yelling for me.

That's it. I'm dead.

The heavy door closes, and Dillan starts talking, no longer in danger of being heard. "I thought I'd made myself clear that you belonged to me. I heard the two of you last night in your studio. You came for him, calling his name. No more. I'll cut out your tongue if you ever call another man's name again."

Twisting against Dillan's sudden and tight grip on my throat, I let him know what I think about his warning. "You may as well sharpen your knife then because I'll never scream for you."

"I wouldn't bet on it."

Dillan turns me back around and shoves

me toward a four-door truck with dark-tinted windows. *This is the same truck that passed me coming home from DC. That's how he was waiting for me.*

I dig my feet in, and Dillan throws me over his shoulder. "Stop struggling, or I'll have the cops here in minutes."

My arms and legs go limp, but my grip tightens on the little hammer inside my purse. I pull it from the bag, ready to attack.

A split second after Dillan sets me down and opens the back door to the truck, the art store's back door crashes open. "Iyla!" Nolan yells as his feet pound the pavement.

Taking advantage of Dillan's distraction, I start swinging. The small, steel head makes solid contact three times, and Dillan stumbles back, pulling me with him. My shoulder slams into the side of the truck, but I avoid hitting my head when we hit the ground. Still holding the hammer, I jump up and run toward Nolan.

He catches me and redirects my steps until we're racing around the building, through the alley, and back to his car. Once inside, he squeals the tires, getting us out of there.

Nolan is quiet during the ride, but the white knuckles on the steering wheel speak loudly of his mental condition. I'm not doing so great myself.

The car doesn't stop until we reach a security gate at a military base. Nolan shows his military ID and my license, and we're granted admittance. The next time we stop, we're parked in front of a small cabin.

Nolan gets out, comes around to my side, opens my door, and pulls me to the cabin's entrance. He jabs a code into the keypad and steps through the door, pulling me with him.

The door hasn't even closed before, I'm yanked against Nolan's trembling chest. "Nolan?"

"Shh. I need a minute."

Since I feel the same, I shut my mouth and squeeze him a little tighter. The worst of the shudders subside, and Nolan releases me but doesn't stop touching. He backs up to the sofa and sits down, pulling me astride his lap.

Nolan's hands lift to cup my cheeks, and he looks straight into my eyes. "What happened at the art store?"

"Dillan snuck up behind me. He said he planted meth in your car on Monday and that he'd report it if I didn't leave with him."

"Dammit, Iyla." He kisses me hard. "Don't you ever make a deal with this bastard for me again. I can handle any shit he throws my way, but I cannot handle him hurting you."

Softer now, he adds. "I've waited too damn long to find you just to lose you again."

"I'm sorry." Tears spring from my eyes, and Nolan reaches up to wipe them away, "Don't cry, baby. And thank you."

"Thank you?"

"You were trying to protect me with your life. I don't take that lightly. Just don't ever do it again."

Nolan guides my head to his shoulder, and we sit in silence for a long while.

After we've calmed some, I sit up and look around. "What is this place, and why are we here?"

"This is a safehouse on base, established by our commander."

The cabin is small but comfortable, with an eat-in kitchen, living room, and two doors that could lead to bedrooms. "Safehouse? On base? After seeing the armed men guarding the gate, I hate to imagine why it's necessary."

Nolan groans. "It's six very long stories. I'll tell you all about them one day. For now, do you want or need anything?"

I shake my head.

"Ok. Not that I'd presume to make decisions for you. The plan is for the two of us to stay here for a few days so you're not alone in a place Broderick can get to you. After checking in with my commander, I'll have one of my team take me home to pack some stuff. The commander will have the Masters at Arms check out my car."

"What are the Masters at Arms?"

"Navy base police."

My eyes widen at my recent mistrust of

law enforcement. "Good police?"

"I'll put it to you this way, if Broderick were to try to get on base without clearance from the base commander, they wouldn't care about his badge. They'd only see him as a threat and would treat him as such."

So, Dillan can't influence them. That's a relief. "Thank you for bringing me here."

"You're welcome."

ESCAPEPROOF

JO CHAMBLISS

CHAPTER 19

NOLAN

Now that my heart is no longer thumping out of my chest, I walk outside to bring in Iyla's things. I take my time, needing to expel my rage for letting that fucker get his hands on Iyla again.

After setting her bags inside, I walk back out to call Fish. He's notably outraged over the attempted kidnapping and the possibility of the cop planting drugs in my car. He hangs up to dispatch the MAs and update the commander, still swearing under his breath.

I wait outside, expecting that the MAs won't be long before arriving. I don't, however, expect Fish to show up a few minutes after the MAs come and offer to be my ride. Nor do I expect Willa to insist on following him in her car.

Hearing all the commotion, Iyla walks outside to see what's
going on. "Oh my god!" she squeals when she notices Ari. Ari runs over and grabs Iyla, essentially cementing her in place. With the little girl wrapped around Iyla's legs, Fish formally introduces his family to Iyla even though they've

met briefly before.

The women and kids go inside, and I talk through the details of what just happened with Fish and the MAs.

"How did he find you?" the senior MA asks.

"We weren't followed, if that's what you're asking."

"We'll check for a GPS locator as well," he says.

Fish and I watch as one of the MAs opens the back door of their vehicle to let a K9 officer out, and the other retrieves a scanner from the trunk.

Their job doesn't take long. A GPS tracker is found under the trunk, and a bag of drugs is beneath the passenger seat floor mat. "You're gonna want to have that floor carpeting shampooed with lemon and vinegar to clear out any traces of the compound and the smell."

I thank the MAs for their help, and they leave to write a report for the commander. "Do you want to check on things inside before we go? I know Iyla probably wasn't expecting company," Fish asks.

"I'm sure she needed the distraction."

We walk in to find Ari drawing a picture for her new best friend while the two women. Iyla is holding baby Christopher, and the sight hits me like a punch to the gut. I'm seeing my forever in this scene, and it's too much to hope for yet.

Fish moves to stand behind his wife and lightly draws his fingers up and down Willa's neck. "We're going to leave so we can be out of there before..." his voice trails off, leaving the rest of his thought unsaid.

Willa leans into her husband. "Ok. I'll stay until Ari finishes her drawing and then take these rascals home."

Moving to kneel beside Iyla, I bite my tongue to keep from saying something about her looking like a natural with the baby. Instead, I look down at Christopher playing so happily in her lap. "I think he likes you."

I kiss her temple and stand back up. "We'll be back as soon as we can."

"Please be careful."

"There's nothing to be worried about. I promise."

Fish and I walk out, and he passes by my sedan. "We'll take my truck. I don't want this asshole spotting your car again today."

On the way toward my house, I call to update Jasper—again.

"I like your plan," he begins. "But what about the long-term? I'm sure it's not practical to leave your homes indefinitely."

"You're right, but he's angry now and will be even more so when he figures out we both disappeared. I'm thinking he's going to make a move soon, a big one. And I don't want Iyla where he can get her. I'll see Broderick and me both dead before I let him get his hands on her again."

"That's not happening, so forget it."

Jasper hangs up, and I resume looking out the window for signs of the asshole cop.

Fish asks, "How is Iyla holding up?"

"She has her moments, but she's okay."

"You seem to be pretty serious about her."

I shrug casually. "No more than you are about Willa."

Fish laughs. "You little shit. I have to say I'm impressed with her. I still can't believe she attacked him with a hammer. That woman is a fighter, and she helped Ari get her fight back, too."

The area around our houses seems undisturbed when Fish turns onto my street. If you don't count the hideously high grass in both yards, everything looks deceptively peaceful.

My alarm hasn't tripped, so I know my place is secure. I run inside and pack some shit for myself. I'm out in less than three minutes.

When we visit Iyla's house, we do so with guns drawn and check out the place thoroughly. I want to clean up the mess in her studio, but I have to settle for taking pictures of the damage.

Fish whistles at the fury displayed in the art room while I collect some sketch pads and drawing stuff. All in all, we're back on the road in less than ten minutes.

Willa has already left by the time Fish

drops me off at the cabin. "I wish there was more I could do for her."

Acknowledging his help with a handshake, I confess, "I've said the same thing. I'll see you in the morning."

I carry our stuff inside and find Iyla in the kitchen cooking. She looks up and gives me a feeble smile. "Willa took me to the commissary while you were gone."

"Whatever you're making smells good."

I set the table, and Iyla and I share a better salmon dinner than I make for myself. "That was fantastic. Maybe tomorrow, I'll impress you with my culinary skills."

Iyla chuckles softly. She's missing the boisterous laugh I've heard from her before. "Hey, you've had a shitty day. Let me handle cleanup while you take a long shower."

Iyla kisses my cheek and stands without comment, likely agreeing because she's still in shock.

The dishwasher is loaded, and the counters are wiped down when Iyla emerges from the bathroom. A puff of steam follows her out to the living room. Iyla sits beside me on the sofa, and I swing her legs onto my lap. "I have to report at five in the morning. I could be gone most of the day."

"I'll be fine. Thanks for grabbing my sketchbooks and pencils."

"You don't have to thank me. I'm just sorry

I put you through today. I should have driven straight to base. If I had, Broderick would have never had the chance to get his hands on you."

"Nolan, don't—"

Still angry at myself, I interrupt her efforts to absolve me. "I'm going to get some sleep. My commander says this could be a busy week."

She presses her lips together but doesn't try to talk me out of my self-recrimination. "Ok. I'm going to stay up and draw for a while."

I spend the next three hours tossing and turning, wishing I could touch Iyla, but she hasn't come to bed. I imagine she's scared and angry and fear some of her anger is toward me. My stupid ass failed to anticipate Broderick's move and almost lost Iyla.

Eventually, I'm able to nod off, but wake alone when my watch alarm goes off at four-thirty. Iyla didn't come to bed at all. Still angry at what I almost let happen yesterday, I get dressed and find Iyla asleep on the sofa when I leave.

Little Creek is hopping when I meet up with my team. With all platoons on base at the same time, there's barely a place to park. Our whole - well, almost our entire platoon is warming up to run together.

"Shit! Look at all the holes in this guy," Duck says.

The other squad's medic studies the visible shrapnel damage and whistles. "How is Skin doing?" he asks.

"We're hoping to get some good news today," Bandaid answers.

We set off for a long run, and afterward, all eight platoons gather in front of HQ for Commander O'Reilly to address us all at once. "I'm sure you're aware of last week's attempt on Lieutenant Hill's squad by the arms dealer we're hunting. Intelligence is calling in every expert and favor it's owed to find those responsible. When they do, we're going to take them all out at the same time. Every man here should be ready to move with full gear at a moment's notice until instructed to stand down.

"While I'll personally enjoy getting payback for what happened to our men, this is not some vigilante revenge mission for a hit on a SEAL team. These men put guns in the hands of the worst this world has to offer. Those guns are turned on our allies and friends who protect our shared interests.

"Until you receive orders, you are to carry on as normal. Lieutenant Bennett, I'd like to see your platoon. The rest of you are dismissed."

Clothespin nods to the commander, and our group approaches the steps as the rest of the men disperse. Commander O'Reilly meets us on the sidewalk. "I've spoken with the doctors in charge of CPO Ramsay's care at Landstuhl. They tell me they're shipping Ramsay home on Thursday. Depending on his progress, he won't return to active duty for another two weeks or so.

"Myers, I don't imagine he'll accept that easily, so for his and your sakes, I won't be asking for nor allowing you to evaluate him. I will, however, ask for your evaluation of CPO Lockmore's condition. While this would normally be done privately, I know this group is closer than most and that I'm probably the only one here who *hasn't* been updated."

All the men laugh – except me. Of course, he didn't ask me. Like any other SEAL, the answer would always be, *I'm good to go.*

Bandaid speaks up with laughter still in his voice. "I would consider him clear for duty."

"Even though he looks like Frankenstein's monster?" the commander asks with a smile.

"I'll remove the stitches as soon as we're dismissed."

"Fine. Lieutenant Bennet, they're all yours."

Salutes are issued, and O'Reilly goes inside. Clothespin now turns to us. "Myers, take Lockmore and deal with him, then meet up with us on the tactical range. We need to run some drills with new groupings since we're short a man."

Driving back to the cabin after the day's training, I spend my time thinking about the Broderick situation since I pretty much know what to expect from the Navy this week.

Broderick took quite the chance in trying to take Iyla without knowing if there were cameras in the loading area. What that says to me is that cameras or no, if he got her into that truck, he was never coming back. Since he didn't get her, this could go one of three ways depending on the existence of and configuration of cameras behind the art store. Yesterday could look like an attempted kidnapping, an attack on an innocent man, or go completely unnoticed.

I guess we'll see.

IYLA

I hit a man in the head with a hammer. Three times.

The water from the showerhead pounds over my face but fails to stop the thundering in my head. *I attacked a man with a hammer.* The fact that I did it to prevent my kidnapping may not matter. For everything that Dillan has done, he's been able to make *me* look like the guilty one.

What if he claims that I attacked him for no reason? Any video footage would be damning for me. It's not like he brandished a weapon or hit me or anything. I'd tell people he was trying to kidnap me, but who would believe it? Dillan's boss is already aware of one kissing story, and Dillan has the pictures he left for Nolan. Dill will tell his boss that we're lovers and he was being playful when I attacked.

I could end up going to prison for this. At the time, I wasn't thinking of anything other than getting away. That Nolan and I fled the scene won't help my situation if I am accused.

The shower isn't calming my nerves, so I finish up and get out. Out in the living room, it seems Nolan is suffering self-doubt over what happened, and neither of us seems to be in any shape to help the other. *It's a good thing Nolan doesn't know any of what Dillan said. He'd probably be in a lot worse shape.*

As it is, Nolan goes to bed early, carrying the weight of the world with him. I don't follow, still too worried about a late knock at the door and being hauled away in handcuffs. Fearing the worst--a state-wide manhunt—I pull up local news for Virginia Beach on my phone.

There's no mention of an altercation behind an art store or an attack on an off-duty cop during the broadcast. After the nightly news circuit ends, I check online, searching and scrolling until my eyes are too heavy to keep open.

The cabin is empty when I wake at eleven the next morning. I've spent plenty of time alone but have never felt this isolated. I long to call and talk to my parents but fear my inability to hide the truth from them.

Given how close Willa said I am to a secure beach, I eat a quick bite of brunch and set off for the shore after leaving a note for Nolan.

The walk to the shore is less than half a mile. It's peaceful here, like a private beach. This far north on the Atlantic is not pretty like in

Miami, but I still think I prefer it. Seeing the lighthouses from here would be great, but this is infinitely better than my boarded-up house, where all my artwork lies shredded.

I plop down in the sand and spend the afternoon watching the waves while the breeze swirls around me. And for once, I don't have the urge to draw. *Damn you, Dillan.*

My shoulders are pink when a newcomer sits in the sand beside me. The familiar scent of Nolan's cologne surrounds me as his warmth seeps into my side.

Staring over the water, I say, "I don't think Dillan reported me."

"I've been thinking about that. He wouldn't risk it. If he did, he'd have to explain why he was there, in another city, at the same time we were."

"Or, he could be in a hospital dying from his injuries. If that's the case, pinning this on me will be easy."

"Don't worry. He's not. I had a friend of mine check. My friend is a Virginia Beach detective."

"Oh. It's nice to know I won't be charged with murder."

Nolan ignores my sarcasm. "You're getting burned. Ready to go back?"

"Yeah."

I take Nolan's offered hand and let him pull me up. That's when I notice his left arm and leg. The stiff black threads are gone. "How do they feel?"

He follows my gaze to his healing wounds. "I'm glad not to feel the pull of the stitches anymore."

Nolan escorts me to the passenger side of his car and parks in front of the cabin less than a minute later. He kills the engine, but I place a hand on his to stop him from getting out. "Nolan, I know this mess has turned your life upside down just as much as mine. You don't deserve that."

"Neither do you."

"What I'm trying to say is I appreciate everything you've done. You make me feel safe and cared for."

He turns in his seat and brings my hand to his mouth. "I love you, Iyla. There's nothing I wouldn't do to keep you from harm or make you feel treasured."

"I love you," I tell him sincerely.

Nolan grins big. "Great, now, let's go. I have a surprise for you."

"Ugh. I think I've had enough surprises for a lifetime."

"You'll like this. We're going to make up for our wrecked first date."

Now that I can handle.

I shower to get the smell of the sand and sea off me and put on a red, sleeveless maxi dress. I leave my hair loose around my pink-tinged shoulders and apply some makeup.

Nolan dressed in slate-blue pants and a loose, linen shirt. His slightly longer-than-military hair is styled, but not overly so. The end result has him looking every inch polished and sexy.

Our second attempt at a real date works out much better than the first. We have dinner at the base's golf course clubhouse, followed by a walk on the beach in the waning light.

Nolan holds my hand, stopping occasionally to place his hands on my hips and kiss me. It's all been perfect, but I'm more happy to see he's no longer angry at himself.

Arriving back at the cabin, Nolan locks us in for the night and picks me up, carrying me toward the bedroom.

He nips at my lips softly, but I pull away. "Nolan, stop. I don't want kid gloves—no sweet tonight. I need fire. I need the rush of adrenaline to remind me that I'm still alive and in control of my life. Can you give me that?"

Nolan draws in a deep breath and closes his eyes. When they open again, gone is the gentle soul with the kind face. Muscles flex, lips curl into a sneer, and Nolan's eyes are positively predatory.

"Baby, like most people, you fail to believe I could have a dark side. You want fire, I'll give you fire."

ESCAPEPROOF

JO CHAMBLISS

CHAPTER 20

NOLAN

I shove Iyla against the wall, forcing her legs apart with my knee. The low cut and soft fabric of her sleeveless dress allow me to pull the straps and her bra down to her elbows. This traps her arms in place, giving me free rein to ravish her gorgeous breasts.

Each nipple is licked, sucked, and tweaked until Iyla begs incoherently. Then, with her still pinned, I rip off my shirt, release my belt, and fly. I attack her mouth, fisting her hair to hold her in whatever position I want.

Iyla moans into my mouth as I reach down to cup her through her dress. Our tongues duel and tangle as my fingers caress her over the red cotton fabric.

My engorged dick starts beating with each thrum of my heart, and I rip my mouth away from Iyla's sweet lips. Spinning her around, I march her back out to the living room and shove her down onto the back of the couch.

Iyla's heels put her at the right height, and I pull her dress up, exposing her sweet ass. I give the round globes a squeeze and drag her panties down her sexy legs. On my way back up, I slide two fingers through her drenched slit, sending a jolt through her and making her jump.

Those fingers keep moving until they circle the tight bud of her ass, and Iyla bucks at the contact to the forbidden place. "Shh."

She's never done this before. I keep playing at the virgin entrance, even as I grip my dick and rub the head up and down over her clit. Iyla squirms like she's trying to get away and closer at the same time.

Faster and faster, I move until I feel she's close to orgasm. Dipping my fingers into her wetness again, I return to her tight ass and press the tip of one finger inside. Iyla instinctually bears down on me and is suddenly screaming through an orgasm.

Not wanting to let up, I plunge balls deep in one thrust and remove my finger from her tight rosebud. I grip Iyla's hips with both hands and hold her in place while I pound into her over and over again.

Iyla comes again, barely managing a hoarse whimper this time. Her inner muscles squeeze me tight and send me crashing through my own monster orgasm. "Fuck, Iyla!"

I bend and brace my hands on the sofa, limbs heavy and spent from taking Iyla so roughly. As I catch my breath, I rain open-mouthed kisses up and down Iyla's spine and across her shoulder blades.

Every sense is heightened and attuned to Iyla—her little gasps when I shift inside her, the lingering scent of our combined arousal. I'm addicted and wouldn't miss a second of this.

Iyla begins to struggle against her binds, so I step back and stand her up. She's unsteady on her feet, weak from multiple orgasms. I pull the dress over her head and remove the bra, freeing Iyla. Both are tossed to the floor unceremoniously, leaving Iyla in nothing but her heels.

With a gentle hand, I lift her chin. Her cheeks are as pink as her shoulders. "Was that enough fire?"

Swaying a little, she gives me a little love-drunk smile. "I think I love your dark side."

Now that Iyla is sated and boneless, I pick her up and carry her to the bedroom. This time, she doesn't protest. I unstrap and pull the sandals from her feet and remove the rest of my clothes to join her.

Leaving Iyla the next three mornings becomes progressively more difficult with each day. Our evenings are calm and filled with discussions of our favorite things in life, cooking competitions, and a mixture of sweet and fiery lovemaking. Topping my list are watching desire burn in her eyes while I peel off my uniform and her Scottish curses when my tongue slides through her pussy.

I'm buttoning my uniform in the dark, early Thursday morning. Iyla is still asleep on her back with her gorgeous breasts on display. Forcing my feet to leave, I'm nearly to the door when I give in to the need to hear her voice. Before today, I've always been careful not to wake her so early.

I stalk closer and lean over with a knee on the bed. "Iyla."

She stirs, but her eyes remain closed. "Iyla," I say again, a little louder. This time, her eyes open. "Nolan, is everything okay?"

"Yes, I just wanted to tell you I love you."

Iyla smiles sleepily, making my heart sing, "I love you, too."

I kiss her temple and quietly back out of the room. Outside, I double-check that my pack is ready, as I've done every other morning since Monday. When the Commander says, "*A moment's notice,*" he means a moment's notice.

With the possibility of being deployed increasing with time, I'm not looking forward to the thought of leaving Iyla locked down, alone on base. One thing I *am* looking forward to is welcoming Skin back sometime today.

A strange and unwelcome sight greets me when I arrive at headquarters. Several trucks are lined up at the back of the lot, and O'Reilly is standing on the steps leading to the front entrance to the building.

All men reporting for PT automatically fall

in as they park and notice the unusual happenings. My head is on a swivel, trying to locate my platoon in the craziness. I spot Fish jogging up and move with him to our usual place in the ranks.

He reads my mind and says. "It's been quiet, right? She's safely on base, and the asshole hasn't even messaged her again. Anyway, I'm betting that this mission will be a quick strike."

"Yeah, I'm sure you're right," I reply without conviction.

The rest of the lines fill in quickly, and O'Reilly's assistant calls for attention. The collection of SEALs quietens, and our commander starts his briefing. "We have identified multiple targets affiliated with the arms dealer's organization. As you've guessed, deployment is imminent. I want platoon leaders to account for your men and report to me in ten minutes to receive your team's assignments. Gear up accordingly. You pull out in thirty minutes."

I don't hesitate. I take off toward my commander to... to... what? Remind him of his promise to look after Iyla? I wouldn't insult his integrity by asking. The truth is, I don't know what I hope to accomplish and change my trajectory to rejoin my unit.

"Lockmore! Turn around."

It seems that the commander didn't miss my approach. "I know why you're here. I gave you my word that she would be looked after. In fact, I'm planning to put my best available man on it sometime today. With you guys gone, I'm guessing he'll need something to do."

Skin.

The commander looks at his watch and back up at me. "Now that we've got that ironed out, isn't there somewhere you need to be?"

"Yes, sir."

IYLA

Sitting at the small table in the cabin's kitchen, I absently stir my coffee, still thinking about Nolan's sweet wake-up.

Despite the circumstances, these last three days have been great. I've not received any messages from Dillan, and the time with Nolan has been unbelievable.

I worry, though. I've had to temporarily take down my online gallery as all my stock was destroyed. I'm answering requests from hospitality and agricultural execs but not booking anything for the immediate future.

I can paint anywhere, but it would take more than what I have with me. What I need is to bring my studio here, or at least some of it. Maybe Nolan could enlist the help of one of his teammates, whom I will owe big time when this is all over.

Around five, I'm working on concept sketches for a repeat client based on pictures they sent yesterday. Once again, I'm thankful Nolan thought to grab my sketchbooks and graphite pencils.

Thinking of Nolan makes me smile and gives me an idea. I should put on the best thing I have here and surprise him with a candlelit dinner.

While I'm looking through the fridge for dinner options, a knock sounds at the door, making me jump. I roll my eyes at my paranoia as I cross the room. *You're on a secure military base, Iyla. Get a grip.*

A peek through the peephole has me squealing. I throw open the door, glossing over the red, angry skin and patchwork of bandages. "Leo!"

He's not all smiles and charming personality like before. "Hey, Iyla. May I come in?"

"Of course, you can. When did you get back?"

"Ah, about thirty minutes ago."

I look around him, expecting to find Nolan, but only see Leo's Mustang.

"Well, what are you doing here? Shouldn't you be at home resting?"

He glances up at the sky and groans. "I did enough of that in Germany."

I move back to let him in, and he and I sit in the living room. "I'm sorry you were injured. Do you hurt?"

Leo shrugs a shoulder but won't meet my

eyes. "Not so much. It tingles a lot, itches some. I'm told those are signs of healing."

"Aye. My mother has always said the same thing. I'm glad you'll be ok."

"Ok, as I can be."

"That, I understand."

The SEAL looks a little sheepish. "Yeah. Judge told me about you being left at the altar. Don't be mad at him. He's my best friend and wanted me to understand the dynamic between you two."

I pat his right hand. "I don't mind that you know. It just goes to show that not all scars are visible."

"Another thing my team knows well."

"Speaking of your team, where's Nolan?"

Now Leo looks nervous. "That's actually why I'm here. He and all the others were called away this morning."

"Oh." *I might have guessed.*

"I'm to be your protection until they get back. And don't tell me that I should be resting instead. Being useless is so much worse than the healing."

"Then I'll just say I'm sorry you got stuck with the job. I don't need much protecting here on base. What I do need are my art supplies. Work is beginning to pile up."

"I think we could remedy that. I couldn't take you with me, but if you give me a list, I could pick up what you need from your house."

"Oh. No, I couldn't let you do that, not by yourself. I'd planned to ask a couple of the others to go."

The withered look on Leo's face breaks my heart. "Please, let me help. Otherwise, I might go crazy. My team just left to go on a mission without me for the first time since I joined them. I feel like shit that I'm not there to back them up. Let me help Nolan by helping you."

There's no way I could refuse now. Pasting a smile on my face, I say, "That would be pure barry. For now, can I fix you some supper? I'm getting right hungry and would like the company."

"I don't know what pure barry means, but I could eat."

Leo keeps me company in the kitchen, and after dinner, the two of us talk until late.

I don't know if it's jet lag or his burns, but by nine, he looks busted. "You look like you could use a good night's sleep. If you don't just *have* to go home tonight, you should take the guest room."

Leo stands and nods. "I think I will. Good night, Iyla. I'm glad to see you safe. This group has suffered enough."

He walks away, leaving me stunned, and I seem to recall Nolan saying something similar.

ESCAPEPROOF

JO CHAMBLISS

CHAPTER 21

IYLA

Leo is in the living room attempting pushups when I get up the next morning. He appears to have been at it for a while if his sweaty and haggard appearance is any indication. *He's pushing himself too hard too soon.*

He pops up to his knees when he notices that I've walked in. "I made coffee but be careful. It's strong."

"I like strong coffee. Have you had breakfast?"

"No. I was going to do that after a shower."

"You made the coffee. I'll make breakfast while you shower."

He gives a little salute and turns to go. Before he disappears into the bathroom, I call out to stop him, and he looks back. "If you need help with bandages, ask. I've gotten pretty good helping Nolan."

Leo turns around and comes closer. "How bad is he? I haven't seen him, and my commander didn't say any more than that he has been cleared for duty."

"He's ok. None of the holes were too deep. His stitches came out a few days ago."

Skin nods, relieved. "Judge saved my life. Did you know that?"

"No. He only told me that you were hurt."

Leo snickers and drops down into one of the dining chairs. "He saved us all. First, he put himself between me and a man he had a bad feeling about. Judge somehow figured out that something bad was coming and started yelling for all of us to get off the boat.

"The next thing I know, I'm on fire and can't see. Judge picked me up, carried me up the stairs, and threw me overboard. I didn't see what happened next, but when the team found me, Judge was missing. "I floated in the cold ocean with my face, neck, and arm still feeling like they were on fire, unable to search or even tell the team what happened. The other guys found Judge about five feet down and slowly sinking. He'd been knocked unconscious and had drowned, but Bandaid was able to start him breathing again."

I silently absorb the story, completely dumbfounded and with tears streaming down my face. "He's a good man," Leo says.

"I know," I whisper back.

Leo gets up to shower, and I stare in shock a minute longer. *Yeah, my instincts were right. I somehow knew not to let Dillan get too close but fell fast and hard for Nolan even though I fought it.*

Pancakes and bacon are nearly done when Leo walks back out, carrying a shirt and a bag of medical stuff. I manage to hold back a cringe at seeing the extent of his burns all at once.

He looks embarrassed when he says, "I tried, but I couldn't hold down the gauze and manage the tape with just one hand."

I can't speak for imagining the pain he must have felt, is still feeling, so I nod and turn the stove eyes off, removing the last of the cooked bacon.

Leo sits down on the sofa, and I take the place to his left. From shoulder to wrist, his arm displays burns varying in severity. Some are faded to pink. Most areas, including his cheek and the spot on his neck, are somewhat healed, with dark purple and red skin and some peeling around the edges. A few places on his arm look awful. I ache for him, for what he went through.

"It's ok, Iyla. It doesn't hurt anymore."

I can't help the fact that my eyes well up or that the sniffles start. Blinking away the useless tears, I follow Leo's instructions for dressing the grafted skin.

"Where did they take the grafts from?"

"My ass."

My eyes snap up to his, and the tears spill over as I burst out laughing. I bandage the worst places, and Leo pulls on a long-sleeved shirt before we relocate to the eat-in kitchen.

After breakfast is eaten and cleared away,

I try to talk Leo out of going to my house again or at least waiting for someone to go with him. He won't hear of it. "You need these things. I'm going to get them. End of story. Now, sit down and make your list."

I do as he says but keep it to a minimum for Leo's sake. *I wish I'd never said anything at all.* The stubborn man leaves, and two hours later, I hear his loud engine returning.

The trunk of his car pops open as I walk outside to unload the supplies. The first words out of his mouth when he opens his door are, "I met your cop friend. He's a real peach. He had a big bandage on his forehead."

"Oh god. What happened?"

The two of us each lift a container out of the trunk and start walking toward the cabin. "So, I pack all the stuff you asked for and start making trips to the car. A police car pulls into the driveway behind me, and the cop gets out and asks where the owner of the house is."

Leo breaks into a surprisingly good Scottish accent and continues. "I told him, 'Not here. She's out of town looking for a new place to live while I get to box all her *shite* up.' The guy's face went to stone, and he asked who I was."

"What did you tell him?"

"Only that, 'I'm her brother and the one who's going to kick the *arse* of some *wankstain* that scared her away from here.'"

I nearly drop the box I'm carrying. "You

said that?!"

"Yeah. He didn't seem too impressed. I asked Deputy *Browndick* what he needed you for. All he said was that he needed you to sign your statement from an incident that happened… blah, blah, blah."

"Damn. Now, I wish I'd just bought all new stuff. Seeing someone at my house will probably start him up all over again."

"Iyla, I don't want to scare you, but I got the impression this guy never stopped. His type never does. My Commander filled me in on what Judge and Fish told him. I can guarantee this Broderick guy has just been watching and waiting."

"Feck, Leo. Don't hold back. I can take it," I say sarcastically.

My sardonic tone doesn't deter him. "I'm not telling this to scare you but to warn you not to drop your guard."

"Oh, good. Because I don't need any help in the being scared department. I'm doing just fine freaking myself out."

We get all the supplies inside and have just begun unloading when I get a text notification on my phone. *God, I hate it when I'm right.* I pick up the device and confirm my fear. It's Dillan.

The message reads, *Who said you could leave?*

"Feck."

NOLAN

All platoons of SEAL Team Two are trucked to the Naval Auxiliary Landing Field Fentress near my hometown and then divided up to load onto three planes. To this point, all I've been told is to bring wet gear. Whatever we're doing will be on the water.

Both squads of third platoon get situated on a C-17, and Clothespin, our platoon leader, wastes no time diving into our assignment. "Our job is to create a diversion at the arms dealer's private home compound. Security's too tight for us to nab him there without extensive planning. We're to flush him out where he'll be more vulnerable to capture. We're calling it Operation Rip Tide. Ours, along with operations by all other platoons, are to be carried out at the same time to keep any one part of the organization from warning the others."

Having given us the overall objective, Clothespin spreads out satellite images of an expansive home set on a lagoon. The home is surrounded, not by a wall, but by a simple open-board fence. *They must have great faith in their security team.* On the lagoon side of the property, a fancy speed yacht is moored to a private dock.

"Our target is in Portugal. A helo from Rota will take us to meet a civilian vessel off Sao Jacinto. Once we board, the smaller boat will enter the lagoon and anchor half a mile from this property.

"Job one is to place a charge on the target's yacht that will disable its props. Use a long-range remote trigger so the Navy ship can render her dead in the open ocean. That's how this thing ultimately gets wrapped up. All we have to do is ensure the house's occupants evacuate via the yacht."

The platoon leader points to a spot on the satellite view. "How we'll do that is by blowing up the main gate. Camera coverage is bound to be thorough around the perimeter, so we'll employ long-range everything. We'll use RPGs to take out the gate supports and block the front exit. Who's as good as Ramsay at aiming a grenade launcher?"

Chips from Clothespin's squad speaks up. "I've practiced with him. He's a good teacher."

"You're it then. I don't want anyone else firing toward the house. The security team is bound to be good, and I want to avoid having our muzzle flare giving these guys targets for return fire. Not to mention, the guy's wife and kids are in the house.

"The grenades are only meant to dissuade anyone from leaving out the front, and the eight-foot fence guarantees the only remaining exit is the boat. Everybody got that?"

We all answer in the affirmative.

"Good. Now, I want to hear problems and solutions. Go."

"Security has infrared capabilities and can spot us in the woods." Duck offers his hypothetical scenario.

"Have your mylar blankets ready to use. Then you'll be invisible." Devil answers.

"They still try leaving out the front," Wrench predicts.

All eyes go back to the satellite view. "These are some pretty big trees," Fish points out. "We could knock one of them down to block the driveway."

"Good. Devil, you take a second launcher and be ready to fire. Better yet. Don't wait. Take down this middle tree when the gate blows."

"What if they don't leave, say they hunker down in a safe room or bunker we don't know about?" Bandaid asks

"Valid point. Being a coastal house, any saferoom they have would be above ground. I say we start walking grenades closer and closer to the house as soon as the front gate blows. The man won't risk his family taking mortar fire in any above-ground structure, no matter how fortified it might be."

No one else mentions potential obstacles, so Clothespin begins wrapping up final details. He selects five additional men to the two already assigned to the frontal attack. Wrench and Fuse are tasked with setting charges on the boat.

The rest of us will spread out in the woods to the north and south. We'll watch the sides and back of the property and track movement through the house.

"Any resistance is to be dealt with from the north side by the snipers. I don't want a crossfire situation that gets one of you dead. We herd these people to the boat and let them go. Now, until we land, I want you guys to get some rest."

An hour later, I'm still awake, thinking through ways I could set up Broderick to either put his ass behind bars or at least have enough to blackmail him away from us.

Clothespin gets up and walks over to sit by me where Skin would normally be. "You're supposed to be asleep."

"Having a little trouble with that, sir."

"I heard about your woman. Unless you can handle the thought of dying on this mission and leaving her to deal with that monster alone, I'd suggest you figure out a way to knock off for a while."

He's right. Dead, I'm no good to anyone. "Yes, sir."

My platoon leader returns to his seat, and I lay my head back against the cargo net to sleep for a while.

The plane lands seven hours later, and each platoon is offloaded and immediately funneled to its next mode of transportation. Ours is a Sikorsky Super Stallion. The giant helicopter will fly us the three hundred miles to meet our decoy, a black yacht owned by none other than

Knot Corp, a private military firm.

Two and a half hours after taking off, we reach the yacht waiting thirteen miles from shore. The fifteen of us fast-rope down to the sleek boat, and the Stallion continues toward a Navy vessel waiting farther out.

On the deck, Sadie Phelps and Aaron Hosfeld, Knot's most senior operatives, welcome us aboard. They're dressed to impress, wearing a revealing gown and tuxedo.

We met the two a few months ago when Sadie was the subject of a rescue mission in the Philippines. Aaron tracked her locator to a shack in the jungle and worked with us on her extraction. It was the same mission that we thought we'd lost Ink.

"It's good to see you guys again," she says to Fish. Being the leader of her crew, Sadie lays out the plan for the last leg of our mission. "You men are to hide out below and gear up while we get the boat into position."

Gesturing to other formally dressed people milling around, she adds, "We'll pose as a party crew on deck for appearances and to act as spotters for the Navy ship. The USS Arleigh Burke is waiting another five miles out from this location. They'll start moving in to intercept your boat when you reach the target. I trust all the remote triggers have been coordinated so we've got no chance of losing them, right?"

"I set them all myself." Wrench reports.

"The Stallion is delivering one to the Arleigh as we speak."

Sadie salutes with her flute.

"Champagne?" Chips asks while leering at the deadly contractor.

Aaron scowls at Chips, and Sadie shakes her head. "Sparkling grape. And it's just as nasty."

"All right, you men get below so we can get moving," Aaron orders, still scowling at Chips.

We do as he says, and the private military contractors above start up the engines, music, and laughter.

By the time Sadie comes down to let us know the boat is in position, we're geared up, painted, and ready to go. "It's showtime, fellas."

Chips stares at her ass as she leads the way up a back hatch to the launch deck. Ink thumps him on the ear and warns, "She's taken."

"I don't see a ring," the ambitious SEAL counters.

Ink snickers. "Remember that big bloke in the tux standing next to Sadie? Let's just say I wouldn't let him catch you with your eyes on her ass."

We reach the darkened stern deck and make a final check of our equipment. "Good luck, men," Sadie bids, and we slip silently into the water.

At only a half-mile, our swim would be

considered easier than training, except we're all loaded for bear. We remain on the surface until we reach the point where the snipers and frontal assault groups split off, about halfway between the boat and the dock behind the house.

At this point, the rest of us complete our swim submerged to avoid detection should someone walk out toward the dock.

GPS wrist devices alarm when we've reached the approximate location of the private dock, and Wrench and Fuse branch off to set the charges.

Left are Duck, Clothespin, Taco, and me. We swim another quarter mile and beach way beyond the tree line at the edge of the target's property.

Our dive gear is removed and hidden, and we disappear into the dense forest.

The sniper group was the first team to check in, having had the shortest distance to travel. They're set up on the opposite side of the house from where we'll be. *"Kraken to Poseidon. We're in position."*

"Copy, Kraken," Clothespin answers.

Wrench and Fuse can hear our transmissions but will only be able to reply using Morse code. Soon after Kraken checks in, Wrench reports reaching the yacht. To preserve the air in their tanks, Wrench and Fuse will go ahead and set the charges and then surface to keep an eye on the boat and back of the house.

"Leviathan in position," comes the announcement from the front assault team a few minutes later.

My group is the last to get set, having had to travel the farthest. Clothespin fans the four of us out, indicating that Duck is not to go beyond the corner of the house. He reports that Poseidon is in position, and now, we wait for the pre-set go time decided upon by the Pentagon.

Two hours. That's how long we have to wait. This is partly because we expect most people to settle down for the night by then but also to make sure all strike teams in Europe and Africa can get in position.

I'm not a big fan of long waits. A lot can change in two hours. Fortunately, the only changes I observe are lights being switched off inside the house.

The long wait finally passes, and Clothespin checks in with his strike teams, "We go in five minutes."

Each man responds with his mission call sign, and the minutes and seconds tick down until Clothespin keys in again. "Leviathan and Kraken go in five, four, three, two, one. Fire!"

The rocket-propelled grenades whistle as they fly to their targets, and the corresponding explosions shake the ground. Two seconds after that, everything shakes again with the felling of the giant tree.

The explosions wake the house, and the

security team spills out of the front and back exits.

"Poseidon, Security is opening the garage."

"Verify absence of the target or family and hit the closest ride with an RPG! Leviathan, start walking grenades toward the house!"

Gunfire erupts from inside the front door, but there's no way these guys have identified a target. They're wasting time and ammo firing blind.

In the melee, I hear Clothespin through my earpiece. "Family is evaccing from the back. Loch Ness, confirm they're headed for the boat."

In code, Loch Ness responds. *Affirm.*

"Leviathan, cease fire and relocate. Kraken cover."

"Copy."

Loch Ness breaks in with an update, still in code. *Boat loaded, Family plus 5.*

"All teams hold," Clothespin orders. "If security advances on your position, neutralize and relocate."

"Loch Ness reporting boat is away," Wrench says, no longer in danger of detection.

"Party Barge, do you copy."

Sadie's voice comes in loud and clear. "We copy. Alerting Ghost Ship."

"Rip Tide, continue to hold," Clothespin orders, using the mission codename.

Over the next ten minutes, I hear two separate bursts of gunfire. After each occurrence, the SEAL involved reports his status.

At the fifteen-minute mark, we've had no other contacts, and Clothespin orders everyone to fall back to the lagoon. I take a shooting position to cover Duck's advance and catch movement behind him in the trees when he's ten feet away. "Poseidon, get down!"

Duck hits the deck just before I spot the muzzle flash. The bullet slams into the house, and I return a ten-round burst to the shooter. The full moon allows me to see the man fall, and Duck and I double-time it to catch up with the rest of Poseidon. Duck reports our status, and within a minute's time, we've joined the other two men at the water's edge.

Since our return trip will be made the same way we came, I cover Poseidon while they don their diving gear, and they do the same for me.

We've just met up with the rest of the platoon when Party Barge checks in. "Poseidon, Ghost Ship has claimed another victim."

Mission Accomplished.

We swim the rest of the way back to Knot's boat and pull anchor to meet Ghost Ship, AKA the *USS Arleigh Burke.*

Sadie and the others have changed into black tactical clothes by the time we reach the battleship, and the two operatives see us off. "Gentlemen, until next time."

I watch Ink and Aaron shake hands, and then the yacht speeds away from the Navy ship.

The trip back to Spain on the Arleigh takes

about twenty hours. Since we're the last group to return from assignment, our plane is loaded and ready to take us home when we arrive at Naval Station Rota.

CHAPTER 22

IYLA

Leo reads Dillan's new message and looks contrite when he hands the phone back. "Iyla, I'm sorry. Riling him up was a bad idea."

"No. You were right. Dillan was waiting for *anybody* to show themselves. And I can't hide here forever. I'm only worried about what his next move will be."

"Try not to think about it."

Right. No problem. I almost say it out loud, but then I start imagining what all a SEAL has seen and experienced. Leo probably knows what he's talking about.

Deciding to try his suggestion, I sigh and set up my portable drawing board on the dining room table. I'm laying out the various types of media he brought when Leo removes a book from one of the boxes. "I hope you don't mind. I grabbed an art book to look through."

"I don't mind at all. What kind of art do you like?"

He smiles sheepishly. "Actually, I have no idea. Call it a new interest. Until recently, I only cared about expertly painted faces and well-sculpted bodies."

I laugh at his comical confession and ask, "Oh yeah? What changed?"

"I grew up." Leo walks away quietly and settles on the sofa with his book.

I mourn Leo's easy smile, saddened by the rueful creature he's become. I hope one day soon, he'll find a reason to smile again.

Needing to refocus, I resume setting my tools about me. When finished, I set up my laptop to display another set of pictures. This time, the subject is a custom fountain company's favorite installation to be used for an artistic logo.

Everything is positioned just so. I'm comfortable in my chair, and the lighting is good, but I can't seem to get started. My mind simply does not want to settle down and work. I flip through all the client's pictures again, hoping something will click, but I get nothing.

Unable to concentrate on the concrete or still images of the cascading water, my focus keeps shifting to the man in the living room. Even though I've only met him one time before, it's hard to imagine him being the womanizer he described.

The Leo I see is grounded and kind. Maybe at one time, he was that boy, but something recent changed him. And I don't believe it was the fire.

I pick up a pencil and begin laying down lines, filling up the page with the image of my new friend.

He's on the edge of the sofa, book on the table before him, studying the masters of beauty, fantasy, and the macabre. Being that I'm sitting to his right and that he's in that long-sleeve shirt, his wounds aren't visible. Though angry and swollen now, I can't see the scars spoiling his good looks once they've healed and faded. Still, I don't think he'd appreciate seeing them immortalized on paper.

I reference him periodically until I've gotten the forms down, then I fill in details from memory and add shading. In working so intently, I lose track of time and everything else. I don't notice that Leo has gotten up and is standing behind me until he speaks. "Me?"

"Shite!" I jump and scream.

"I'm sorry. I didn't mean to scare you. Why did you draw me?"

Hand over my heart, I will my heart to settle down. "You're a captivating subject."

He runs his right hand over his head, unconvinced. "Maybe before—"

I stop him with a hand up. "Think what you want, but I'm the expert."

Leo laughs and rolls his eyes. "What are you cooking for dinner?"

I know a dodge when I see one, but I don't want him to be uncomfortable. So, I allow the change of subject. "What are you hungry for?"

His eyes drift closed, and he sighs. "A big-ass steak."

"We'll have to go shopping."

The dreamy smile fades, and Leo swallows. "I… can handle that."

We load up in his car and drive to the commissary. What should be a simple and quick stop quickly becomes uncomfortable. Despite this being a military base, which I'm sure has seen its share of injured sailors, Leo doesn't miss the shoppers' gawking stares. He has to know the burns on his face and neck will heal and fade, but for now, they garner a lot of attention. And each gasp or pointed finger has Leo retreating a little deeper into himself.

I hate that.

Leo is quiet during the ride back to the cabin. I don't know him well enough to know the right thing to say, but I figure whatever I *do* say is better than what he's telling himself.

"They won't always stare," I whisper.

"Won't they?" he snaps.

I rest a hand on his arm, squeezing supportively. "Some might. Those that matter won't."

"Maybe."

Leo sounds skeptical but covers it up by changing the subject and bragging about his grilling skills.

Saturday morning comes late for me after the big dinner and a marathon poker session that saw me losing all my chips… three times.

Leo leaves the cabin to run some errands off base, and I sit down to get some actual work done. At two, I get a strange phone call that I'm not entirely convinced isn't a prank. "Hello?"

"Ma'am, this is Al with Pane in the Glass. We've got a work order from an Iyla Dunsmore for an emergency repair of a broken picture window, but no one is home. This is the number listed on the order."

"There must be some mistake. I'm Iyla, and I haven't called anyone about a broken window."

"Um, I'm standing at the back of the house right now. The window is completely shattered. I'm guessing a wild animal did it because everything inside is wrecked."

A lead weight settles in my stomach. "What exactly is wrecked?"

"It looks like a bunch of art stuff."

"Give me the address where you are."

The man rattles off my address, but I'm still not convinced. "Sir, could you text a picture of the window to this number?"

"I can, but I'll have to hang up to do it."

"Ok."

I pull the phone away from my ear, and Leo walks in and freezes at the look on my face. Before he can ask what's wrong, I get a text. The picture I've just received is my studio's picture window smashed to hell.

"Dammit!"

My phone rings again, and I answer the glass man's call. "Hello."

"That your place?"

"It is. Can you hold on for a minute?"

I place my phone on the table and wake up my laptop. Opening my internet browser, I run a search on the glass company and find that they're legit.

Deciding to include himself in the conversation, Leo picks up my phone and puts the call on speaker.

At his questioning look, I pinch the bridge of my nose and say to both men, "I'm not in a position to deal with this right now."

"Well, ah, you'll need to do something. Bad weather is expected tonight, and you have a big, gaping hole in the back of your house. Whoever called this in for you gave us accurate measurements, and I have the glass on my truck to make the repair right now."

I look to Leo for guidance, but he has no solution to offer. "Ok. What do I need to do?"

"Um, since you didn't call this in, my first suggestion would be to call the police about a possible break-in."

"NO," Leo and I both say at the same time.

"Okaaay." The guy says nervously. "So, like I said, I'm prepared to fix the window now, but since this is obviously a... non-standard situation, I'm going to need some proof of ownership, ID, and a credit card number before starting the job. My boss will fire me if I do an unverified job and end up getting stiffed."

I look to Leo again, who takes over logistics planning. "We'll be there in thirty minutes. Give us your name and truck number," Leo orders the guy.

When the call ends, Leo says, "You verify this guy's ID with the glass company. I'll let the commander know what's happening."

I make the call, and the glass guy checks out, but that doesn't mean I'm any less nervous about going. This screams of a setup, and I'm no idiot. What I am is over a barrel.

Leo walks back into the room a minute later and grabs his keys off the table. "Commander O'Reilly isn't thrilled. Truthfully, I'm not either. The only reason he's not refusing outright is the damage that tonight's expected storms would do to your house. Given my current shape, he'd prefer us not to go alone, but with all of our guys deployed, there isn't anyone else he can send with us in an unofficial capacity. Since it appears we don't have a choice or the support of local police, he's provided me with a list of ass-covering measures we're to take."

"For instance?"

"Verifying the technician's identity was number one. You are to remain inside and invisible the whole time we're on site. I'm to check in with him every fifteen minutes, and I'm quoting here, 'our asses are to clear the area not one fucking second after the technician leaves.'"

"All of that makes sense."

Leo holds his ground, still not convinced. "Iyla, I don't like this. I'd prefer leaving you here or stashing you somewhere safe while I handle this guy."

"I'm not disagreeing with you, but I also wouldn't feel good about you being there alone. Besides, you heard the tech. He needs proof of ownership. I have to go with you."

"Fine, but if something happens, your safety is priority one. If I tell you to do something, you do it without question. Got it?"

I shake my head, no, completely unable to cope with the reality of what he just said. Seeing my reluctance, he takes hold of my shoulders, squeezing them reassuringly. "I'll be with you every second."

Leo then steps back and pulls up the right side of his shirt, showing me a pistol holstered at his right hip and a large knife sheathed on the other side.

Come on. You can do this, Iyla. After my inner pep talk, I let him put me in the car but grab a ball cap from the back seat and pull it low on my head in case Dillan's on patrol.

Leo and I make it through town and to my house without incident. Upon our arrival, the glass man exits his van and walks toward us with the necessary paperwork. He's barely gotten started when Leo interrupts and insists we take the conversation indoors.

My SEAL bodyguard holds out his hand for the keys and uncovers his gun to be ready for anything. The glass guy starts to sweat, so I tell him a little white lie to ease his worry. "Don't worry. My brother is a Navy cop. He's just being careful."

The man relaxes, and Leo finds nothing out of place during his search except for the broken glass.

"Um… if it's all right with you, I'll get started as soon as you fill out this form, show me some ID, and let me get a credit card number."

I fill out the few blanks on the form and sign it, show the guy a utility bill with my name and address, and finally, give him my credit card. With all the red tape finally out of the way, he starts removing the broken glass, and I step into my studio to clean up the shredded art.

Leo follows me in and silently helps. The task is demoralizing, seeing work I've poured my heart and soul into in tatters on the floor.

I clear the shredded papers off the floor while Leo pulls knives from the walls. All my drawings of Nolan are gone. My favorite, the first one I did, is pulled down last, but not before I notice the red writing on it. Leo scrunches it up in his hand, and I know it's to keep me from reading the message.

"Wait. What was that?"

"Nothing."

"Don't lie to me, Leo. I want to see."

Reluctantly, he hands me the crumpled paper. I open the destroyed drawing and read, *You've fucked my woman for the last time.*

The paper slips from my fingers to the floor, and I drop my head. Leo pulls me into his arms and strokes my back while I cry big, mournful tears. I don't even care that the glass man can see me falling apart.

"Come on, Iyla. Let's get you out of here."

Leo leads me to the kitchen and searches through cabinets for coffee makings. He finds what he's looking for and starts the machine.

Minutes later, I'm handed a cup of the steaming brew, and Leo tries to lighten my mood. "Those were... interesting drawings of Judge."

I have to chuckle at Leo seeing naked drawings of his long-time friend. "Did he pose for those?"

"No. I did them from memory. Did Nolan tell you how we met?"

"Nope."

I'm not sure I believe him, but I tell Leo the story anyway. "The day I moved in, the movers took out his mailbox shortly after Nolan came home. It was after what he calls the locust mission."

"Ugh. Don't say that word around me."

"Anyway, I saw him drive up, so I knew he was home. He didn't answer when I rang the bell, so I walked around the house, thinking he might be in the backyard. Well, he was."

"Let me guess. He was in his fancy outdoor shower."

"Yep. My first introduction to Nolan was to his bare ass."

Leo barks out a laugh. "That's beautiful!"

Someone knocks at the back door, making me jump, but we can't see who it is because of the mat board taped to the glass. Leo lifts the cover on the deck door, peering out to confirm it's the technician. He opens the door to the man who asks us to check out the finished installation. I stand to go with them, but Leo holds up a hand to keep me in place. "You stay here. And lock the door."

Without argument, I do what he says and walk back into the art room to watch the men through my brand-new window. The glass man hands some literature to Leo and points to certain features.

Leo leans in to inspect something a little closer, and I hear a sudden crack of sound. Leo's reaction is instantaneous. He draws his gun and crouches down low. He looks to be going for the steps when another crack breaks the silence.

The glass man begins to stumble and sort of melts to the ground. Leo grabs at something on his back but can't reach it. I run back into the kitchen and open the door to help him, but he yells to stop me. "No, Iyla! Go. Get out of here!"

Leo reaches into his pocket and pulls out

his keys. He tries to throw them, but his arm isn't working right. He then walks toward the stairs, holding out the keyring toward me.

Leo doesn't make it. I scream, terrified, as Leo collapses to the stairs. I open the door to pull Leo inside, but before I get one foot out, Dillan emerges from behind a thick rose bush about thirty feet away. I slam the door closed and grip my phone tight, knowing there's no one I can call.

Dillan continues to advance until he's standing over Leo's still form. "Come out, Iyla."

I don't move from my spot. I can't. Dillan props the rifle against his leg and pulls a pistol from the back of his jeans. "I shot your brother with a tranquilizer dart, but if you don't come out, I'll shoot him with something he won't wake up from."

When I still don't emerge, Dillan cocks the gun and points it at Leo's head. My eyes drift closed, and I apologize to Nolan for what I'm about to do. Shaking fingers open the door, and I step through the opening, sliding my phone into my pocket as I do.

"That's a good girl."

Dillan lowers the gun and reaches out his hand.

"Please, may I check on him? He was seriously burned recently. I don't want him to bleed to death if one of his grafts split open."

"I'll allow you that. I'm not completely heartless."

Moving slowly, I walk down the steps and kneel beside Leo, keeping my back to Dillan. With my right hand, I pull the neck of Leo's shirt open to expose his shoulder bandage. As I do, my left hand pulls his phone from his pocket.

I lean even farther over him to appear as though I'm looking down the inside of his long-sleeved shirt at his arm. That's when I shove his phone down the front of my pants.

"He looks to be okay," I tell Dillan.

"Then let's go. I'll need your phone."

I can't let myself be taken. I'll never see my parents or Nolan again.

Allowing my hands to shake, I pull out my phone and allow it to drop. "I'm sorry."

Bending low, I fake reaching for the phone, grabbing the rifle instead. I come up swinging and catch Dillan in the neck. Then, I do the only thing that comes to mind. I run.

I don't have a way to leave as Leo's keys fell under the stairs. There's no escape for me this far out in Nowheresville, but... I can provide proof for Nolan to use against Dillan at my murder trial.

I turn from my original trajectory — the woods — to run behind Nolan's house. If I can get close enough, his cameras will activate and video Dillan making chase.

ESCAPEPROOF

JO CHAMBLISS

CHAPTER 23

NOLAN

Our plane lands at Oceana at nineteen thirty, and I'm down to about a three-minute chopper ride, one-minute walk, and two-minute drive before I see Iyla again. Three Chinooks sit, warming up for our short taxi to Little Creek when the loading ramp of the C-17 opens.

Eagerly anticipating returning to Iyla, I grab my gear and jog to the nearest bird. The helo lifts off as soon as it's full, and we soon land at Little Creek.

Commander O'Reilly waits nearby when the Chinook doors open, no doubt to congratulate us on a successful mission. However, when I step out of the bird, he points directly at me and gestures to follow him away from the rotor noise. That's when I notice we're not on the helipad. The chopper landed in the grass behind HQ.

O'Reilly's dark expression sends a shiver surging down my spine, a chilling precursor to words that will forever alter my brain chemistry. I hurry to catch up with the commander, and of course, all of my squad comes along.

By the time I reach O'Reilly, I've already experienced a torrent of emotions, dread being predominant. The commander's bearing is a carefully balanced blend of empathy and resolve, but his eyes tell another story. He's fucking scared, and now, so am I. "Five hours ago, Ramsay and Iyla met with a glass tech at Iyla's house. Someone had smashed the giant window in her art room, and the repair couldn't wait because of the coming storms. The glass company and tech both checked out. I instructed Ramsay on precautions to take, including leaving when the repair man did and checking back in with me. I haven't heard from Ramsay since."

Grief threatens to crush me, but a spark of determination keeps me on my feet. My friend is alive, and I will find Iyla. Broderick has no claim on her. She belongs to me.

With gritted teeth, I stiffen my spine and take off, running toward my car. Iyla needs me. Footsteps thunder beside and behind me, and I realize it's not just me running toward the parking lot. At my car, I dig my keys from my pack and then discard the heavy bag on the ground.

The door automatically unlocks when I grab the handle, and I dive in, reaching inside the console to get my phone. It takes an eternity for the damn thing to turn on so I can try Iyla's number. The phone boots up, but a security alert from over an hour ago pops up on screen before I can access the keypad.

Fear tightens like a vice around my heart as I start the attached video. The clip begins with Iyla hauling ass across my backyard, only to be caught from behind by Broderick.

She tries to fight him off but quickly finds herself pinned to a tree. Broderick rips Iyla's shirt from her body, grabs her face to keep it still, and forces his tongue into her mouth.

I've seen enough. "I'm going to kill him. I'm gonna kill that son of a bitch!"

Me and three other somebodies climb in my car, and then I'm jabbing my finger into the start button and screeching out of that parking lot.

We're driving through the gate when I notice Fish's voice yelling into his phone. "Omen, I need you to trace a phone now!"

A second later, he's yelling at me, "Judge, what's Iyla's number?"

I stumble over the numbers, unable to answer for trying to keep this fucking car on the road and my fear of what's happening to Iyla. "Stone, get his phone!"

A hand reaches for the phone perched on my thigh, and a second later, Commander O'Reilly calls out the digits to Fish. His call is then placed on speaker, and I hear the familiar voice of Chase "Omen" McDaniels, founder of Pantera Security and former Army Ranger. "I'm running the trace. What I want to know is why the hell I wasn't contacted before now?"

I don't answer our old friend because I don't know.

Precious seconds pass, and I hear Omen say, "Got it! The phone is stationary at... Judge, it's at your address, or to be more exact, it's about eighty feet to the west of your property."

I floor the accelerator at the news and hear Omen again. "Now, one of you needs to tell me everything."

I mostly ignore the conversation between Omen and the men with me, only answering when asked a direct question.

"This asshole ditched your woman's phone. I'm not Cle or Squid, meaning I can't hack into shit, but when you find her phone, see if you can get in and give me the number he's been using to message her. I can trace it and hopefully give you a target."

"We'll do it. Stone out," the commander replies.

The dark clouds threatening chaos over the area finally open up as Iyla's house comes into view.

Coming up on our street, I shift into manual, drop to low gear, brake, and flick the steering wheel. I drift through the turn, sliding onto Iron Horse Road. I enter Iyla's driveway using the same maneuver and skid to a stop right behind Skin's Mustang and the glass van.

Two more cars squeal to a stop behind me,

but I'm already out the door, running up Iyla's front steps.

The door is locked, so I kick it in, finding the inside to be as dark as the outside. I flip on the lights to find the place unoccupied and undisturbed.

O'Reilly, Fish, and Ink appear beside me, holding firearms. "We do this right." O'Reilly barks. "Clear every room. The rest are checking around back here and at your place."

In no time, we hear yelling from the back of Iyla's house. Still, we finish checking the interior, which ends up being a waste of time. No one is here.

Before walking through the back door, I throw the switch for the floodlights, revealing what had the others yelling. Two bodies are sprawled out in the back yard being soaked by the downpour, one man in a service uniform... and Skin. He's lying face-down, half on the stairs and half on the ground.

Fuck no!

Bandaid tucks his gun away and leans over Skin, pressing a finger to his carotid. "He's got a pulse. Strong."

"What's wrong with him then? I don't see any blood or bruises," O'Reilly says.

Holding Skin's head, Bandaid instructs Fish to turn him over. "Careful... There."

The doctor points to a metal cylinder with a fuzzy neon top. "Tranq."

"Call an ambulance. We don't know what was in it."

I stand up and face my commander. "If you do that, the cops will come with them."

"Lockmore, you've got two victims here and video evidence of an assault and kidnapping. They have to believe you now."

"Fine, but I'm not waiting. I need to find Iyla's phone."

And the Dead Man Walking. I move around O'Reilly to start the search, and he calls out to two of the men with us. "Murphy, Delano, go help him."

It takes a while in the dark and pouring rain, but I find the phone about ten feet from where Skin fell. The device will do us no good. There's a bullet hole right through the center.

Even with the setback, there's no way I can stand here and do nothing. I split off from the group, running toward the last place I saw Iyla. Splashing through the low spots in the lawn, I curse the rain falling even harder now.

The lawyer side of me laments the water, washing away trace evidence that could lead me to where that bastard took Iyla. I locate the tree shown in the video, but nothing that points to where Broderick took her. All I find is Iyla's destroyed shirt.

I'm ready to run off into the woods just to be looking somewhere, but I'm stopped by a restraining hand on my shoulder.

"You need to slow down and think," Devil warns. "Running around blind isn't going to help. Anyway, you're a lawyer. You can't be the man that wrecks evidence. And you're going to want that evidence to fry this guy."

I jerk out of his hold, ready to fight. "I don't want shit because Broderick won't face a jury. This judge is going to kill him with his bare hands."

Devil only stares me down as thunder rolls. "This isn't you, friend."

Glaring at my teammate, I growl. "It fucking is now."

Incoming sirens pull my attention away, and I jog back to Iyla's house to confront the jackasses that allowed this to happen in the first place.

O'Reilly is talking to a deputy, and EMTs are working on Skin and the other guy when I reach Iyla's back porch. The commander and deputy look my way, and I recognize the name clipped above his badge. *This is the same man Iyla went to for help.* "So, asshole, believe us now?"

I know I have fire in my eyes, which is probably why O'Reilly shoves a hand against my chest to push me back. The cold rain running down my face does nothing to cool my temper, but I respect my commander enough to stand down.

"I want to see this video," Deputy Birch insists.

The commander gestures to the covered porch, and the group gets out of the rain. I pull out my phone and call up the security feed, making myself watch the entire clip this time.

After Broderick holds Iyla and kisses her, she attempts to strike him with her knee, but he blocks the blow.

Then, he hits her.

The asshole backhands her across the mouth hard enough to send Iyla spinning to the ground. With Iyla lying on the ground holding her face, Broderick stands over her, saying something as lightning flashes in the background.

Deputy Birch hands me his phone and demands, "Get me that video."

He turns to another deputy, spitting out orders as he walks away. "Give me your phone. I've got to call the Sheriff."

I open the cop's text app, message my phone, and reply with the video attached. The file is sending when I get another message. *I know where you are. If you want to see her alive again, leave now. On foot. Alone. Walk through the woods beside Iyla's house until you reach the highway, then turn south. Keep walking until picked up.*

How the fuck am I supposed to do that?

I look around the group to see that everyone is focused on one thing or another. It might be possible to slip away unnoticed, but not if I take my time about it. Going alone is stupid, but I can't risk Broderick hurting Iyla. And everything I've seen from him indicates that's exactly what he plans to do.

Slowly and carefully, to not attract attention, I step inside the house, having made my decision. Opening the settings on my phone, I change the screen timeout to thirty minutes and open the messaging app again, leaving Broderick's message on display. Next, I place my keys, gun, and phone on the kitchen table. That should point my team in the right direction while allowing me a good head start.

I pocket the cop's phone and walk to Iyla's studio that faces the woods. Sneaking out from here should be easy in the dark and with the rain drowning out any noise I might make.

Just before I open the window, I spot Iyla's purse lying on the floor. It gives me an idea, and I reach for the yellow canvas bag. I find what I'm looking for and finally jump through the window into the storm.

IYLA

My cheek stings after the blow from Dillan. I stare up at him from the ground while lightning flashes in the sky like a bad omen.

"I think I rather prefer you willing and begging."

"I wouldn't give you the satisfaction."

He pulls me back up to a standing position, stroking a hand over my lace-covered breast. "You will."

Dillan drags me through the woods for what feels like miles but is likely less than one. The dense forest abruptly opens to a dirt road with an orchard beyond. I worry about being exposed to commercial pesticides, but the rain must have cleared any particles from the air.

Dillan turns me to the left, and I spot his truck parked several yards away. I'm shoved toward the vehicle, and the back passenger door is opened in a sickening case of déjà vu. Anticipating a fight, Dillan bear hugs me and tosses me inside, shoving me down to the floorboard. My hands are cuffed behind my back, and the door is slammed closed.

Our ride isn't a long one, and judging by the bumpy surface, we're still on the dirt road. The truck comes to a stop, and Dillan must anticipate my plans to attack with my feet. He opens the door at my head and pulls me out by my arms.

The sun is beginning its descent behind the hills, but there's still enough light to see that we're in the middle of nowhere with no paved roads, much less streetlights. We're standing in front of an old-fashioned barn with stairs leading up to an enclosed loft.

Dillan directs me toward the stairs with a grand sweeping motion. I take a step back, and he grabs my bicep roughly. "No. You need to stop fighting this. You're mine, and you need to start acting like it."

"Yer aff yer fecking heid. I'll never belong to you."

Dillan reaches behind me, yanks me by the hair, and pulls me flush against him. Grinning suggestively, he stares at my mouth. "Such venom coming from the same lips that begged to worship mine just a week ago. Kiss me, Iyla."

I laugh at him. Actually, laugh. "You have no leverage over me now."

"No? How about we go back, and you can watch me finish off your brother?"

I laugh even harder. "That's not my brother. He's a bodyguard. You have nothing and no one you can use to control me. And that's what you're about, isn't it? Any idiot can take from an unwilling woman. It takes a truly superior being to make the unwilling woman want to submit. Well, guess what? I'm stronger than you. You'll never break me."

Dillan's grin hasn't faded, "You're right. You are strong, stronger than the others. That's why I chose you. You're wild and untamed. That'll make your inevitable submission so much sweeter. You're also right about me being a superior being. However, I want you to know I won't hesitate to use *force* if I feel you need it."

Dillan emphasizes his point with the thrust of his hips. Lightning flashes, adding an exclamation point to his dark promise. "Go inside before you get your first taste of punishment. I promise you wouldn't like it."

The color drains from my face at his threat. I turn for the stairs before Dillan gets the idea to throw me over his shoulder and discovers that I'm smuggling Leo's phone. Up to this point, I have been stalling the best I can, hoping to give O'Reilly or someone time to find me, but it's time to play it cool.

Inside the finished and furnished loft, Dillan releases my left wrist from the cuffs and attaches my restraints to a decorative iron apron beneath the built-in dining bar. Dillan walks away then, sitting on the sofa and leering at me. I don't understand. Despite what he said outside, I expected to be fighting against being violated, not being tethered to dining furniture.

Then it hits me. Dillan is using my own words against me. *It takes a truly superior being to make the unwilling woman want to submit.* Dillan's in it for the long game. He's going to try to get into my head.

I huff in anger and fear and flop down onto one of the bar seats. *Hurry up, Commander. Leo and I need your help.*

Rain starts falling on the tin roof, and I can only imagine Leo lying soaked on the ground. I'm afraid he'll develop an infection or something will go wrong with his grafts.

The rain also reminds me that it's been several hours since I last used the bathroom. And now that I've thought about it, I can't stop.

An hour passes with me ignoring Dillan,

and I'm fidgeting in the seat and squeezing my thighs together. I scan the room as a distraction, seeing Dillan's smiling face in the mirror over the bar.

Judging by his arrogant contentment, Dillan knows about my predicament and is enjoying this. "I have to use the bathroom," I finally admit.

Dillan smiles broadly. "That's a privilege. You haven't earned any yet."

Earned — I know what that means, and he can go to hell.

Several more minutes pass until, finally, I can bear it no more. "What do I have to do?"

Dillan stands and swaggers over to me. He pulls me upright and says, "Ask me to touch you."

I recoil from his sickening demand, and a tear runs down my cheek. Shaking my head, I answer, "No."

"Iyla, pretty soon, you'll need food, a bath, and clean clothes. All of those things must be earned. Don't make yourself suffer when there's no need. Ask me to touch you, and I'll let you go to the bathroom. Don't, and you'll have an accident. Then you'll need many more privileges to clean yourself up."

I taste bile in the back of my mouth and blood from where I'm biting my tongue. Through tears and gritted teeth, I say, "Please touch me."

Dillan's hands slide up my waist, causing

me to cringe and suck in a deep, shuddering breath. When his revolting touch reaches my breasts, a tormented sob escapes my lips.

My eyes remain squeezed shut throughout the whole ordeal until the cuff on my hand is released. "See? That wasn't so bad, was it?"

I don't dare say what I'm thinking.

Dillan closes the door to the bathroom once I'm inside, which surprises me. I rush to relieve my bursting bladder and try Leo's phone. I've got to get a message to the SEAL commander but can't get past the screen lock. There's not even an option to place an emergency call.

Dammit!

Remembering that Dillan is waiting outside the door, I stand and do up my jeans, flush, and start the faucet. While the water runs, I search the small bathroom for a place to hide Leo's phone. I've already lost my shirt and fear it's only a matter of time before Dillan finds the device in my jeans.

Finding the sink pedestal hollow, I wrap the device in a towel to silence it in case it rings or vibrates and tuck it inside the cavity near the floor.

Dillan knocks on the door. "Time's up in there."

I wash my hands quickly and turn off the water. Dillan doesn't wait for an invitation or even permission to come in. He opens the door and pats down my pockets. "Just checking,"

My knees nearly give out in relief that I successfully hid Leo's phone before it was discovered. Dillan pulls me back out into the central area of the loft and, once again, chains me to the bar.

As the storm ramps up outside, I start hearing what sounds like police radio communications. They're coming from a large walkie-talkie type thing with lots of buttons.

I can't make out all the police code used by those on the radio, but I understand enough to know that a report of two men down and a kidnapping has been called in from my house.

O'Reilly must have gone looking for Leo and me when we didn't check in. As I listen to the vague and coded communications, Dillan is in the kitchen preparing some food that he'll expect me to earn by letting him do something sick and depraved.

A female dispatcher relays the reported information to the sheriff's office, and I think I recognize the answering voice. It's the same guy that accused me of trying to get Dillan in trouble.

Deputy Birch's reply to the female dispatcher dashes any hope I had of a rescue. "These are the same damn people. I'm not wasting one minute on their bullshit claims."

"Sir, the call came in from a man claiming to be a Naval commander. He says he has video footage of the kidnapping."

Video footage... There's only one person that

has access… that has to mean… "Nolan!" I scream and jump up from the chair, stretching to try and reach the radio. I've almost got it when Dillan kicks it off the table out of reach.

His face is furious as he glares at me. "I warned you about calling another man's name."

Dillan pulls out his phone and begins tapping out a message. "Stop! What are you doing?!"

"I'm removing the final barrier between us. Don't go anywhere. I'll be right back."

CHAPTER 24

NOLAN

My boots squish and splash through Iyla's side yard as I run in a low crouch to the tree line on the east side of her house. Inside the woods, I stand and run at full speed, undetectable in the dense foliage.

I break through the treeline and turn right to head south on the two-lane highway stretching from my town to the next. I'm still considering my crazy, dangerous idea and am working through all the variables as I move.

Everything Broderick has done so far is to manipulate Iyla into doing what he wants. Own, manipulate, control. He threatened me twice to ensure her compliance, and I'm betting he used Skin the same way. Broderick's got her now, so he shouldn't be interested in me unless Iyla refuses to do what he tells her. *You fight him, baby. Don't stop.*

I'm coming for you.

Just like in this last mission, I hear Clothespin's voice in my head. *Problems and solutions. Go.*

Hypothetical one. Broderick needs me for leverage. Initially, maybe, but that makes the least sense in the long run because he can't keep me around forever.

Two. He means to kill me outright. If he succeeds, he has Iyla. If I fight and win, whether Broderick dies or lives, I might not ever find where he's taken her.

Three. Broderick takes me to Iyla with the intent to kill me in front of her. In that case, I'm likely to be bound, or worst-case scenario, tranqued.

All theories considered, I figure I have a sixty–seventy percent chance of being taken to Iyla once picked up and a one hundred percent chance of being used to achieve complete control over her. The only question then is when Broderick plans to kill me.

Solutions to these scenarios would be finding and exploiting Broderick's weaknesses. That he's willing to risk bringing me around exposes Iyla herself to be his weakness. Exploiting that weakness means I'll be employing my shitty plan.

Pulling Iyla's inhaler from my pocket, I remove the canister from the mouthpiece and roll both parts into the underside of my left uniform sleeve. So Broderick doesn't suspect anything, I also roll up the other sleeve. Broderick will never know I've got the inhaler, even if he pats me down.

With the medicine secure, I step off the

pavement into the strawberry fields on the opposite side of the road. All the plants are soaked by the continuing rain, but I hope there's enough pesticide on the leaves to transfer to my stomach and legs.

I hold up my arms to keep the poison away from my hands and rolled-up sleeves as I bend and rub my body over the plants. I'm back on the road a second later and set out at a jog to put some distance between the men at Iyla's house and me.

About two miles up the road, I pass an old farmhouse with an equally old Buick in the driveway. Another half-mile or so passes, and I hear the approach of an engine. The Buick slows and pulls alongside me, and Broderick's face appears in the driver's window.

"Hands up and walk behind this next house."

I do as he says and walk around the broken-down shack. Broderick follows me up the drive, leaving his lights on when he gets out. "Turn around slowly."

When I face him, I'm not surprised to see a gun pointed in my direction. Broderick approaches cautiously and snaps a cuff around one wrist, bringing it down behind my back before locking down the other.

I'm patted down as I expected, and the deputy's phone is tossed into the woods. There's nothing left to find except the micro tools in my watch band, a gift from Fish to all of his squad.

Thank you, man.

Gesturing with the gun, Broderick points to the back of the car and opens the trunk, ordering me inside. The old car backs out of the rutted drive onto the smooth highway seconds after Broderick closes the trunk. It's not long before he pulls off again, and the old sedan bumps along a dirt road.

I don't recognize the location when the car stops and the trunk opens. The only structure in sight is a pole barn with an exterior staircase leading to a loft apartment. "Get out."

I maneuver my legs out of the cavernous trunk and make a show of it being awkward with my hands being secured behind my back. With me now upright, Broderick moves to stand in front of me. "I thought she left, but it was you. You took Iyla and hid her away."

His right fist flies at my face, making solid contact. "I told you not to touch Iyla again."

I lean forward and smile with my split lip. "I didn't just take her, I made her scream for me, and she loved every fucking second."

Broderick yells and commences beating the shit out of me. I take every punch, kick, elbow, and knee strike he delivers, only pretending to be weakened by the blows. I can't fight back yet. Not until I know that Iyla is here. And I have to protect the inhaler hidden in the fabric under my bicep.

The cop delivers some serious shots but,

lacking the stamina of a SEAL, soon wears out. "I could kill you right now, but I need Iyla to watch so she knows you're gone. Now, get up. I don't want to have to carry your ass."

I push up from the ground, groaning and appearing to have much difficulty. At the stairs, I lean against the wall for support to further convince Broderick that I'm licked. The asshole cop opens the door when we reach the top and shoves me through. Iyla screams, and I let both of them see me stumble.

Just before I hit the floor, I launch from my faux-wounded crouch and make a break for Iyla, praying I don't kill her. "Iyla, I'm so sorry," I bellow.

Broderick rushes over and yanks me backward, landing me in a chair. Iyla has already started coughing when Broderick lands his next blow to my stomach. Iyla screams and sputters my name between coughs and stretches, trying to reach for me or stop Broderick.

After a left hook to my right eye, Broderick backs up and shakes out his fist. "See what you did, Iyla? This man is going to…" he stops mid-sentence and turns around after finally noticing Iyla's distress.

Her coughing worsens to the point of wheezing, and she slumps to the floor with her arm awkwardly still fastened to a metal bar.

Now's my chance. I'm only half faking when I start freaking out and going on about her asthma. Being a cop, Broderick would know there's no faking severe asthma symptoms. Especially once her lips begin turning blue. *Please, let me get to her before then.*

With Broderick distracted, I pull the metal pick from my watch band, working at the cuffs while keeping up the panicked talk. "Oh, god, you've got to help her! Where's her medicine?"

Broderick releases Iyla's cuffed hand, picks her up to lay her on the bar, and checks all her pockets. "She doesn't have anything on her!"

"What?! If she doesn't get her asthma medicine, she'll die!"

I scream the last part to mask the snick of the cuff opening. Now, I have to get this asshole out of the way. I leap at Broderick, and he turns at the last second, shock evident on his face. "How?!"

Off-balance due to his last-second redirect, my fist glances off his jaw, and the two of us hit the floor.

Broderick gets his hands around my throat, but I catapult him over my head into a grandfather clock. He rolls out of the way just in time to avoid being crushed by the wood and glass cabinet when it falls. We both jump back up, and Broderick grabs a lamp, swinging and hitting me with it but leaving himself open.

I land a jab and cross into his stomach, followed by an uppercut that sends him stumbling back into the wall. Broderick reaches for the gun holstered on his hip, and I rush him, slamming both fists into his chest. We struggle to grab the gun and end up on the floor again.

We both have a hand on the gun's grip, him pulling, me pushing. Meanwhile, I keep landing blows to his middle at half-strength because of the awkward position.

A loud thud sounds across the room, and I look up to see that Iyla has fallen to the floor. The momentary pause is enough for Broderick to pull the gun free, but my competing grip sends it sailing across the floor.

Having been on top of the pile, I dive for the gun, and Broderick slams a chair against my back. The wood frame shatters, launching broken spindles fly all over the place. The impact is violent and takes my breath just long enough for Broderick to jump over me.

I grab his foot and yank, sending him crashing to the floor, but he still has enough reach to grasp the pistol. As he comes up with it, I grab one of the broken chair spindles and stab it into his thigh. Broderick roars but continues to swing the gun around.

Grabbing another large sliver, I jump up and, with a yell, shove the wooden stake into his chest. Broderick's eyes go wide, but he's not dead yet, so I grab the gun, snapping his wrist.

With a deformed wrist and blood pouring from his leg, chest, and mouth, Broderick still manages a triumphant grin. "You don't win. Iyla is going to Die With Me. I... told you. She's... mine."

"She was never fucking yours."

I feel no remorse when I put a bullet between his eyes.

With Broderick no longer a threat, I toss the gun away, strip out of my uniform, and unwrap the inhaler components. Iyla's lips are blue, and her chest barely moves when I kneel beside her. I put the inhaler in her mouth and watch her chest, depressing the canister as she attempts to breathe in.

"Come on. Come on, Baby! Breathe!"

I spray the medicine two more times, and the door to the loft explodes inward, "Police!"

"Get in here! We need an ambulance Now!"

The place fills up with police, SEALs, and eventually, paramedics. Someone pulls me away, and I watch helplessly as the medics place an oxygen mask over Iyla's face. Worried that I might still have that shit on me, I yell out to my guys on the way to find a bathroom, "I need clothes!"

I take off through the place, looking for a shower, and grab the hand soap off the sink when I find a bathroom. I scrub hurriedly and cover myself with a towel, not bothering to dry off before running back to the main room.

The medics and Bandaid are hovering over Iyla, where they've placed her on the dining table.

A green mask leaks smoke over her nose and mouth, and Bandaid listens to her lungs with a stethoscope. He looks up at me, and his face is grim. *It can't be that I've killed her. Please, God, no.*

"Start an IV. Give her adrenaline."

The medics share a look. "Sir, you're not affiliated—"

"Then get out of the fucking way, and I'll do it myself!"

O'Reilly steps into my view and holds out some dry clothes to me. "Go put this on. She's in good hands."

I don't want to move, but the firm set to his jaw says he won't entertain otherwise. On the way back to the bathroom, I spot Deputy Birch standing next to an older man wearing a sheriff's badge. *Getting dressed can wait.*

Not caring that I'm standing nearly naked before the Sheriff of Chesapeake County, I point a finger in Birch's direction, "You'd better pray to God she lives."

IYLA

A cacophony of voices pulls me from sleep, and I wake wearing a hissing and bubbling mask. *Nebulizer.* I open my eyes in the bright light to see that I'm strapped to a gurney. The small space is crowded, and I only recognize one face, one of the SEALs.

"There she is." He smiles with water dripping off his hair. "Iyla, do you remember me?

I'm Bowie Myers, Bandaid."

I nod at him, but that's all I can do with this mountain sitting on my chest. It looks like I'm in the back of an ambulance with the doors open. It's still raining, and Nolan is nowhere in sight.

Reaching over with my fingers, I tap Bandaid's leg to get his attention. "What is it? What do you need, Sweetheart?"

I spell out *Nolan* against the blanket using my finger.

"Except for worrying to death about you, he's fine. He'd be here now, but the sheriff wouldn't let him leave."

With my hand against Bandaid's knee, I form the flip-off signal, making him laugh. "Yep. I'll bet he feels the same way."

"You ready to go, Doc?" someone asks Bandaid.

"Let's go," he answers.

The ambulance doors close, and I tap on Bandaid's leg to get his attention one more time. He glances at me, looks down at my hand, and watches as I scratch out the name Dillan. The SEAL doctor's gaze returns to mine, and he reports, "Dead. I confirmed it myself. He'll never touch you again."

I tap him one last time.

Bandaid laughs again when he looks down and sees me giving him a thumbs-up. At that point, I close my eyes and concentrate on breathing.

At the hospital a short time later, a call pulls Bandaid away from the emergency exam room where I was placed upon arriving. He pats my hand with a wink and disappears from the room. The next face I see is Nolan's.

He has a patched-up cut on his cheek, a black eye, and a split lip, but I don't think I've ever seen a sight so wonderful. I lift a hand to caress his face, and my voice is craggy when I try to talk to him. "I thought he was killing you."

Nolan adjusts the oxygen tube at my nose and shakes his head. "I had to let him think he had me beat so he would drop his guard and focus on you."

"So, the asthma, it was intentional then."

Nolan drops to a knee beside the bed and takes my hand. "I'm so sorry that I took a chance with your life, but it was the only thing I could think of that would give me a chance to save you. I even hid your inhaler in my uniform to help you after getting Broderick out of the way. Can you ever forgive me?"

It's my turn to bring his hand to my face. I hold his palm against my cheek and look into his warm eyes. "If you hadn't done what you did, I'd still be his prisoner. I would rather be dead than to have spent another minute under his control. There's nothing to forgive."

Nolan pushes off the floor and touches his lips to my forehead. "Thank you for fighting and staying alive."

A sharp knock sounds on the door before Bandaid and a hospital doctor walk in. The doctor wearing a lab coat says, "Your O2 levels are good. As long as you promise to follow up with your doctor, I can let you go home now."

I give him a nod. "I will."

"Good. I'll have the nurse come back and discharge you."

The emergency doctor leaves, and the Navy doctor walks over and taps me on the knee with a wink.

"Bowie, how is Leo? He's ok, isn't he?"

"Skin's ok. He woke up a short while after the paramedics showed up at your house. Of course, Judge was gone by then, having taken the deputy's phone. That's how we found you, not by tracing the deputy's phone, which only led us to an empty farmhouse, but by realizing you must have taken Skin's phone without Broderick knowing. Once we had a lock on Skin's cell, we came running."

"Where is he now?"

"Well, he's… here."

My head snaps up to look at the clock on the wall. *Nearly one am.* "What?! Why?"

Bandaid shrugs. "He wouldn't leave until you were found and then until he knew you would be okay. He made the commander drive him here in his Mustang. I tried to send him home with the others two hours ago, but he refused to leave. Now that you're going home, I bet he will, too... after he gives me a ride back to base. Oh, and speaking of rides..."

Bandaid pulls a set of keys out of his pocket and tosses them to Nolan. "Fish thought you'd want your car here. It's parked outside."

Nolan lets go of my hand to shake that of his friend. "Thanks, man. For everything, but especially for saving Iyla."

"Hey, you did that yourself."

Bandaid tosses another wink to me and passes the nurse on his way out the door. "Sir, you can go get your car, and we'll meet you out front."

Nolan bends down and kisses me on the lips. "See you in a minute."

The door closes behind Nolan, and the nurse makes a tsking noise. "Whew. That one looks like he had a rough night, too."

"I cannae even begin to tell you."

My IV is removed, and since I'm still in my own clothes, I slip into my sandals and transfer to the waiting wheelchair. The nurse rolls me outside to where Nolan is waiting by his car, and the grin on his face is loving, brilliant, and just about the most beautiful thing I've ever seen.

He helps me into the soft leather seat and leans in to kiss me as if he can't bear to wait another minute to taste my lips. I grab onto his shirt to keep him from pulling back before I'm ready because there was a moment in that loft when I thought I'd never touch him again.

Behind Nolan, an elderly and slightly annoyed man says, "Can't you get her home before you start all that?"

Nolan pulls back laughing and turns to address the old man. "Yes, sir."

I lean back against the seat and close my eyes as Nolan shuts my door and walks around to his side. When he's seated, I reach over blindly to lay my hand on his thigh, needing to touch him as much as he needed to kiss me.

Nolan lifts my hand to his mouth and places it gently back on his leg, covering my hand with his own. As the car pulls out of the hospital drive, I've got something on my mind that's bothering me, but I'm reluctant to bring it up.

Nevertheless, if he's headed home, I need to say something now. "Nolan?"

"Yes, Iyla."

"I know this probably means I lack fortitude, but I don't want to live in Chesapeake anymore. Too much has happened, and… I don't want to live in a place where every memory of my short time there is spoiled by what Dillan did. I'm going to put my house on the market. I don't… I don't know… What I'm trying…"

Shit. How do I tell Nolan I don't want to make love with him in his garden shower while staring at the tree where Dillan forced his tongue past my lips?

Nolan squeezes my hand, and his eyes take on a distant look. "You're not leaving Virginia, are you?"

"No. I just… I can't be where he was."

Nolan pulls off the road and stops suddenly. With the car in park, he reaches over and takes my face in his hands. "Then I'll move. I want to be where you are, Iyla. I'll put my house on the market and start over somewhere else. I don't care where that is. Just promise you won't leave."

My face is a canvas painted with a peaceful contentment I'd only ever dreamed of experiencing. Hoping Nolan hears forever in my voice, I answer, "I promise."

Nolan pulls me toward him for a sweet kiss and releases me to start the car moving again. As he reaches for the gear shift, I stop him with a touch to his arm. "Nolan, would you maybe want to look for a place together?"

His face shines with a megawatt grin. "Hell, yes, I do."

ESCAPEPROOF

JO CHAMBLISS

EPILOGUE

NOLAN

A home with Iyla.

And she looked so nervous when she asked. That makes me smile again. If the woman has any doubts that I'm a complete goner, I need to do a lot better job convincing her.

I turn the car around toward Little Creek instead of going home. Our stuff is still at the cabin, so it makes more sense to go there anyway.

We will, however, need to make some arrangements for the short term. I have no doubt that Iyla was serious about not returning to Chesapeake. I wouldn't expect nor ask her to do anything more than make day trips to pack and clean out.

I'll worry about all that tomorrow. For now, all I want is to be in a soft bed with Iyla, a locked door between us and the rest of the world.

I take Iyla to bed inside the cabin, holding her carefully but firmly as though she might slip from my fingers if I don't. Despite being exhausted, neither of us seems to be able to fall asleep. I'm tracing my fingers up and down her graceful back. "Iyla."

"Yes?"

"Thank you for saving my friend's life."

Iyla nuzzles her face against my neck. "He was trying to do the same for me but never got the chance."

She lifts her head and adds, "Leo's a good man, but I think he's just now learning that about himself. I'm also afraid for him. He took it rough when we were out in public. Don't let him think his life is over."

"We won't."

"Nolan."

"Yes, Iyla?"

"I love you."

"I love you, Iyla."

I brush her hair away from her face and neck, and she's asleep in minutes.

A knock on the door at ten the next morning has me sneaking out of bed to keep from disturbing a still-sleeping Iyla. No one could blame her. Her life has been a living hell the last two weeks, and she nearly died last night.

I've been awake for hours, content to hold her warm body safe in my arms, but it appears that time is over. Pulling on a pair of sweats, I leave the bedroom and close the door. A quick check through the peephole has me nearly ripping the door off its hinges to get it open.

"Dammit. It's good to see you, man."

Skin stands on the doorstep holding a bag

from the bakery on base. "Yeah. I'm glad you're not dead." He looks down at his feet and kicks at some invisible object. "I'm sorry I fucked up with Iyla. We were so careful."

"Hey, knock that shit off. No one saw this bastard coming. He was smart. I think even smarter than us."

I back out of the way and gesture inside. "Come in. Iyla's still asleep, though."

Skin follows me into the kitchen, and I start making coffee.

"How is she?"

"She'd rather burn down her house than spend another night in Chesapeake."

"That good, huh? What are you gonna do? *You* still live there."

"Not for long. We're both selling and getting out. What about you?"

Skin won't look at me. "I hear my arm will function just fine."

I duck into his line of sight and give him a look that asks, *And?* "What about your head? Are you still one of us, or will you quit?"

"I'm a SEAL... even if my love life is now a rerun of *Beauty and the Beast*."

"Well, I'm not much into Disney princesses, but I'm pretty sure that one turned out all right."

A door closes, and a yawning voice asks, "Is that coffee I smell?"

Not knowing Iyla's state of dress, I grab a

towel and throw it over Skin's face.

Iyla walks into the room wearing one of my shirts over a pair of denim shorts. Her hair is a messy pile on her head, and she's absolutely gorgeous... and decent. "It's safe to look, Skin."

My friend pulls the towel off and throws it at me. Realizing he's here, Iyla squeals and runs over to hug him carefully. "Leo! God, I was so worried about you! Your bandages. I'm sure they got soaked. You aren't going to end up with an infection, are you?"

Leo Ramsay shakes his head, bemused at Iyla's reception. "Nope. All good. In fact. Bandaid had one of his other Navy doctor friends visit the hospital to look me over. He looked under the fresh bandages Bandaid put on and took them off. Said I don't need them anymore."

"That's great!"

Mine and Skin's phones sound off at the same time, sending me into high alert. The last time that happened, we spent the rest of the day pulling bodies off the floor of the Atlantic.

I retrieve my phone from the bedroom as Skin reaches into his pocket. My thumbprint unlocks the screen, and I drop my head with a sigh, reading the message. *Dinner tonight. Bandaid's house. Assignments below. Command performance.*

I walk back out to see Skin still staring at his phone blankly. This type of announcement comes as no surprise. It's our team. This is how we do things after a mission, and I wouldn't change it for the world.

Skin, however, looks like he wishes he was back in Germany.

My friend finally looks up from his phone, mumbles something about checking on us, and rushes out the door.

It's painful watching him run away like that. I guess Iyla was right. He does have a long road ahead of him.

FIVE MONTHS LATER

SKIN

"Fish, forget it. I'm not going."

My team members, led by my squad leader, Christopher "Fish" Hill, stand around my car watching me worm my way out of attending the Navy's biggest annual celebration.

"You're going to miss the Navy ball, your favorite chance to impress the ladies?"

I turn away and throw my gear into the trunk of my Mustang to keep from saying what I'm thinking. The rest of my teammates murmur their shared surprise, which I ignore. *That's me, all right. Mr. Impressive.*

Fish holds his ground, crossing his arms and making an annoyed sound like he knows what I'm thinking. "Those scars don't define you. When are you going to stop hiding behind them and live your life again?"

My team goes deathly silent at Fish's

audacious question. When no one—not even Judge—calls him out, I realize they're all in this together. This is some kind of fucked-up intervention.

I grit my teeth and slam the trunk closed, carefully weighing what I want to say. I'm angry, but these are my brothers. I can no more harm them with words than I could cut off my own arm. Still, I do my job. My personal life should be just that, mine. Shoving off the trunk lid, I wheel around to stand toe to toe with Fish. "Is that all, Lieutenant?"

My squad leader stares me down but remains silent. Since he's not in a position to make me listen to his bullshit pep talk, I back away from him and yank open my door. Without another word to any of them, I drop into the seat and speed out of the parking lot.

I feel shitty leaving like I did, but they just don't get it. They'll be living it up tonight, dressed to the nines with their women in gorgeous gowns. They'll be dancing, taking pictures, laughing, and having a good time.

What would I be doing? Sitting at the table watching. I'm the odd man out in this group these days, and no woman would give me the time of day with this patchwork of dark purple scarring running up my left arm, neck, and cheek.

I actually believed everyone who told me that not all of the burns were severe and that the swelling would go down and the scars would diminish. The swelling went down, sure, and the scars flattened out, but now, they're this angry, translucent purple. They're more visible now than a week after the explosion.

Maybe they'll fade in time. Maybe they won't. In the meantime, I watch my friends live the lives I'd kill for, knowing no woman will give me a second glance. In just the few months since the explosion, my squad has seen more pregnancy announcements and weddings than I thought possible.

At each new delivery of happy news, I felt like I'd taken a knife to the heart. Over all that time, all I've accomplished is making a toddler cry at seeing my jacked-up face.

Maybe I'm paying for all the shit I've pulled over the years with the too-casual relationships with too many women. Now that I'm ready for the real thing, I'm too fucked up for a woman to even look at me. *Except for Iyla, though she doesn't look at me the way she looks at Judge.*

Since meeting Judge's woman, she and I have been like brother and sister. If I had a sister, I imagine she'd be a lot like Iyla. As Ari is with Hawk, Iyla doesn't see my scars; doesn't even register their existence. She's the only one, though. Iyla tells me that the right person won't care about my scars. I desperately want to believe what she says, but it's impossible when the scars are all people see.

"You're a captivating subject... Think what

you want, but I'm the expert… They won't always stare… The ones that matter won't. The ones that do, don't matter," she'd said.

Iyla is right. The ones that count, my team, the kids, Willa, Rory, and the others, don't treat me differently. I'm the one that's pushing people away. My own brother doesn't even know about my burns. What does that say about me?

The Mustang automatically shifts into sixth gear, and I sigh audibly as the engine levels out. I wish I could do the same. *Maybe Fish was right. Maybe I am hiding behind my scars.*

When I get home, I consider sending a message to Fish. I was an ass to him and the others about this Navy ball shit and don't want to let it ruin their evening.

I change out of my uniform to some jeans and a short sleeve, white graphic tee and finally pick up my phone to type out a text to my leader. *You're right. I'm working on it. See you Monday.*

On the way out the door, I grab a ballcap and my keys. It's time to rejoin the land of the living.

The parking lot at Dune is almost full when I pull in for the first time since coming back from Germany. I pull the ballcap on, adjust it low on my head like I've been doing lately, and get out of the car. At the last second, I remember what I said to Fish, and the hat, my crutch, gets tossed back in the car.

I don't see my friend Nicky, the owner,

behind the driftwood counter when I pass through the entrance. It would be just my luck if I picked the one day a decade he takes off work to show up for a drink. While searching for the plucky bartender, one person who notices my entry is Chelsea, a woman I've occasionally hooked up with.

She sashays over from her high-top table on the right side of the bar and rubs her hand over my crotch. "Where have you been, lover?"

This isn't the first time she's greeted me this way, not even close. My usual response is to palm her ass and see if I can identify what she's been drinking by tasting it on her tongue.

For some reason, though, tonight, the woman's presence grates on my nerves like nails on a chalkboard. I pull her fake claws from my dick and answer in a bitterly, "Getting blown up."

Chelsea laughs at the suspected joke but stops when she notices I'm not smiling. She backs up a step and inspects me from head to toe in the low light, pausing on my left cheek, exposed arm, and the left side of my neck. "Oh my god."

She takes another step back and says, "I'm glad you're ok." Then the sexy and shallow beauty rushes back to her table and her flawless friends.

I fight off a groan and the urge to walk right back out to my car. Forcing one foot in front of the other, I travel to the far-left side of the bar to take an empty seat on the end.

Nicky comes out of the back a while later and does a doubletake when he spots me sitting alone. "Where the hell have you been?"

Same question. Same answer. "I got blown up."

Nicky laughs as he walks over but pulls up short, swearing when he notices the still-healing burns. The usually suave bar owner clenches his fists and speaks coldly, using a tone I've never heard from him. "I hope your guys killed every last mother's son of them."

I don't say anything. Nicky nods somberly, then turns around and pulls a bottle of twenty-two-year-old Tomatin scotch from a locked case on the top shelf. After pouring a double over ice, he slides it my way. "On the house. You look like you've paid enough."

I tip the glass toward him in thanks and take the first sip. Mercifully, that's the end of it. Nicky is one of the few people outside the Navy that know I'm a SEAL. I'm glad he isn't an overly emotional guy and won't waste time digging into my mental state or ask why I'm not two drinks in with Chelsea or some other woman by now.

He's not uncaring, just pragmatic. The man is also loyal and business savvy but with a wicked sense of humor. I guess that's why we get along as well as we have the four years that I've been coming here.

Over the next hour, I'm approached by a

few people who know me as a regular at Dune. The guys notice the scars and find some excuse to leave, not accustomed to discussing topics more profound than who they'll be banging later that night.

The women who stop by to say hi start out eager enough but quickly change their minds upon seeing I'm no longer the catch of the day. *I used to be, and I damned well knew it. They don't call me Skin for nothing. Or didn't.* Those days are long gone.

After each body walks away, I sink deeper and deeper into myself. I used to be just like them. The realization sickens me. The longer I drown in my self-loathing, the more I want to get out of here. But I figure I've earned the punishment for being just as shallow as these fandans. *Thank you, Iyla, for teaching me that word.*

I decide to tough it out and keep sipping on my drink, determined to be unaffected by these people who can't handle being around me now that I'm flawed.

Those that matter won't see them. Those that see them, don't matter.

God, I hope Iyla's right.

Shortly after the fifth woman walks away, a feminine voice a few seats over mumbles to herself, but I pick up on what she says. "Geez, picky much? What was wrong with that last one?"

I don't know why, but her mumbled

words piss me off. I turn in her direction and say, "Excuse me?"

The woman looks up and over to me, mortified that she spoke out loud and that I heard her. She's dressed pretty much the same as I am, which looks out of place among all these women working their attributes to attract attention.

Despite her jeans and t-shirt, a quick scan of the word bomber reveals smooth skin, flawless nails, glossy hair, and perfect, if understated, makeup. The woman opens her mouth to speak, but the first sound she makes is an embarrassed squeak. She clears her throat and tries again. "I didn't mean to say that out loud."

"Well, you did."

TWO MONTHS LATER

I raise my glass to Ink, sitting in the lounge at the front of Canvas, his tattoo shop. I'd been thinking about something that woman said weeks ago sitting at the bar at Dune. She suggested I look into getting a sleeve tattoo to cover the scars.

My response had been an absolute hell no at the time. Besides the Wendigo tattoo the eight of us got a few months ago, I've never wanted anything on my skin. Now, my whole team is here, checking out the finished ink job.

Ink knocks his glass against mine, and the lobby TV snags my attention. The screen is showing the muted local newscast. My focus locks onto a familiar face, and I don't notice Ink tapping my right arm.

"Skin, are you still with us?"

"Holy fuck. It's her."

"Who's her?" he asks, turning around.

"Shut up and turn the sound on!"

Ink looks from the door to the TV and jumps up to grab the remote. He backs up the broadcast to the story's beginning and turns up the volume. *"Mira Canaveri, daughter of Adrian Canaveri, Italian foods magnate, has been reported missing. She was last seen entering her apartment in Norfolk two days ago."*

The news anchor's face is replaced with a video plea from the woman's father. "I want my daughter home safe. I will pay a reward of two million dollars for information leading to her whereabouts."

Another man who could be FBI steps up next to answer a reporter's question hurled at the worried father. "There were no signs of foul play, but Miss Canaveri is the daughter of the owner of Migliori Pasta. We are operating under the assumption that she was taken against her will."

"You know that girl?" Fish asks.

I nod absently. "She told me her name was Mira."

"What happened?"

"We had one night together — the night of the Navy ball. I begged her to stay, but Mira left the next morning. I haven't seen her since."

But I never stopped looking.

THE END

Jo Chambliss Books

Ranger Mine series (read in order)
Remember Me - Omen & Sam
Forget Me - Squid & Erin
Lose Me - Shark & Ava
Find Me - Hyper & Cle

Waterproof Navy SEALs
(can be read in any order)
Shatterproof - Fish & Willa
Flameproof - Devil & Rory
Crashproof - Bandaid & Charli
Blastproof - Wrench & Everly
Soundproof - Hawk & Cailyn
Fadeproof - Ink & Dallas
Escapeproof - Judge & Iyla
Foolproof - Skin & Mira
Bulletproof - O'Reilly & Cass

Knot PMCs
Knot Guilty
Knot Innocent

To connect with Jo, check out her socials
www.jochambliss.com
Instagram @authorjochambliss
Tiktok @jochambliss
Facebook @jochamblissbooks
Facebook fan group, Jo's Blissaholics

ESCAPEPROOF

JO CHAMBLISS

ACKNOWLEDGMENTS

To Rose Lipscomb of Flawless Fiction. My characters make this fun.
You make this easy.
Your work with wrongly accused service men and women makes you a hero among heroes.
The world may never know about those you've helped restore their freedom, but to those you've helped, your work has meant the world.

ESCAPEPROOF

JO CHAMBLISS

ABOUT THE AUTHOR

Jo is an Amazon best-selling author living in a suburb of Birmingham, Alabama with her husband, two kids, and a cat ~~that's trying to convince her to let him move in.~~ that has now moved in.

She's a huge fan of the romantic suspense genre, favoring the works of Cynthia Eden and Susan Stoker. Her favorite kick-ass military stories are written by Andrew Peterson

Milton Keynes UK
Ingram Content Group UK Ltd.
UKHW011823190923
428965UK00001BI/41